FARNSBEE SOUTH

by *Helen Hudson*

TELL THE TIME TO NONE

MEYER MEYER

THE LISTENER AND OTHER STORIES

FARNSBEE SOUTH

FARNSBEE SOUTH

Helen Hudson

HOLT, RINEHART AND WINSTON
New York Chicago San Francisco

Published simultaneously in Canada by Holt, Rinehart
and Winston of Canada, Limited.

Library of Congress Catalog Card Number: 77-138866

First Edition

SBN: 03-085997-2

Designer: Nancy Tausek

Printed in the United States of America

To the memory of Mary and Olga

". . . to whom the miseries of the world
Are misery, and will not let them rest."

Keats, *The Fall of Hyperion*

FARNSBEE SOUTH

PROLOGUE

It had struck—that memory—like something between the teeth. For years he hardly knew it was there. The days passed over it and the weeks and the months and even a decade or two. But later he found it, still there, still intact, to be probed and pulled and tasted again. If he had the stomach to experience it twice.

It had happened long ago in a strange country, for his father had been a man given to mountains and tunnels and detours, a man who lived beyond borders and outside chronology. He sat with a glass between his hands and his battered doctor's kit between his legs and let the mornings and the evenings pass him by. His son was young. He lived on the bias of his father's life. It was a hot dry country with huge empty spaces where the dust rose and fell, settling nothing, and the people lived and died, proving nothing. Except on that one night, a dark night with the moon tossing among the clouds like a roving eye.

The boy had walked through the tough high grass carrying

the shovel, with his father slightly ahead, a brown burlap sack filled with "instruments" over his shoulder. For he had pawned his doctor's kit long ago, piece by piece, down to the old leather bag itself, complete with initials and bullet holes, to Pete who ran the American Bar on the square.

" 'PQB!' Them's my initials too," Pete had said, a hugh dirty man with a center part to his hair and a side part to his teeth. "But what the hell do I want with a 'Q'? "

"For curiosity," the doctor said. "Or quits, if you prefer. Signifying that I am now quits on you."

"Till the next time, doc," Pete said. "Jes' till the next time."

The doctor laughed and poured his drink. He was always laughing or whistling. When he wasn't drinking. Even on that dark night, walking through the tall tangled grass, he whistled softly. It was the only communication he offered his son except to tell him, waking him in the dead of night, that he would show him something he'd never forget. He handed the boy the shovel and told him to "come on."

They had driven out of town in the official government jeep assigned to his father as medical examiner for the district. They drove in silence till they reached the field of tall grass, then walked single file to the graveyard, where the stones stuck up white and tipsy and the moonlight slithered warily around a corner of the church. His father dropped the sack and reached for the shovel. "Dig," he said. They dug.

"He's been dead several days," his father said after a while, wiping his forehead and reaching for his flask. "Won't be a pretty sight. Or smell either."

They reached him at last and yanked him out, as if by the roots. His father took his "instruments" from the sack—a carving knife, a saw, and an old mayonnaise jar—and gave the boy the flashlight. "Hold," he said. He put on a pair of rubber gloves like a woman about to do the dishes. Then, while his father went to work, the boy held the light and forced himself to watch. Someone else, he thought, must have held the moon, for it stopped tossing and shone steadily on that one spot, as if deliberately focused there.

"Look, boy," his father said. "Look. The Arch Fear himself. Might as well have a look while he's not looking back." But it wasn't death. It was just an ugly heap of mess and dirty rags and a terrible smell, with the eyes still open and one hand reaching out, palm up and the fingers slightly curled, as if it had been holding something. And the sounds of crushing and pounding. The boy turned his head and was sick and turned it back again, forcing himself to watch while the knife hacked and the dead eyes stared. "Essential organs, boy," his father said, holding something up. "Liver and heart and kidneys. And maybe we'll take the brain and the intestines too. For good measure. Known as 'autopsy,' boy. From the Greek meaning 'seeing with one's own eyes.' And smelling too, eh, boy?" He put the essential organs in the mayonnaise jar and threw the rest back into the grave. Then he sat down with his back against a headstone and drank.

The boy picked up the shovel and filled the hole, smoothing it when he had finished, smoothing it over and over, pressing out the bump which might have been the head or the hand and would not lie flat, patting it all over and over to make it fit back into the landscape again, getting down on his knees, finally, to pat it gently with his palms and sprinkle it with grass. But he could not make it look like the other graves. Any more than the man below looked like the other dead around him.

"Leave it be, Rex," his father said, and held out the flask. "To the essential organs," he said. "All neatly put up."

The boy took the flask and put it to his lips. His mouth felt dry as an old rag. But he could not drink. He lay back and watched the moon with the clouds crossing its face.

Later his father was opening a brown paper bag and the light was just beginning to come up—slowly, very slowly, as if afraid of what it might find.

"Breakfast," his father announced, holding out a few dry tacos.

"No thanks."

"Eat."

The boy ate with his back to the grave, waiting for the light, which seemed stuck behind the hills, chewing carefully, swallowing hard. But later, when he thought about it, about the dry tacos and the dirty rags and the hacking of the knife, he was sick. The thing they dug up, he remembered, had looked all chewed away. He woke up often at night for weeks after, to vomit and to wash away the dry dusty taste of the tacos. But it never entirely disappeared. And he remembered how his father had whistled.

They drove back in the dawn in silence with the fields still dark beside the road. But the boy needed no light to see the horror that lay buried everywhere, just below the surface of the earth.

CHAPTER ONE

The Mayflower Memorial Hospital was large and new and private. It looked down on the East River where the barges moved slowly and the old New York Hospital for the Criminally Insane—displaced from the mainland—squatted on its tiny island, staring forever at Manhattan.

Rex Bannister sat on his bed in Farnsbee South, the small experimental psychiatric ward, and stared at his shoes. It was visiting hour, the only time he was ever allowed to be alone. His roommates were in the lounge and the solarium, entertaining friends or staring at other people's relations: Terence with his can on his knee, spitting out what should have been concealed because, waking one morning, he preferred a can of Drano to his usual fare; Garrick with his pad in his lap; and Hartley, roaming the halls, hoping to be offered candy and fruit, along with an embarrassed smile for his strange twisted arm and the twisted words no one could understand.

"Christ, what's the matter with him?" Beverly Ann had said. "He looks like he's got the shakes. Permanently." Still quivering from the shock of his birth. Rex wanted to smash his fist into the placid face of the sky and scatter the zodiac whenever Hartley was around.

But now Rex stared peacefully at his shoes with the toes crowded inside. Everyone and everything was crowded in Farnsbee South, especially the tiny hospital room where four men who had burst the conventions of their daily lives were being forced back again into a mold which would, surely, be even smaller than before. And some of the parts would certainly be lost or mixed up. Farnsbee South was noted for its rapid cures. Even now Rex could feel bits of his roommates adhering to him: Hartley's sticky smile and Garrick's ski cap pulled down low and Terence's can moving up and down, motion requiring little space. And he knew that just beyond the door the other patients were waiting, waiting to offer him great hunks of fear, ripped, still dripping, from their unconscious. For he was still so vulnerable. And they were, most of them, so young.

Indeed, many of them were still students, students who no longer saw any reason to read books or listen to lectures, for whom the twisted neck of the desk lamp was answer enough while an empty chair held all the questions they would ever care to entertain. Sometimes the questions overflowed, driving them out—to the streets and the jails and the psychiatric wards of the hospitals, set up like dorms to receive them. Here they lived, crowded together, in tiny rooms up and down the halls and ate and played and talked and danced in the lounge and the solarium and the occupational-therapy room, with a coffee urn and a Coke machine and the TV always turned on. They had shut out the world but had brought a few familiar pieces to fit between the fantasies. Outside there were large dark patches of emptiness where they might stumble and be lost forever. But here there were always lights and sounds and rooms full of people, young people. A resort for the young who wandered around in jeans and sandals, constrained by the contours of the ward and the contents of the drugs. Even the visitors were young. Family Meetings were often attended by fellow students instead of parents, as if the patients had created themselves. For the parents were too far away, in California and Kansas or the suburbs of sanity, and too busy appeasing the days of the week to drop everything and head East. They might have been proud of the son selected by the university, complete with scholarship, had he not suddenly run through the streets one night screaming that the moon had overflowed.

"Why?" his mother asked his father. "In God's name, why?" How could she know, smoothing the linoleum where her son had sat at the kitchen table eating what she had cooked, that he would turn it into something she could no longer recognize or understand?

"That's the college's problem," his father said. All those baseball games on Saturday afternoon when his son chewed hot dogs beside him and cheered for the Dodgers. There had been no moon then, no hint that his concerns would reach so high and so far beyond his father's filling station and the superhighway to LA. "That's the college's problem," he told his wife. "Don't worry. The college will fix him up." But it was the college, they thought, crumbling their napkins, that had broken him down.

Still, the young were probably better off, breaking down so early. For minds, like bones, undoubtedly healed faster in youth. Certainly they seemed happier than poor Mr. Nuffield, a postman who, after a long career of devoted service, suddenly began, quite deliberately, to mix up his mail. "Let them learn something," he said, shoving the Bixbys' mail under the Kuznicks' door. "Let them see each other's bills and read each other's letters." He was delighted with the thought that Miss Howland in Number 20 might, for the first time in her life, receive a love letter; that Professor Munson would get *Playboy* and Gil Ferrara *The Quar-*

terly Journal of Metaphysics. "Why not spread it around?" he had said when confronted with his crime. This, after thirty years of faithful service. For there was something wrong, he thought, with a system where Number 18 got more mail every day than he could shove into the box while Number 20, right next door, with a neater lawn and no dog and the zip code always given, got nothing but the gas bill and a monthly letter from St. Mary's School for Girls.

So now Mr. Nuffield walked up and down the halls of Farnsbee South with his hands stiff at his sides and one shoulder slightly raised, securing his invisible pack. "Please. The mail must go through," he would say gently if anyone tried to get him to a meal or a meeting. The rest of the time he spent writing love letters to all the Miss Howlands in his zone. He was being sent to Fresh Meadows, the state mental hospital, next month.

But even *he* was probably better off than old Mrs. Schiller, who sat in the solarium gripping the arms of her chair. She did not enjoy rock-and-roll or television or bridge. Sometimes she sat on her bed reading Dante but was reminded that she must "interact." Sometimes she sat alone on the narrow balcony but was told not to "withdraw." "I'm sixty-eight," she announced to Dr. Fensterer, young enough to be her grandson. "I have nothing to say to you." Her husband had died last year and she lived with her widowed mother-in-law and her unmarried daughter, three generations of women separated by terrible gaps where the men should have been. They drank their morning coffee in silence and kept the doors of their rooms closed, though they gathered in the evening to prepare, no doubt, for the long isolation of the night. They sat at the large round dining-room table, their books open, their heads bent, intellectual women who turned to Kant and Kafka and Spinoza and Mann after the dishes and despair of their daily lives. They did not, in fact, turn to each other except to say good night. First old lame Frau Schiller senior, at ten o'clock, nodding silently. Then Gerda at eleven, leaving her mother all alone. Mrs. Schiller was afraid they would go for good in that order, leaving her by herself at the empty table.

But at Farnsbee South the doors were always open and she was never alone. Three other women, aged sixteen to twenty-one, shared her room. There was a huge doll on the bureau and a framed picture of the Beatles. Beverly Ann sat on Mrs. Schiller's bed every night, teasing her hair and talking while Mrs. Schiller, rigid on her back, recited passages of Dante to herself, ashamed that she knew them only in translation. Daphne, an eighteen-year-old bride from Yonkers with enormous topaz eyes which she enjoyed filling with tears, practiced crying in front of her mirror. When tears were not effective, she hid. She had been found in closets and cupboards and behind the TV set with her eyes closed and her thumb in her mouth. The fourth occupant of the room was a biology major from Hunter, convinced that she needed a heart transplant. She spent her time in the therapy room writing begging letters to Marlon Brando and Paul Newman and the Duke of Edinburgh.

"As soon as I'm out of here," Beverly Ann said, "I'm hitching up to Boston. Mike promised to get me a job." A senior in high school, she liked to travel and had already had five bad "trips." Her father was the biggest car dealer in Babylon, Long Island, but Beverly Ann had been hitchhiking since she was twelve. She liked sleeping in trucks and she liked sleeping with truck drivers. She liked waiting on them too, and had been located by the police in various diners between New York and Riverhead. "Or I'll hitch across Route 6. Any time I need money, I'll just tell them to let me off at the nearest diner. I can always get a job," she said teasing her bangs, "around truck drivers. I guess they just naturally go for real brunettes." She had a succession of "brothers" and male "cousins" who came to Family Meeting and bit their nails and kissed her good night.

"'I pass from light/Into the kingdom of eternal night,'" Mrs. Schiller said fiercely to herself. Beverly Ann had been her "buddy" for an eternity. But thank God for Dante. She used him in Group Therapy and Family Meeting too. "My thoughts," she whispered to Rex beside her, "are, *Gott sei Dank,* my own."

But when the group voted down her weekend pass, she beat the table. "Democracy among the ignorant is no democracy. It is fascism. It is madness. These neurotics, these lunatics, these *children,*" she screamed. "What do they know? The Beatles and television and teasing the hair. How can they tell *me* what to do?"

But she was always in the minority, a woman who remembered the Nazis and read Dante and was sixty-eight years old in a country intoxicated with youth, in a ward full of teen-agers. She had not fled from Hitler to be dictated to by children. She was glad Theo could not see her now. He would shake his head and raise his palms as he always did when he was disappointed in her. "But what are you doing, Elsa? *Liebchen?*" he would say. "*Na,* come. Sit down. We must be calm, reasonable." What would he think of her now, surrounded by madmen, cutting her meat with a fork? But she could not sit down, could not be calm, or reasonable. For the moon was waiting above the narrow balcony, waiting to spread her secrets across the sky. She hurried down the hall and saw Rex Bannister, a new patient, fresh from being a reporter all over the world. A tall young man who had disregarded borders and penetrated whole continents. But now he sat on his bed, reluctant to cross the threshold of a hospital room.

Rex, staring at his shoes, realized he had never paid much attention to his feet before, though they had served him well, carrying him in and out of disaster and the television studios of CBS. In those days he had had other things to look at besides his own feet; terrible things, enough to make the rivers stop flowing and the seed stay buried beneath the earth. While he had rushed around, "covering" it all with a pad, tilting at horror with a pencil. As a journalist he was always *there:* when the bombs fell and the hungry rioted and the Arno ran berserk through the streets of Florence. Just as he had been there on the night the grave opened and the stench rose and he heard the sound of a knife on human bone. He had seen the face of a young man with his beard half torn away and the back of a black woman, prone in the street, bleeding over her dead son. He had seen men in uniform with their arms raised, holding clubs or guns, and the sight of braid or badges caused a riot beneath his skin. And that woman at Kennedy Airport, a bunched-up little woman wandering around the parking lot with a soldier's cap in her hands, peering into the empty cars, searching for her "missing" son.

A quiet young man with a copy of Shakespeare's *Tragedies* in his raincoat pocket, Rex occasionally drank too much. Then he did strange things. The night the Americans began to bomb North Vietnam, he had marched outside the American Embassy in London cheering for the USB, the United Sons of Bitches. And once, in a hotel in Lisbon, he had confronted a legislator from Mississippi, a big fat man with a smile that floated like oil across his face.

"Took good care of old Corabelle all her life," he had said, raising his whisky to the sun. "Clothed her and fed her and doctored her when she ailed."

"And buried her, I'll bet, when she died," Rex said.

"That's right, young man. We did." He turned and smiled at Rex. "Yes, sir. Right in the family plot too."

"Right along with the pet poodle and the pet parakeet, I'll bet. Didn't just leave her around to smell up the old plantation, did you? Or put her out with the trash?"

"Why you damned insulting little bastard," the legislator said. "You need a good sound thrashing." And swung.

"And you need a bath," Rex said, swinging back. He landed him in the swimming pool just beyond.

But most of the time Rex had walked quietly through the world with his rage stuffed down in his pocket and his pencil out. Except for that night in Haiti when he had been too drunk even to reach for a pencil and had forced a whole boatload of people to tell their story themselves. It was a night he longed to forget.

"We're not interested in your past here," young Dr. Fensterer had said. "Only the present and the future." He smiled.

Rex smiled back. He was glad to be rid of it. Excess baggage which he had carried around too long. Sometimes at night, in a village or an army post, he imagined noises coming from his bag, as if the socks and shirts were screaming to be let out. But he knew it was merely the sounds of the past which he packed up so diligently each morning. He was glad to give it all up, along with his wallet and his penknife. "You won't be needing that now," the nurse had said.

"You will be given certain medications," Dr. Fensterer went on. "Along with psychotherapy. If all goes well—and I don't see why it shouldn't—you'll be out in three or four months. Dr. Prokosh himself doesn't believe in long hospitalization." Dr. Prokosh was the director whose name, like Freud's, had achieved the eminence of a constant accompanying pronoun.

But Rex was in no hurry. He was perfectly content to sit on a hospital bed, protected by walls from the world and the other patients, those normal-looking boys and girls who wore fear tangled up in their hair. He had seen their tongues stiffen and the pores of their skin open and their hearts roll, like billiard balls, into a far pocket. Even Dr. Sourette, the young Haitian, sitting behind the desk at the nurses' station, looked scared. As though afraid of being caught forever in the huge wheel of the hospital, pinned down among the charts and the order sheets when he longed to be running up and down the hills of Port-au-Prince. But Rex felt ashamed around Dr. Sourette, who reminded him of that one story he had failed to cover. That was his curse, though his wife insisted it was merely his illness, that he was no longer a distinct, discrete person but was spread like a film, receiving impressions. The sound of a drill made his teeth ache and the mention of CARE gave him hunger pains. And in the crowded quarters and insistent schedule of Farnsbee South, he began to assume his neighbor's obsessions and appropriate his roommates' dreams. Would he end cured but transformed, practicing imaginary passes like Bigelow; or sitting perfectly still like Sandra, forever posing for some invisible artist; or praying all night like Joyce, who longed to be called Sister Mary Joseph and walked with her hands up her sleeves?

"I want to be alone," he told his wife. "Just for fifteen minutes a day. Even in the can, there's someone waiting outside." Monitors and buddies and specials and checks.

"It's the new method," Audrey said. "Patient participation."

"Fascism and a shortage of staff," Rex said. "It's driving me nuts."

"Oh, Rex." She was carrying her Bonwit Teller shopping bag and wearing her powder-blue suit and the little fox she always wore for making calls. She was "bearing up," a conscientious girl, the kind who still made calls. It was good of her, Rex thought, to always take that little fox with her though she loathed pets and was afraid of birds. But perhaps the little fox was company for her, so young and pretty, going to see her sick husband. Not sick as other people were sick, so friends could ask questions and send flowers and even visit with her, making a gay little party around his bed, shutting out the sight of the other patients, old and twisted and laid away in a hospital bed to die. But Rex was sick in a grotesque way that had nothing to do with cool drinks and trays and three pillows behind his handsome head. Though he had gotten so thin it looked far too big for him now, all stuffed with crazy ideas.

"Why don't you let me ask Uncle Clement?" Audrey said. "He could get you into that nice place in Tarrytown where there are loads of nurses and the patients wear robes and stay in their rooms and rest. Not like here where everyone runs around and you can't tell *who's* crazy." She had been informed, one afternoon, by an elegant young man in a Nehru jacket that Rex had been sent to the front, to turn back the rebels at Gettysburg. She had

had hysterics beside the coffee urn and demanded to see the director.

"That's another thing," she said now. "That director. Dr. Prokosh. He gives me the creeps."

"He's a genius," Rex said. "Everyone says so."

Though Rex had been at Farnsbee South for several weeks by then, he had not yet met Dr. Prokosh, who rarely came to the ward, conducting its affairs from his office-apartment high up in the tower of the hospital. He made rounds only occasionally, taking the patients, one by one, into the tiny office beside the utility room that had two straight chairs and a narrow window and a light burning constantly. The other patients talked about him all the time.

"My old man says he's the best shrink in the business," Bigelow said. He was a big brawny boy, a college football star who had never had a penalty called against him.

"Of course he is," Daphne said, a girl who clearly felt entitled to the best. She stopped practicing her eye-tearing technique. "Everyone knows he's tops in the business."

"Some business," Beverly Ann said.

"He's a great doctor," Joyce said, nodding over her folded hands. *"And* a great man. Otherwise Reverend Mother never would have sent me here."

"Holy Jesus, *Reverend Mother* sent you here?" Beverly Ann said. "She doesn't trust *Him,* any more, the Great Healer?"

"Of course she does. Dr. Prokosh is just one of his instruments."

"Some instrument," Beverly Ann said. "Blunt. Like an ax."

But the others all agreed that he was a great doctor. All except Terence Drew, Rex noted, who said nothing. He was afraid of doctors, especially shrinks. Especially Dr. Prokosh. A pale young man with a long thin face and a good deal of blond hair, Terence looked, Rex thought, like an emaciated cherub, stretched beyond his limits to fill a space. He maintained a brittle silence on the subject of Prokosh.

But Rex thought of Dr. Prokosh as a tall man with gently

graying hair, moving quietly through the ward, listening with understanding instead of a stethoscope. A neat well-controlled man in a business suit with his wrists sliding smoothly in and out of his cuffs and his eyes looking straight ahead out of the middle of his glasses, not trying to slip to the corners like Rex's. Ever since Rex had been in the hospital, he had felt his eyes somersault periodically and had the sensation that his ears had been stuck on backward, straining for the sounds of the past. The effect of the drugs, no doubt. But Dr. Prokosh's features had certainly never been shaken up or even smudged. His ears would be steady and his eyes focused and his watch always accurate. For he was a man who had spent his life studying, had sat down with himself and his fellows for years, content to examine the world through the narrow but deep passage of the mind. While Rex had rushed about, pushing back the edges of the earth, prying beneath the corners of the sky. A journalist, he had thought to heal the world by exposing it. Indeed, he still carried a notebook and pencil in his breast pocket. But only from habit. He no longer had any desire to report the news—even the big news from Farnsbee South. Or North or East or West.

"Your agent keeps calling all the time," Audrey said.

"Tell him, for crying out loud, that I'm not a reporter any more. I'm a patient in a mental ward." Though the news *was,* in fact, sensational. Why only yesterday, in the middle of Group Therapy and after one of the shortest labors in medical history, one of the new patients had given birth to a Coke bottle. But Audrey would not understand. She was sitting perfectly straight with her feet together as though propped there for a moment, merely waiting to be picked up again and carried away. She had given her name as Audrey Salter Bannister. Not Mrs. Rex Bannister.

"Why don't you divorce me?" Rex said. "You've got grounds."

"Oh, Rex. It's not like you're *really* crazy. Not like the others. You're just stubborn. Like that time in Haiti. They *told* us not to give them any money."

"Of course I'm crazy, Audrey," he said softly. "Only a madman would bother to give away a handful of coins in a country full of beggars." Which was exactly what he had done, that last night, as if to make up for his earlier crime: a handful of coins for a boatload of people. He had seen them coming, the ragged bodies and the outstretched hands, and reached for his pockets. And a black wall had closed around him.

"You're *not* crazy," Audrey said. "How could you be? I wouldn't have fallen in love with a crazy man."

"Oh, but you didn't. Don't you remember? It was Paul you fell in love with. I just bullied you. Right after he was killed, when you were so broken up. Rebound, isn't that what they call it?" As though people simply bounced like balls off tragedy into the nearest pair of hands.

She stared at him blankly. And then, for the first time in weeks, he saw her smile. She was very young, of course. But at seventy she would still want new furniture and the kitchen redone. Because death was not on her calendar. She might weep before the Tivoli's wide screen but kept her eyes dry and sharp for the cleaning woman. When things went wrong there was always someone else to blame. Salesladies shortchanged her and the butcher gave her poor cuts and her children, when naughty, would take after their father. "Don't blame me." Her face would always look bright, as if she had appropriated the sun for her personal spotlight.

"I couldn't leave you now," she said. "Not *now.*" But she sighed and stared at the rings on her finger, the very slim wedding band and the very large diamond from Paul, which she had gone on wearing when she realized there would be none from Rex. "I couldn't possibly think of leaving you."

"Well do," Rex said. "Do think of it." She stroked the little fox at her neck and Rex knew she would. By the time she reached home she would be ready to tell her mirror and her friends: "I had to, you know. For Rex's sake. Even if it does make me feel like an old shoe. My own husband telling me to get out. But he insisted. Part of his sickness, I suppose." Would she, he wondered, go on wearing *his* ring too, after she married someone else?

She got up then, a small girl, though her legs were heavy as if designed for a much bigger person, too heavy for carrying just a shopping bag and a few extra rings and a little fox. They might, perhaps, have staggered a bit under the weight of a dead fiancé and a mad husband. But those sorrows had been swallowed up by the little fox long ago. Rex could almost hear his own life history being ground between its jaws. That was why she carried it, of course. To snap at intruding shadows, leaving her face always in the sun.

She stood up now in her powder-blue suit with her blonde hair and her unclouded face, a bit of sky dropped into his hospital room. But it was a heaven he no longer coveted. Her legs were too heavy. They supported so little. For him there was "nothing left remarkable" to hold his interest or compassion. Only, perhaps, the constant surprise that she should claim the face of the sun, as though Daddy had willed it to her along with his mother's trinkets, had left it hanging up there only because it was too heavy to wear around her neck. But Rex knew she had no such metaphysical concerns. Nor such a monstrous ego. Like the little fox, she was content to snap up what was within reach. Which did not include Rex. He had slipped away long ago. Had, in fact, never really been there at all except for those few weeks right after Paul's car turned over, when his own heart turned over too, at the sight of Audrey in black, looking as though she had borrowed some older woman's dress and was now forced to live inside someone else's life.

He covered his face for a moment, for his eyes were beginning to somersault. His head felt swollen, spreading to encompass the world. They never should have made contact at all, the top-heavy man and the bottom-heavy woman. Audrey was moving to the door now, a well-bred girl ending her call.

Walking down the hall with her, he felt a sudden compassion, for he could see that she too was crowded: her shoulders inside that snug jacket and her toes inside her shoes, with her heels tilting her too sharply toward the future. "Don't bother to come any more," he said. "There's no point." He touched the fox in farewell, the clever little fox that had guarded her so carefully that now she would never grow up to use those solid legs to walk in the rain occasionally and, maybe, even through mud.

"We never should have gone to Haiti," she said. "That terrible place." As though Bermuda might have saved him. As though the Voodoo priest chewing up razor blades in the little room behind his hut, surrounded by black-faced saints, had called down the powers of black magic or served them up in the watery cocoa Audrey refused to drink. She had worn her white gloves in and out of the shacks of Thomonde. "We never should have gone to that terrible place," she said again. It was her only good-bye.

Indeed, he thought, they had had their choice of terrible places: Calcutta and Kingston and Istanbul, a whole world of horrors and all within walking distance of any Hilton Hotel. Still, he had insisted on Haiti. To make up for that story he had failed to cover? Only to fail again. He kept his eyes averted from the nurses' station, where Dr. Sourette, the young Haitian, sat behind the desk. "Repress it," Dr. Fensterer had said. "Remember it," Dr. Sourette seemed to murmur without moving his lips. And Miss Reed, walking by, punctuated by cap and pin and the rounded toes of her shoes, smiled slightly. "Accept it," she might have been saying, for her footsteps made no sound.

Walking back along the hospital balcony, Rex thought of the balcony of the hotel where he had stood with Audrey the day they arrived in Haiti. They had been married a little over a year then and they stood with the sun blazing down on them and on the rooftops of Port-au-Prince, frosted pink and blue and set in a tissue of trees. "It's lovely," Audrey had said. And it was. Looking down from a distance. Until he noticed two men standing in the bushes just beyond the hotel fence, two skinny black men in faded shirts and jeans and large straw hats, their arms outstretched, palms up, over the rail. Rex felt in his pockets. "Don't," Audrey said. "You'll never get rid of them." He emptied his pockets and ducked into the room. He never went out on the balcony again. But he knew they were there, were in fact everywhere, all over the island, all over the world, with their eyes raised and their hands out, waiting. It made his mouth go dry. They were even here in Farnsbee South, pushing and shoving against him, eager to hand him their stories. He felt the pad and pencil burning a hole in his chest. But he was not a reporter any more.

He fled, when he could, to the safety of his room, to stare at his feet or the wall. The drugs distorted his vision so that he could not read. Instead, he deciphered the wall. Until Beverly Ann, passing by, screamed: "OK, big shot. Come on out and interact like everyone else. Even if you do think you're too good for anything but a press conference at the White House."

"Na, leave him," old Mrs. Schiller would say. And Mr. Nuffield, shifting his invisible pack, would promise a *very* special-delivery letter very soon for Mr. Rex Bannister. But when Miss Reed told Rex gently but firmly to come out and start effecting his own cure, he went stiff with fear. For he knew the other patients were all staring at him, waiting for him to take down their stories. All except Verna, a new patient, a small black silent woman, too busy listening to the voice of the Lord to indulge in earthly chatter. She had not spoken a word since she arrived.

"You may never be completely cured," Dr. Fensterer told Rex. "In the ordinary sense of the word." It was a chemical imbalance which made it impossible for him to maintain his equilibrium on a planet that was forever whirling through space and shrinking at the edges. Though it gave the illusion of stability and permanence and a rationale that sent out little green shoots every spring.

"It can, of course, be controlled," Dr. Fensterer went on. "So you'll never know there's anything wrong." He smiled.

Rex nodded. He would like to know more about his chemistry. It was an aspect of himself he hadn't considered before. But Dr. Fensterer, he knew, had many patients waiting. He went back to his room and stared at the wall. And tried to think of himself as a collection of chemicals with the formula gone slightly berserk.

And upstairs in his tower suite, surrounded by records and books and primitive masks, Dr. Arnold Prokosh opened his files at "B" and pulled out the tape marked "Bannister."

CHAPTER TWO

In Farnsbee South the walls were painted many colors. None of them white. Stripes rode the couches and rugs stretched across the floors and long thick curtains hung ready to cover the view from the seventh floor. The TV lectured all day on how to brighten linoleum and whiten teeth and cover the gray in laundry or hair. Sickness was bound up inside the skull and pushed down beneath the skin. Between the walls, the residents moved from lounge to solarium to therapy to bed, like guests on a ship, passengers who had come aboard from Flushing or Times Square or the BMT, leaving the wind and the dust and the chewed-up gum on the streets. The long one-legged buildings stretched intolerably to the sky, threatening to topple over onto the citizens below, who nevertheless continued to vote and register for the draft and deposit the exact fare.

Rex, sitting in the lounge beside Terence, remembered the streets where the fire hydrants stood patiently between the Cadillacs while young executives played leapfrog over them on their way to lunch. But the hydrants had suddenly become the bent backs of old men waiting on the wrong corner for a bus which refused to stop. And far below, Rex felt the rumble of the subway, rushing eternally back and forth, carrying whole segments of the population who sat underground, reading ads and newspapers, sucking Lifesavers from the vending machines, calling Miss Subways from the nearest booth; men who knew all the station stops and even their sequence and how to cross from east to west without danger of assault from above ground upon the senses or the sympathies. Even time might be suspended, a wave of darkness which never broke but remained forever poised at the crest between Sunday and Monday.

Still, it was better to be above ground, Rex thought, if only for the daylight, which was not, he remembered with satisfaction, generated by Con Edison or any subsidiary thereof. And he was grateful for his bed on which other men had lain before him, brave men who, in the end, had made it back down into the city, defying the cigarette ads and the sirens and the emptiness of a left trouser pinned up against the wind. How had they summoned the courage, those men who had once lived in this room, to watch the cars, with their passengers boxed up inside, roll steadily up to the light? To see the leaves die and the cracks widen on the walks and the revolving doors turn endlessly on the same spot? Beside him, Terence spat into his can, an ex-Latin teacher holding Virgil on his lap and moving his lips slightly as if to prove he could still take something by mouth.

In the center of the room the chairs were arranged in rows, like seats in a theater. As though the performance were continuous.

"It's a circus," Beverly Ann said. "Without the popcorn. Wait'll you see."

Rex nodded and glanced around. Most of the other patients were playing cards or guitars or ping-pong. Or tic-tac-toe on the far corner of the sky. Except for Garrick writing and Verna listening to God and Terence reading Virgil and spitting the irregular endings into his can.

"Mostly clowns," Beverly Ann went on. "Except for one 'living statue.' " She pointed to a pretty girl who sat rigidly all alone beside the coffee urn. She had long blonde hair and might have had an address stamped across her mouth. "Like she was a model or something stuck on the cover of *Vogue*," Beverly Ann said. "That's all she does is pose. Hey, Sandra," she yelled. "This here's a famous world reporter. He wants your life story."

But the girl only stiffened and kept her eyes on her own reflection. "I am sitting here," she told herself. But she was also sitting over there in the coffee urn and she knew she was sitting in dozens of studios and billboards all over town. And maybe even in galleries and living rooms too. But she must not think of those other Sandras. She was not responsible for them, for how they looked or what they did or didn't wear. Still, she knew that at that very moment someone, somewhere, was examining her fleshtones. But there was nothing she could do about it. Except to go on sitting perfectly still. It was the thing she did best. The only thing she *could* do. She had been trained to it.

"Christ," Beverly Ann said. "Pardon me for breathing. Or am I supposed to do it for her?" She turned on her heel. "Jesus, a zombie. In here we've got everything."

"Never mind her, darling," a husky voice beside Rex said. "She's nothing but a cheap little bitch from the provinces. Blows her lines and upstages everyone and can't do half a scene without taking off her clothes." Rex felt a long bony hand on his wrist. He turned and saw a pale thin woman in a red-velvet dressing gown and false lashes. An ex-actress who had obviously taken many final curtains. She had once enjoyed a mild success as Desdemona on tour and still wore her long blonde wig in the ward. "*I* have a story for you, darling," she went on. "A marvelous story. I'm Alicia Hunnicutt, you know. You probably saw me on stage before my husband started spreading lies about me. When

I was the toast of Cleveland, with the mayor and the whole city council lined up outside the stage door. Every night and Saturday matinées. They even named two hotels and a city square after me. That was until Orin here got so jealous he broke up every performance for a month. Didn't you, darling?" She turned to smile at the silent sandy-haired man beside her who came faithfully every day and fetched various articles for her from her room or the drugstore and even from the department stores downtown. He wore tan suits and always carried a book which he bounced gently, like a child, on his knees.

"Oh, yes, I have a wonderfully dramatic and tragic story for you, darling," Mrs. Hunnicutt said.

"But I'm not a reporter any more," Rex said. "Not any more."

"Of course you are, darling. You'll never stop being a reporter any more than I'll ever stop being an actress. Or Orin here will ever stop being a jealous husband. Will you, darling? Years ago he was a playwright on his way up. But now he's a complete failure who hands out other people's books at the public library, don't you, darling? Because he was so jealous he couldn't let me out of his sight long enough to finish the first act. Could you, darling? And he's still wildly jealous. Honestly, darling, I don't see why they don't put *you* in here instead of me. Just like that little bitch," she screamed suddenly, pointing at Sandra. "Copying my hairstyle and learning my lines and trying to steal my scenes." She burst into tears suddenly and sat with her head down, letting the thick blonde hair, someone else's glorious hair, hide her face. Until her husband lifted her gently and, with Miss Reed's help, led her away. But just before she reached the door, she turned an anguished face on Rex. "Tell them," she screamed. "You *must* tell them. No one here will listen. Dr. Fensterer's too young and Miss Reed's too jealous. And Dr. Prokosh is too ashamed. He never comes. You *must* tell them. 'Falsely, falsely murdered.'" She stumbled out between her husband and Miss Reed, murmuring broken phrases—". . . a divided duty . . ." ". . . a fury in your words but not the words . . ."—playing out the tag end of her drama on such a small dreary stage that the lines were not worth remembering.

"Not bad. For a matinée performance. From an old has-been," Daphne said. "But I could do much better and I've never been to the Actors Studio. Wanna see?" She stood in front of Rex, opened her eyes wide, and held her breath until the tears began to roll down her cheeks. "Don't forget to put *that* in your story. Front page in the *Daily News*. And say I'd be sensational in *Funny Girl*."

Rex got up and started for his room. Terence, attending to Aeneas, let him go. Beside the coffee urn, the girl, Sandra, was still staring at her own reflection. She lifted her eyes as he passed and, for a moment, he was afraid that she too was about to give him some copy to go with the photographs. But she was looking past him at the clock on the wall. At the door he almost collided with Bigelow, who had just completed an invisible forward pass. "Tell Sandra it's time for her ten-minute break," he whispered. "She'll believe *you*." When Rex told her she turned her head and smiled.

In the hall, he passed a tall man in a black suit and very white cuffs, a quiet man who walked slowly but steadily. His hair lay flat on his head and his clothes were smooth, with no wrinkles or gaps for misapprehension. Dr. Arnold Prokosh, Rex thought, staring, wanting to take him all in, a man who could, without tools or even touch, mend the broken connections of the mind and straighten out the twists. His hands were smooth and white, as if he kept them in surgical gloves, ready always to perform the most delicate incisions. He was walking steadily down the hall, all the way down to the end where paranoia and aggressions and terrifying delusions sat waiting for him in the lounge.

"Good morning," Rex said.

"Good morning." Rex Bannister, Dr. Prokosh thought, recognizing the voice. But he would have recognized the face too, he realized. Scalloped and scored, the face of a martyr with no one to stick in the knife. He nodded and walked on. Rex turned gratefully into his empty room.

On his bed he sat with his face to the wall, a face that had been stamped by "Passport Control" and chipped by impressions all over the world. After two hours in a new country, his skin felt tender. On long assignments he stopped shaving. But he shaved regularly now that he spent his days in Farnsbee South, as if by close and frequent shaves he might present a continually new face to the ward, a protection against the limp wrist and the sudden moan and the minds dripping at the edges. For he was no more reconciled to Farnsbee South than he had been to the rest of the world, a world he had been around so often it might have been his own backyard. He had wandered through it as he pleased, a handsome young man, leaning across the desk in Dar es Salaam and Saigon and Hanoi, with much dark hair and never a hat against the rain. And his jacket always open. Looking now as if he had been dropped, quite suddenly, in the middle of a hospital bed with his shirt buttoned up and his eyes on a blank wall.

It showed him many things, that wall: cups without saucers and shoes without laces and pitchers with broken spouts; trees growing upside down, their branches shading the dead, their bare roots rising to scratch the living; man-sized babies in enormous prams pushed by dwarfs with huge heads and short pants; empty phone booths, their doors closed, their dials whirling; sidewalk displays with real people set out for sale, the price tags pinned to their lips. Sometimes he saw scraps of poetry: "the lonely of heart is withered away," "this scalloped shell of silence," "sea-deep till doomsday morning." Sometimes merely signs: "Members Only," "Fly Eastern," "Shrink Hemorrhoids," "Closed." And the signs on the three lavatories in a Southern airport: "Men," "Women," "Colored." He saw doors slammed, gates shut, windows barred. He saw the women of Haiti sleeping on the stones of the marketplace with their bare feet turned up, growing calluses on their soles. For what else would grow in that rocky soil? And he saw an open palm, lying in a hole, waiting.

He longed for the sight of something pleasant: the islands of Greece with the mountains wading into the sea that summer before he was married, when anticipation still filled his suitcase. But the wings of the Nike were gone and the pillars lay on their sides among the ruins and the peasant women wore black kerchiefs over their mouths because of the dust and the deaths they had known. He tried to picture Audrey as she had looked to him when he first knew her, all "fire and air" wrapped up in a bit of blue sky. But all he could remember now were those selfish unused legs, fat with indulgence, good for nothing but to wear nylons and shift gears. He remembered the shock he had felt when he first saw her in shorts in the brilliant sunlight of Haiti with her legs deadly white as if they'd just been unpacked.

Actually, he remembered her best in hotel beds in the morning, flushed and disheveled, with the sun dammed up behind the curtains, not bothering to comb her hair or even open her eyes when breakfast came, any more than if it had been served by the little fox. They had spent almost the whole first year of their marriage in hotels, going where the news took him, because Audrey could not bear to be left behind. Though Rex came to believe that what she really couldn't bear was marketing and cooking and cleaning house. The hotels took her in and pampered her, offering her constant service and constant company and no responsibilities beyond choosing between the fricassee and the fish. She was the eternal guest, forever on holiday.

"What did you do today?" he would ask when he came back in the evening.

"Nothing much."

He believed her. She was a girl who would always be doing "nothing much." While he did more and more, rushed out earlier in the morning and came back later at night, as if everything would stop if he were not there to "cover it." Like some Recording Angel. As if by reporting the horrors he could, somehow, destroy them. He was obsessed by the need to expose it all, expose what he knew lay everywhere, just below the surface. Or was it, also, that he longed to close the door as soon as possible, for as long as possible, on that dull little story in his own room?

The trip to Haiti had been their only vacation, the only time they had spent a whole day together since their marriage. Rex had spent their honeymoon at the front. Audrey took it very well as soon as he promised to leave her in San Francisco in a room with a view, with French restaurants across the street and elegant shops in the lobby and Alcatraz right in the middle of the bay. As long as he didn't expect her to stay in some horrible dive in Hong Kong or Singapore. Or alone in some dreary little apartment. That was before she realized that there would always be a "front," that she would always be alone in a three-room flat on East Seventy-seventh Street with nothing but Rex's by-line outside the door. Though even an apartment was like a hotel with Audrey. They ate most of their meals out and had the rest sent up, even breakfast: coffee and Danish and cream cheese and jam, served to Audrey in bed by Rex or the delivery boy from Al's. She accepted Rex's coming and going as she accepted the breakfast tray, though she occasionally complained of a stale roll. And Rex would feel his heart pound with anger or pity, he was never sure which, that she expected so much—or so little. She kissed him hello and good-bye and devoured Danish in between. "Tell me. Did you talk to the Rockefellers? Did you see the Queen? Were the Burtons nice? Tell me. Tell me." That and where to have dinner and whether to wear the beige or the blue, her hair up or down. And he, fresh from the sight of bare feet, would be outraged by her mules, so coy beside the bed, so elegantly flimsy, just high heels and a bit of fluff to take her to the dressing table and back. Since Audrey, his fluctuating fits of pity and anger had become more violent: the pity that made him tuck her hand under his arm and the rage that made him want to shake it off again.

"Pity?" Dr. Fensterer had asked quietly.

"Pity," Rex said. It *was* pity, wasn't it—and guilt—that had made him take her, at last, on a vacation? Two weeks of sunshine and a silent typewriter and her husband always beside her. Then why not to Bermuda or Nassau as she had wanted? Why to Haiti, where he knew there would be few tourists in August and no beaches and a dozen stories to report? To make up for that one story he had failed to tell? That one act he had failed to perform? And had, thereby, betrayed Jacques and a whole boatload of people, his good friend Jacques who put him to bed on nights when the moon shook with palsy and the buildings lined up to block his way and a single star began the long descent into his pocket. Jacques had brought him scraps of information too, sneaking down from the Ibo Lilly, defying the soldiers, to stand beside him at the bar of the Villa Franca, dropping news from the side of his mouth. But when Jacques asked for help, Rex put his glass down and wiped his lips.

"But what can *I* do?"

"You are an American. You can persuade the authorities to let us in."

"I'm a journalist. Not the Secretary of State. Or even an ambassador."

"You are an American."

"Hardly even that. Certainly not a good one."

"You at least speak English. You could interpret for us."

"But it's crazy. They'll never let you in. And I couldn't help you. I'd just get thrown out of Haiti forever for trying. And I'd never be able to write another word of how things really are here."

"They make a difference, your stories?"

Rex looked at him. Then shook his head.

"But *this,* this could make a difference."

"But it won't work. And I have no authority, no influence at all. Less than none. I'd fail miserably and they'd only send you back."

"If you fail, nothing will be lost. For us. Sooner or later we will be caught and killed anyway." He stared into his glass for a moment, not looking at Rex. "But either way, my friend, I will not blame you. You, at least, have something to lose."

"All right," Rex said. "I'll come."

But he was frightened. The fate of two hundred people was in his hands. He had never been responsible for anyone else before. Two hundred political refugees without passports or visas or rights of any kind. They were planning to escape in a freighter from Haiti to Puerto Rico, from hell to dry land. Only Rex knew how muddy the land really was, how slimy and full of quicksand, where good men sank to their knees and would never stand upright again.

The night they were to sail, he got roaring drunk. He wandered around the square in front of the President's palace, shouting to Duvalier to come out and explain what had happened to the hundreds of citizens who were picked up by his soldiers regularly and never put down again. "You eat up your children, eh, Papa Doc? Like Cronus, eh? You gnaw them for breakfast and chew them for lunch and swallow them down for dinner, eh, Papa Doc?" When the guard came he was standing with his head between the rails of the palace fence, insisting over and over that it was impossible to sail to Byzantium in a shoe. They locked him up for a few weeks to let him sleep it off. Then they sent him home. A lenient punishment because he was an American or because they did not understand English.

He learned later that the boat with its passengers had been sent back after three days. But he never found out exactly what had happened to the people. For weeks, months, even years, he would wake in the night imagining that boat crammed with refugees, stuffed like rags in the hold, to emerge, one by one, at Port-au-Prince. One by one they would walk down the gangplank to be picked off by the waiting soldiers. Sometimes they were shot but more often they were speared like fish or hoisted by a gigantic hook and dropped, to save burial, into the sea. Sometimes he was one of the passengers waiting to disembark. But whenever his turn came, another refugee would step in front of him to be hooked or shot or speared in his place. And sometimes he was one of the soldiers waiting, with his finger on the trigger, for Rex Bannister to come ashore. But he never did.

He had not gone back to Haiti again. Not until that summer with Audrey.

"Haiti?" she had said. "Why Haiti? No one ever goes there!" Poor Audrey. A nice girl in powder blue with a fox forever at her throat. But she had gone meekly, wanting only to keep the air-conditioning way up and the sun out, to wander through the tourist shops by day and the tourist cafés by night. By the end of the week, Rex felt stifled and walked with his head in a paper bag. "Oh, Rex. Look at that darling pair of sandals. Could we buy them? And that adorable little basket. And those beautiful bowls!" The women sat behind their wares, crosslegged on the ground, waiting for darkness and death and Audrey's decision. But Audrey never noticed them.

"And you never pointed them out?" Dr. Fensterer said softly.

No, he had never pointed them out, had never really let her into his thoughts at all, had merely kept her on his arm. And tried, periodically, by violent extravagant gestures, to shake her off. If she wanted to dance, he danced her until she was exhausted. If she mentioned buying perfume, he would stop suddenly in the middle of the street and dash into the nearest shop and demand it by the pint. If she wanted a rum punch, he made them put half a fruit salad in it while he drank his neat, strumming the table. And then, for a little while, he felt calm again. Until that night, at the end of their stay, when he shook her off forever.

They had just come out of La Gaie Creole, where there had been phony native dancing and fancy foreign tourists. It might have been an act at the Music Hall. Rex's mouth felt dry and he longed for the hotel bar and another drink. But before they reached their car, they were surrounded by a horde of vendors and beggars, hundreds of them it seemed, slipping from the darkness with their hands out, empty hands stretched out under the sun by day and the moon by night; hands that were never filled unless by their own labor. Some of them carried bowls and carvings and hats and baskets.

"We really should take back one of those little wooden statues," Audrey said. "For the mantel." She was wearing a new blue dress and little white gloves and pointing. All over the world, Rex thought, fingers were pointing. "I'll take that and that and that." In Greece the tourists took possession of the ruins and the relics and left the dust and the poverty behind. He put his hand in his pocket as much to stop the shaking as to find his wallet.

"OK," he said. "How many?"

"Not *here*. Not *now*. In one of those shops in town. Tomorrow."

"No," he said. *"Here. Now.* If you want any of those damn 'native products,' you'll damn well get them from the natives. Not from some lousy white bloodsuckers downtown." He was shaking and his head was spinning inside the paper bag.

"Rex, please. Stop shouting. You're attracting the whole crowd."

But Rex kept on shouting. "Now, damn it. Now. And here." He took his fist out of his pocket and offered the men his money. "OK," he told them. "Take what I owe you. The lady wants a little piece of your native life to take home with her. So take what it's worth to you, a little piece of your life, a piece of your soul, your quaint black native soul for the white lady's mantel. Here, take it. Take it all." And he began to fill the open palms. But they kept coming, hemming him in closer and closer. Soon all his money was gone, but still they kept coming, pressing against him with their hands open. He began to give them pieces of his clothing and was about to offer up his arms and legs when the wall closed around him and he too became something on which the moon shone, stretched out on the ground with his palms up.

But when the soldiers came he punched and kicked, shouting

at them, the bastards, to leave him alone. They sent him back to Seventy-seventh Street to rest and relax as the doctor ordered. Audrey went back to her mother in Westchester. But there was no rest for him. He spent the days alone in his apartment with the shades down and the phone disconnected and the newspapers piled up outside his door. And an open bottle at his elbow. He sat at the typewriter in pajamas and trenchcoat, typing up the stories no paper would ever print: of two old black women kept, out of benevolence, in a cage in Mississippi with the knowledge and approval of the entire town and the state welfare commission; of the soldier who went through basic training with a lump as large as an onion on the ball of his foot and spent his leave in a hospital having it removed—so that he died in Vietnam smooth-soled and unblemished; and of that small boat from Port-au-Prince that had attempted to sail to the face of the moon only to be shoved down again to the backside of the earth.

For weeks his only contact with the outside world was the delivery boy from Al's and the eleven-o'clock radio news, taken with his nightcap so that he would not, he told himself, have to drink alone. He carried on a running comment with the newscaster, refuting his facts and impugning his intelligence; calling him a lying bastard and a goddamn toadying son-of-a-bitch, the invective mounting with the disasters and the casualties. And ended by chanting the commercial, along with the announcer, to the tune of "God Bless America."

But one night after he had been home for about two weeks, the commercial changed. For the main news that night was of a protest march to Montgomery, Alabama, led by a Baptist minister named Martin Luther King. And suddenly Rex wanted to be *there,* in Montgomery, Alabama, with the marchers and Martin Luther King. And that night the eleven-o'clock news had a brand-new sponsor and a brand-new announcer, a voice from as far away as the past and as long ago as Haiti. It was the voice of Jacques, speaking from the depths of the sea. "Read Bannister," he said. "His stories not only *are* different. They *make* a difference. Read Bannister. Every day. In the important newspapers of the world. Get your Bannister now." Terrified, Rex rushed from the apartment in his pajamas with the radio still on. He got into his car and drove. Fast. All night.

After that he left the apartment every night, just before the eleven-o'clock news and Jacques' voice announcing that Bannister's stories made a difference. He raced up and down the highways of Jersey and Westchester and Connecticut. All night long he drove, with the traffic rushing along around him; mad humped creatures racing before him, behind him, beside him. Going—where? Why? To do what?

And then one night, forced to sit for hours in a long line of stalled traffic because of a three-car wreck, he found the answer. Waiting patiently, he heard the sirens and saw the flashing red lights and realized, suddenly, why the cars around him had been racing so madly, so continuously, all night. And were now content to stop, merely panting or moaning a bit, waiting to be led back to the paddock and the barn. For the thing they had pursued all night was there, at the head of the lanes with the wrecked cars and the bashed bodies and the sudden violent finish. They had run it to ground. That was why they came down the highways every night, from the cities and the suburbs and the ruts of the countryside. Crazy to start a fire or cause an accident or commit a murder. Rushing to create news for the morning papers. And he understood that it was no longer enough simply to *report* the news. He must somehow *prevent* it. That was what Jacques had been trying to tell him every night on his eleven-o'clock broadcast.

Rex changed his routine. He still left his apartment every night before eleven and drove along the highways leading out of the city. But now he drove slowly, stopping at phone booths along the way to call Washington and Rome and Hanoi. He warned Medgar Evers to beware of his driveway and John Kennedy to stay out of Texas and Malcolm X out of Harlem. He phoned

Rome to demand that the Pope sanction birth control and commanded the mayor of Los Angeles to return the Dodgers to Brooklyn. On and on he drove, dropping twenty-dollar bills into the toll machines for the needy of White Plains and Scarsdale and Greenwich. And in between, he called Audrey. "Don't worry," he told her. "A ceasefire in two days. I guarantee it. Roger." And drove on. But remembered Audrey wasn't worried about Vietnam. He stopped and called again. "No more starving in Haiti, ever. I've fixed it with Papa Doc. Over." He drove on. And realized that Audrey didn't care about the starving anywhere. He stopped again. "Relax," he told her. "Paul isn't going on that sales trip. I've fixed it. I'll deliver him to you, safe and sound, in twenty minutes. Repeat. Twenty minutes." Audrey had hysterics. Her mother called the cops.

In the beginning in Farnsbee South, Rex tried to phone constantly: to Jacques, warning him not to sail, the forecasts were bad; to Duvalier, demanding amnesty for all prisoners; to himself on Seventy-seventh Street, reporting that Rex Bannister was hiding in the hold of the ship, afraid to come ashore.

But the hospital came at him with its pills and its needles and he felt his veins expand and his membranes melt and his will ooze away. He collapsed gratefully at last, flat on his back, face up on the bed, declining the pillow, as if preparing for the grave. And waited for the world to go away. When it refused, he turned over, accepting the pillow but only to bury his chin, resenting it still, this attempt to cushion the night. Until that too passed and he sat up and allowed the weeks to slip over his head, sitting quite still so as not to jostle them lest they return again, bringing back Bloody Monday and Black Tuesday and Ash Wednesday; careful not to bump his fellow patients, ready with their memoirs. For he knew he had been locked up in Farnsbee South to get everyone's life story and would not be allowed out till he did. But he did not want to hear their stories, the tales of twisted cauls and missing genes and coins forever rolling away down the curb. Besides, he had no wish to get out, to suffer the weather and the daily obituaries and the constant intersection of the streets. No, it was better to stay here and be quiet, neither coming nor going, binding nor loosing, speaking nor listening. When possible. Which was very rare. He seized his chance when he could, sneaking back to commune with the wall or to sit next to Sandra, who had no desire to tell him anything.

At bedtime when his roommates returned, he was still watching the wall. They undressed in silence. Hartley, the schoolboy, unable to go to school, unable even to be a boy, capable merely of dragging a crooked path from womb to grave, stood still while Terence helped him to unhook and unbutton and untie. Then he lay down, careful to hide his withered arm beneath the covers. He closed his eyes, with his head toward the bedside table where he stored whatever scraps of food he managed to collect during the day. For he never got enough to eat. The meal was always over and even the dessert cleared away before he was halfway through the main course. He hadn't had dessert since he came, except when he sat next to Bigelow or Garrick. But just before dropping off to sleep he opened his eyes and looked at Rex, who had picked up his paperback Shakespeare. "You like books?" Hartley mumbled. "My mom can bring you real ones. Lots. She sells 'em." He said it proudly, as if bragging about her ability on the trapeze. "Wish she'd bring me food instead." And Rex remembered the large woman who had sat next to him briefly one afternoon during visiting hours, a widow from Springfield, New Jersey. But Hartley was out on a pass.

"I have this book for him," she told Rex. "Usually I come in the evening because of the shop. But today. . . ." Today was the anniversary of her husband's death. So she had closed the store and brought her son an old edition of *Fanny Farmer's Cookbook*. It was the only book in stock remotely suitable. "Sounds awful," she told Rex, "but I wish it was a tea room instead. At least I could eat good and bring him some food and feel decent for a change. Most of those books I'm ashamed to sell." Her husband had taught her that books were a man's best friend. But hardly a lady's. She might as well go live with the hippies in Greenwich Village. They had nothing to say to her, the people in the latest books. What did she care about their problems—adultery and murder and perversions and drugs—she for whom sex was as remote as chicken pox and murder less terrible than the sight of her son's twisted arm, held up at his side as though waiting for someone to take it and lead him away. She could have murdered her husband quite cheerfully for dying so young, for leaving her all alone with Hartley and a stock of dirty books. She spent her life among the perverts of her novels and the patients of a mental ward, and there was no comfort in the cash register.

Once a week she drove to the hospital for Family Meeting. "And what's the point of *that,* I'd like to know? Listening to everyone else when Hartley can hardly talk, not so's anyone can understand him anyway. If I have to listen to that Daphne Kisch or Kitch or whatever one more time, I'll go nuts too. You'd think she'd be ashamed to tell it all right out like that. And her husband too. Fighting in public that way in front of all those strangers and nurses and Dr. Fensterer. And Hartley just sitting there, picking his nose and waiting for refreshments. They want to know will I let them give him shock treatments. How do I know? They say he's not responding and they can't keep him much longer."

She looked at Rex. She was a sturdy woman who kept her tweed coat buttoned up as if to distinguish her from the patients. Rex stared resolutely at his feet, as if by not seeing her he would be absolved from hearing her too. It was not, in any case, he told himself sternly, a story he could use. The pencil in his pocket dug its point into his chest and the pages of the pad seemed to be riffling themselves. But he merely rose and nodded and went for his four-o'clock medication. She had left then, with a sigh, still holding the book, had gone off on her long return ride to New

Jersey without a word of hope from anyone, not even Rex.

"I know your mother," Rex told Hartley. "I met her once during visiting hours."

"Did she bring me anything to eat?"

"Just to read. Sit next to me at meals from now on. I'll help you hang on to your plate."

Hartley smiled and closed his eyes. His mother would be all right. He had left her with hundreds of books full of cops and detectives and agents of all kinds. They would take care of her. And the new patient with the chipped face would take care of *him*. Even better than Bigelow or Garrick. For Garrick kept his eyes on his pad and Bigelow was forever holding his ball. But this new man wore sneakers like a boxer or a basketball player. Hartley turned on his side, content, ready to welcome his favorite dream before falling asleep, a dream in which he lifted his mother's entire stock in two strong arms and dumped it all into the sterilizer in the utility room. Then he locked up the store forever and took her rowing across the Hudson to Palisades Park. She sat facing him in the bow, making huge sandwiches and unwrapping enormous slices of cake. And behind him the ferris wheels and candied apples on their long sticks turned slowly.

Terence put his can on the bedside table. In the morning, Rex thought, the pillow would be soaked. Christ, the poor bastard was literally running at the mouth. By dawn all his juices would be gone. He'd be nothing but a dry shell to be pumped full of liquid again through an ugly little tube, pumped like a tire and sent rolling through the ward for another day. Terence propped himself on one elbow and opened his Catullus.

Only Garrick Troy never seemed to go to bed, a tall gaunt man with a smile like a mouthful of glass. He was always writing. He wrote as other men breathe—to stay alive. He had begun almost from birth, when he had been nearly smothered by his mother, a tiny greedy woman who forced him to share her womb with a twin brother. Garrick had escaped as soon as possible, elbowing Grant, his twin, aside, a desertion which left him feeling guilty for life and upbraided regularly by his mother. "Kicked his little brother out of the way, that's what he did," she would say, a small fierce woman, with a clenched right fist. "And almost killed me in the process." Though Garrick was convinced that he himself would never have survived that dark cramped passage had it not been for a line of iambic pentameter, shouted defiantly at the world on arrival at the top of his infant lungs. He had, as a consequence, dedicated his life to poetry and his younger brother. Nothing else seemed to touch him, only the words that floated down the hall all day and through his head at night, words to form a silver skein to protect his beloved twin. Garrick mailed him his poems in manuscript as soon as they were finished. And wrote all the time to blot out the memory of that small accusing woman, even typing at night on the silent electric typewriter, a gift, he told Rex proudly, from his more worldly brother. And kept his cap pulled down low lest he be mistaken for Grant, who had never in his life seen the inside of a mental institution. Not even to visit his brother. Rex wondered what it was Garrick could possibly be writing in the dark, for he continued to type long after the lights were out. Garrick, as if sensing Rex's gaze, raised his head and gave him one of his rare smiles, lit up by the light from the hall.

Whatever it was he wrote, Rex thought, it would undoubtedly make better reading than Audrey's notes to him. The last had been stuck in the toaster as though waiting to be slipped under a poached egg; a note telling him she'd gone back to Tarrytown and Mother and to please forward her mail and her sheared beaver from the Elite Cleaners. Rex gave her coat to the Salvation Army and threw away her mail—magazines and bills. She received no letters and no appeals. She was on no donors' list. She would go through life without ever being asked to give a penny to anything. He smiled back at Garrick, typing in the dark. Did it matter what keys he hit?

Rex lay for a long time, watching Garrick's fingers and listening to the sounds of the ward: Mrs. Hunnicutt moaning, "'Kill me tomorrow; let me live tonight'"; Joyce intoning her "Hail Marys" and Mrs. Schiller descending silently into the third round of hell. And, just before he fell asleep, he thought he heard Jacques' voice once more, giving the eleven-o'clock news. "Today Rex Bannister, one-time ace journalist, now assigned to Farnsbee South, has failed to file any stories at all. For two weeks. That brings the count of unreported horrors by this reporter alone up to the unprecedented high of. . . ." Rex, stiff and trembling, tried not to listen. The voice stopped abruptly.

"Dr. Prokosh," Terence said. "Christ, someone must have turned the intercom way up by mistake. Or to remind us that he's still there, still listening."

But Rex hardly heard him. It was Jacques' voice, he knew, reminding him once again who he was. "But I'm *not* a reporter," Rex moaned. "Not any more. I'm a patient in a mental ward. Not a reporter. I don't have to file any stories. Not any more." Over and over until Miss Reed arrived with a sedative.

Upstairs in his tower suite, Dr. Prokosh spoke calmly through the intercom to his staff in Farnsbee South, urging greater vigilance. For he detected a certain tension in the atmosphere below. But when he turned the set off, he was aware of a distinct sense of uneasiness. As if he, the Father Confessor, had, by some strange twist, been overheard at his own confession.

CHAPTER THREE

"*How* come Sandra never interacts?" Beverly Ann said in the lounge one morning. "All she does is sit there. Like she was posing all the time. Like she was a model or something."

"Maybe she is," Bigelow said. "She's pretty enough."

"Well, she's no model here."

"Yeah," Daphne said. "That's right. She's no model *here*."

"Just a nut like the rest of us."

"Only prettier," Bigelow said. "Much prettier. And you're just a nut too, don't forget. A jealous nut."

Rex looked across the lounge at Sandra. She was sitting perfectly still but hardly posing. Merely huddled up, clutching an illusion. She reminded Rex of that bunched-up woman at the airport, clutching a cap. Though Sandra was only a model who'd lost her pose, not a mother who'd lost her son. Rex felt a wrench of pity and reached for the pad in his pocket. "Mind if I try a sketch of you?" he said, pulling up a chair. Much easier than writing her story.

She looked up, startled. "Oh," she said. "Oh." Someone to give her a pose at last. But not like the others. For his eyes were wide open, not squinting like the others. As if he wanted to see her whole, not in pieces or lopsided like the others. All her life people had been duplicating her, on canvas and film and, sometimes, even in stone. In the interests of baby food and toilet paper and bras and gin. Or just to fill an empty space. There were so many Sandras, smiling and smoking and emerging from the bath. While the original got dimmer and dimmer. To sit at last in Farnsbee South, gripping the arms of a chair. Someday she would fade away completely. But this man was not like the others. He was smiling and waiting.

"Why would you want to sketch me?" she said.

"Because it would be nice to look at *you* instead of a blank wall. Or somebody's dirty socks."

"Nude or dressed? Full-length or torso? Legs for stockings or head for hair color?"

"You," he said. "Just you. To look at. I like looking at you."

He was looking at her now as if he really did, looking at her face and smiling, not frowning or murmuring grimly "Christ, the chin's all wrong," as if she were something to be corrected or improved. He was not staring at her chin. He was staring at ***her***.

"Don't be selfish, darling," her mother had said. "We're poor, baby. Poor. Mummy's only got two hands so you'll have to lend a hand too." Lend a hand. Lend a leg and a breast and thigh. Lend it all. For Mummy's hands were sticky with clay that never took the right shape, though she had been working it for years. But the clay always hardened too soon, perhaps because of the whiffs of bourbon Mummy blew on it all the time. It was hard being a woman alone, even an attractive talented woman with hair to her waist and a walk designed not merely to get her from here to there but to take all eyes along with her. Her own eyes were large, suggesting limitless tears, and, indeed, she would willingly have wept for a whole neighborhood of women too busy to do it for themselves.

"I don't normally let her pose in the nude," she told Mr. Traeger, "though I realize it pays more." Imagine her in-laws seeing Sandra at the Whitney in *that* condition. For Millicent Carr had deserted the son of a wealthy prosthetics maker (a form of applied art, he had pleaded) to live for Truth and Beauty in the Village, shaping her heart's desire on a potter's wheel with her baby daughter beside the kiln. "But for you, Traeger, darling, I'll make an exception." Her life was riddled with exceptions. And the bourbon was in low supply. "Mr. Traeger is such a gentleman, darling," she told her daughter. "And *such* an artist. Besides, it's your only talent. We must make the most of it. And you'll make such a sweet Bathsheba."

So Sandra learned to sit perfectly still and stare at the afternoon pinned to the wall while people, who were mostly legs beneath an easel, stared at her. She looked at a crack in the ceiling or a hole in the curtain and made her body go stiff while the minutes crawled across the floor. Once, when they forgot to tell her to take a break, she had been unable to move and they had carted her off to the hospital encased in her pose, a rigid Ariel wrapped up in a white sheet.

But after a while, she realized that no one really saw her—only pieces of her. They talked to each other and laughed and joked. She might have been a dish of apples. Only when she moved did they notice her—with surprise and annoyance. She learned not to move, to become a hard shell inside which she sat perfectly still, examining her half-moons. "She's superb," the artists said. But they refrained from intimacies. She was, they felt, merely to be copied. A perfect model. Such a slight pale girl, it was easy for her to sit still. There was so little of her, mostly bone and a mantle of hair and large dark eyes forever in search of something more interesting than her own nails and the back of an easel.

Wherever she went, the pose went with her. The perfect model. But only that. She expected to be stared at. Could tolerate only that. If more was required, she fled, leaving her petrified body behind.

She had barely spoken a word in the ward for almost a month, until Rex asked to do her portrait. It was a question she could understand. And he had smiled when he said it. She allowed him to sketch her face. He kept his pad on his lap so she could look at him and he talked while he worked, asking questions he expected her to answer, so that she forgot to go rigid, forgot she was a model and became just a girl talking to a man at one end of a long room.

"Who's the man who comes to see you?" Rex said, shading the left cheek.

"That's Marcus."

"And who is Marcus?"

"My husband." A respectable young man, an accountant who had never counted on visiting his wife in a psychiatric ward.

"Maybe they'll let you go home to him soon," Rex said.

"Oh, no. I don't want to go home. Ever." She did not smile. She never smiled. The artists had not wanted her smiles. She learned to save them for the ads.

"What's the matter with him?" Rex said.

She shook her head. "Such a nice young man, baby," Mummy had said. "He'll take good care of you." For when she finally gave up clay for a second husband, she had married off Sandra too. What else could she do with her? The second husband was not an artist and just seeing Sandra opposite him at meals, holding her still silent pose, made him feel creepy. "My God," he said, wiping his brow. "It's like eating with the Mona Lisa. Without the smile."

So Mummy invited a serious young man to tea one Sunday and told Sandra to pass him the sugar. He was a CPA with "prospects" and had helped Mummy with her exemptions. In return, she gave him her daughter.

"Won't it be marvelous, darling?" she said. "No more posing. No more worry about whether you *should* eat and whether you *can*. Now you can even move around as much as you like. And get nice and fat."

But Sandra did neither. She did not get fat because meals were a torment. In her mother's house, where they were mostly skipped, she had never learned to cook. But Marcus, she felt sure, expected something more than cheese and wine and slugs of bourbon. Such a big man with a giant-sized bottle of mouthwash always in the medicine chest. Just seeing the arms of his chair with all that empty space between them, waiting at the head of the table, made her want to cry. And how could she possibly move around when she had no idea in which direction to go?

But he was a patient man. "You'll mold her, Marcus," Mummy had promised. Was that what he anticipated, someone he could put together like the figures of his columns to add up to his expectations? But after a week he realized that, far from being malleable, she was already petrified. "A perfect little Ingres," her mother had said. Good only, she might have added, to take to parties for public viewing.

"She should be on a pedestal in the Louvre," someone said. "An exquisite little Psyche. But how do you get her home?"

"In a taxi, of course," Marcus said proudly. Not everyone could boast his own private little Psyche.

But she was afraid of him. When he sat at the desk in the evening, his shoulders were so square and his neck so thick. And there was no redress from his straight columns in which the zeros were perfect circles and the ones inflexible. So for her too there was no respite, no "break." She sat behind him on the couch with an open book, tormented by his rigid back, feeling slack and soft with no hard shell to protect her any more. Her half-moons were floating away. For what pose did he wish her to take?

"She is very young," her mother had said. "And has had a demanding career. In which, you know, she rose to the top in no time at all. A mere skip and a jump. A remarkable child. But has had no time to find herself."

"I'll find her," he promised. But how could he when he hardly ever looked? Sometimes, sitting opposite her at dinner, he took off his glasses. But his pale blue eyes, so big without the glasses, were like drops of ink. How could they see her? They could only blot her out. And if they *did* look, it was not even for the purpose of duplicating her, of transferring her to paint or clay or stone, but simply to shatter her, like the numbers, into workable parts. "I have no patience with improper fractions," she imagined him saying. "They must be reduced." So she sat slack and oozing on the couch. I am disappearing, she thought. Soon there would be nothing but the soggy pillows and a slight puddle on the floor. Only in bed at night did she go rigid.

She went back to modeling.

When he found out he took off his glasses and obliterated her. "Now that you are my wife," he said. But she did not know what it meant to be his wife. Except, perhaps, to be silent and still but with no one to give her a pose.

One day she closed all the kitchen windows and turned on the oven and lay down on the floor. And waited. Death would give her a pose. The final pose. But they carried her out and melted her down and when she awoke she was a mere glob again, covered by blankets and an added layer of shame. She stared at the ceiling and went stiff.

"I like it here," she told Rex.

My God, he thought.

"Except when Marcus comes."

"Have you told Dr. Prokosh?"

"No. Just Dr. Fensterer. He says I must adjust. It's part of my cure."

Like Leda adjusting to the swan. "You must tell Dr. Prokosh," Rex said.

The other patients were crowding around now, examining the sketch. "Not bad," Bigelow, the football player, said. "Only she's prettier than that. Much prettier." Nothing about the bone structure or the chin. Just "pretty." Miss Reed smiled in agreement. She had been young and pretty once too, but it had not served to soften the space she filled. She wore starched uniforms and walked with her back very straight. Around her the air seemed rigid. Even Beverly Ann raised a respectful eyebrow when she learned that Sandra was a professional model. "And me thinking she was a nursery-school teacher. Who didn't know anything but baby talk."

Rex tore off the sketch and handed it to Sandra. "For you," he said. "Not for perfume or beer or Pan Am or sprays. Just for you. To remember me by." Which was not, he thought, what Sandra needed to remember.

After that, Bigelow sat next to her at meals and meetings and Beverly Ann borrowed her lipstick and Joyce brushed her hair. Even Hartley paid homage, leaving bits of doughnuts and cookies on her bed. She began to enjoy her life in the ward except for visiting hours, when Marcus came and sat beside her. Then she went stiff, not posed but simply freezing into any position. Marcus never looked at her. They sat side by side, staring straight ahead like two strangers on a subway. She waited, patiently, for him to get off. As soon as he left she went to her room and looked at Rex's sketch of her. It was the only picture of herself she had ever really seen.

At Group Therapy they took their usual places: Bigelow next to Sandra and Daphne next to Beverly Ann. Dr. Fensterer sat at one end of the long table and Mrs. Schiller, as though poised for flight, sat at the other, near the door. Verna, her thin black body tense, sat near the window, away from the group, listening no doubt to the Lord. As He had commanded. Which she did, remaining steadily at her post at one end of the couch with her eyes fixed on one corner of the ceiling. As if the Lord were perched on the molding, whispering endlessly into her ear. Every now and then she would raise her right hand and make a sign with two fingers, a silent and secret assent. She had given her name as Hagar, handmaid of the Lord. And kept her children locked up.

Garrick, beside Rex, had his ski cap pulled down and his pad on his lap. He was writing with his left hand. For his right had been paralyzed ever since Verna arrived. Though he avoided looking at her, he was always aware of her, small and tense, raising her right hand periodically and reading his poems, he knew, before he ever wrote them down. Though her eyes were fixed on the Lord.

"I don't see why in hell Garrick's allowed to go on writing all through Group Therapy," Beverly Ann said. "I'm going to get my manicure set right now." She got up.

"Sit down," Dr. Fensterer said. And sighed. "All right, Garrick, let's have your pad till the session's over." Garrick, who had heard nothing, went on writing until Daphne poked him. He looked up, bewildered, then passed his pad down the table. Rex, beside him, saw his head sink on his chest and his arms go slack at his sides. Rex's own pad was there, useless, in his breast pocket. He took it out surreptitiously and laid it on Garrick's lap. Garrick raised his head and smiled his slow jagged smile.

"And Cover Girl Sandra Mishkin," Beverly Ann said. "Still not talking."

"Just posing," Daphne said. "Like she thinks she's still a model."

They could not know that though Sandra was still quiet, she was not posing. She was listening. The day Rex had given her his sketch, she had pinned her long hair up into a large topknot, flat as a disk, which revolved slowly to the words: "I like it here. I like it here."

"Shut up, Beverly Ann," Bigelow said. "She'll talk when she's ready. A lot sooner if you stop bullying her." He clenched his fist. "You're too damned timid, Sandra. That's what it is. Assert yourself. Stop letting everyone walk all over you."

"Well, I'll be damned. Superman running for a touchdown. Only now he's carrying a torch instead of a football."

Bigelow blushed. He was tall with a full pink face but there were other things he wanted to carry beside a football. The football had, in fact, carried *him*. Right into Yale, where Father wanted him to go. He played brilliantly but would have preferred to sit in the stands with a girl eating hot dogs, watching her chew, not caring who had the ball.

"You'll never get into a decent college any other way," Father had warned. "And I'm not paying to send my son to any half-assed institution. It's Ivy League or nothing, boy, so get your arms around that ball and keep them there." Which Bigelow did only to discover, on Saturday afternoon, that that was absolutely all he had to hold on to. On the field his body behaved, taking him through the walls of flesh, past whirling arms and legs and around the ends. On the field the ball was a dream to be pursued and caught and carried across the goal. In the shower he felt spent, could barely lift his arms, felt dazed and empty as if it had been his own heart they had been tossing around the field. During the week he wandered through classes and down corridors, carrying books he did not understand.

"I'd like to be a farmer," he told Sandra. "Raise cows and chickens and big fat dirty hogs. And lots of kids. Work in the fields all day and go home sweaty and dog-tired and wash up and put on a clean shirt for supper. Weekends I'd lie on my back in the grass and take the kids fishing on Saturday afternoon and my wife to town on Saturday night." Driving back it would be dark and peaceful, with her head on his shoulder and nothing but the moon and the stars through the windshield. In the ward he walked slowly, with his shoulders sagging and his empty arms hanging down as if they were too heavy for him. Except for practice periods, when he carried his invisible ball.

"What happened?" Sandra said. "How did you get here?"

"I ran. All the way."

It had been the last game of the season, an easy game. In the lockers during the half, they spoke of papers due and skiing weekends and exams coming up. There would be no more practice, no more Saturday afternoons. He would wander through the week carrying three books from one room to another with no goal posts in sight.

For the rest of that game he played brilliantly, in a daze. He heard nothing but the signals, saw nothing but the ball—and the minutes on the board. For when zero appeared, he too would be reduced to nothing. In the last ten seconds of the game he caught the ball and ran. He ran thirty yards down the field and over the goal line. And kept on running. Through the exit and out of the bowl and across the park and on into town. On and on he ran, carrying the ball into the middle of the city, carrying it for God, for Father, and for Yale. Carrying it like his own heart in his hand, carrying it he knew not where or why, only that he could not give it up and he could not stop running. When they caught him at last, his hand was rigid. They had to drug him to get the ball. But they had given him nothing else to carry instead.

"Maybe you *can* be a farmer," Sandra had said. "When you get out of here." It would be nice to live with fields and grass and a bolster of hills at her back. He was staring at her as if trying to imagine her in a cotton dress with bare feet, scrubbing the family wash in a big tub beneath the trees.

"He's right," Rex said now. "Stop bullying people, Beverly Ann."

"And you stop trying to shut me up, for God's sake. We're supposed to *express* ourselves here, aren't we, Dr. Fensterer? This isn't a shitty little Cub Scout meeting, for crying out loud. Is it, Dr. Fensterer?"

At the far end of the table Dr. Fensterer rubbed his cheek and waited for twelve o'clock. There were times when he longed for the peace and quiet of orthodox analysis, with *one* patient on the couch and himself in an easy chair out of sight and in control. In fact, there were times when he wished he had followed his initial impulse and concentrated on rocks. He was still very young and still spent his time off examining the igneous intrusions of the surrounding countryside. But rocks, he knew, had no need of him.

So he had devoted his life to people instead. But the intrusions that split his patients' minds still bewildered him. He must check on the medication for Beverly Ann. She was getting terribly high.

"All right," Dr. Fensterer said. "All right."

"All right nothing," Bigelow said. "I thought this place was supposed to be so great. Everybody so friendly and free coffee and Coke and lots of help with your problems. But Christ. . . ." He stood up.

"And right now we're supposed to be helping Sandra," Rex said. "So sit down."

Bigelow sat down. But Beverly Ann continued to shout. "She's not making any progress. She's not even trying. She hasn't said one damn thing at Group Therapy or Family Meeting since she came. She just sits there. Like now. Like she's too good for us. My father's paying good money for this rotten. . . ."

"Oh, shut up, Beverly Ann," Joyce said, taking her hands out of her sleeves. "If you're sexually frustrated, say so. Don't keep taking it out on us." She crossed herself and slid her hands back up her sleeves. She had been a nun for over a year, a girl for whom "sex" was merely a word on an application form. But she did what she could, since coming to Farnsbee South, to justify her nightly penance, forcing herself to commit—by word or deed or even thought—at least one venial sin a day for the pleasure of lying spread-eagled on the floor of her room beneath the arms of the crucifix. Besides, in Farnsbee South she was not really herself, only Joyce Gambardella, who could type one hundred words a minute and cut a clean stencil. Her real self, Sister Mary Joseph, was still at St. Ursula's polishing the candlesticks and sweeping between the pews, a strong eager girl ready to dust mountains and burnish the sun if need be. She lowered her chin over her sleeves and smiled at Sandra. But Sandra was sitting perfectly still, listening to the disk on the top of her head.

"See what I mean?" Beverly Ann screamed. "You call *that* participating?"

"Looks more like posing to me," Daphne said.

"It's twelve o'clock," Dr. Fensterer said, barely repressing the "Thank God." He stood up, said "Good morning," and hurried out.

The others stood up. "Thanks," Garrick said, returning Rex's pad. "I've included a sonnet for you." Rex glanced at the tiny illegible scrawl, fourteen lines of it. But whether it said something beautiful or nothing at all he could not tell. He slipped it into his pocket.

In the dining room the patients ate mashed potatoes, a constant staple, as if the diet kitchen hoped to keep them permanently sealed up. But the cracks kept opening, allowing memories and complaints to spill out and mingle with last night's gravy. The sight of it made Rex's eyes whirl and his brain swell, pressing against his skull. He longed for the peace and quiet of an empty room with the world reduced to images on a salmon-colored wall. But Miss Reed stopped him at the door. He must join the others, stay with the others, interact with the others. Suffer and hallucinate and despair with the others. Across the room Terence, sitting alone, raised his can to Rex in a mock toast. The others sat around small tables. Mrs. Hunnicutt, pushing her food away petulantly, complained that it was worse than the mess she got on tour. Rex sat down between Hartley and Mrs. Schiller. Opposite, Joyce laid down her knife and fork in the form of a cross on her plate and put her hands up her sleeves.

"You really a reporter?" she said. "For what?"

"Free-lance," Rex said. "Used to be."

"No such thing. That's just what they try to make you believe here. Like me. Telling me I "used to be" a nun. Well, they're crazy wrong. I *am* a nun. I'll always be a nun. Only not at St. Ursula's."

She had not lasted terribly long at St. Ursula's. A bouncy country girl, she had entered the convent joyfully, ready to weed vegetables or polish woodwork or scrub floors for her Lord. She could kneel for hours, exulting in the gloom and the silence, with the candles flaring up to where He hung, compassionate and forgiving, as Mr. Looney at the typing pool never was. Scolding her so harshly that the other girls raised their black-rimmed eyes and tittered; girls who never noticed the grass or wondered what lay hidden in the folds of the hills. She had loved the meals at long wooden tables where the nuns ate with a careful silent grace to the rhythm of St. John the Divine. Not like her colleagues at Looney's, who crowded the tables at *Gigs* and shouted and grabbed for the ketchup. Poverty, chastity, obedience, these she had embraced cheerfully. She did not need money or sex or the freedom of the Looney Type-Rite Service. The mountains were hers, patient and dependable, flinging their cloaks down to the very chapel walls. She was free to examine the breadth of her soul instead of the width of a page. And the dittoed arches of the nave.

Only the silence had been a problem. She had, time after time, burst into song while scrubbing the chapel, had exclaimed too exuberantly at lunch at the soup like a ladle of sun in her bowl, had thanked a sister too profusely for reminding her that matins were over or her wimple too loose. Poor Joyce even talked in her sleep. And Sister Mary Joseph could not break the habit. In the end, they had been firm. Her spirit was too ebullient, could not be confined by the starched coif and the heavy robes. He who had suffered beyond the limits of pain could not stand so much effervescence. "We require that you find happiness through control and discipline and submission," the Mother Superior had said, an old woman with her soul so perfectly at rest it might have been a kitten curled up in her lap, content to see nothing beyond the folds of her black habit. "But of course," she added, "that is not for everyone." And stroked the edges of her thighs.

That night Joyce went to the chapel for the last time and gazed up at Him, hanging there in lonely silent agony. But His eyes, she realized now, were not on her. They were turned up and away. He had not, it seemed, suffered for *her*. He was actually sterner, more inflexible even, than Mr. Looney, who deducted the torn stencils and wasted envelopes from her paycheck. But *He* was ordering her out, out of His house and back to the typewriters and the carbons and the tyranny of the BMT.

She knelt before the altar for a long time but she could not pray. Instead, she watched the candles until their points seemed to grow longer and longer, burning their way up through the darkness. At last she got up and, standing on tiptoe, thrust her tongue into the flame.

"So you see, I'm not crazy at all," she told Mrs. Schiller, who was sitting back, shaking her head. "I don't know why they sent me here. I could have managed so well in the convent without a tongue."

Mrs. Schiller reached out and patted her hand. *"Armes Kind,"* she said.

"And there's nothing worth talking about here, is there? Just fighting with Beverly Ann and trying to explain to Dr. Fensterer why I don't want my family to know where I am. They think I'm still at the convent." She paused and stared at the cold hard lumps of potatoes. But what she saw were the mountains looking over the convent wall at Sister Mary Joseph shelling peas in the garden. "And I really am too. That's why I must keep doing my offices and practicing silence. But it's even harder here." Where silence was considered a felony and Beverly Ann was a constant temptation. She sighed.

Mrs. Schiller patted her hand again. *"Doch, doch.* But you are young. You can make a new life."

Joyce turned and looked at her. She was terribly old, and so thin on top, as though her bosom had fallen into her lap. "I'm twenty-three," she said. "What new life? I can be a typist or a nun. And they won't let me be a nun." She crossed herself, put her hands back up her sleeves, and bent her head over her mashed potatoes.

My God, Rex thought. My God. Why not let her be a nun?

Why not let her pray for us sinners now and at the hour of our death? Instead of shoving her into a mental ward and back into a typing pool to duplicate trivia. He cut up his meat and pushed his plate toward Hartley. He looked around and saw Bigelow, a frustrated farmer forced to carry the ball for the entertainment of Saturday crowds instead of a hoe for his own salvation. He saw Beverly Ann, a schoolgirl by law and a tramp by nature, with a father who tried to keep her in line like one of his used cars, waiting to be resold. Across the room Terence raised his can again, to what? To him, Rex Bannister, forever angry with the world, a would-be reformer reduced to a mere reporter and now nothing at all but a chemical imbalance? But Rex found himself wondering about Terence.

"Tell Orin to bring me a filet mignon from Sardi's," Mrs. Hunnicutt moaned. "I can't do a matinée on this slop."

"You're doing pretty well as it is," Beverly Ann said. "Besides, I thought a real trouper could do it on spotlights and greasepaint."

"Na, leave her alone," Mrs. Schiller said.

There was a sudden silence as Dr. Fensterer walked into the room. "I have an announcement to make," he said quietly.

"Storm warnings," someone muttered.

"It has been reported," Dr. Fensterer went on, "that one of the visitors has been bringing marijuana into the ward. That is, of course, strictly forbidden. He has been permanently banned from the hospital."

"Ban you," shouted Beverly Ann, jumping up. "And stuff you too. If Norm isn't let back in here, I'll tear the joint apart. I'll tell my father. I'll tell the mayor. I'll tell Prokosh. And I'll get you fired so fast you'll wish you were on the longest trip of your life. I'll. . . ." She was standing up, leaning across the table and shouting. Suddenly, she spat into Dr. Fensterer's face. Two nurses hurried up and led her away.

"That means, I'm afraid," Dr. Fensterer said, wiping his cheek, "that all passes are canceled, as usual."

"But I have a job interview tomorrow," Terence said. He was standing now, clutching his can.

"I'm sorry," Dr. Fensterer said. "But you know the rules." He sighed and left the room.

"Christ, what *are* the rules?" Rex said.

"Just that," Terence said. "For certain infractions all passes are automatically canceled. For the entire community. Everyone. I've missed two job interviews already this month."

"And I haven't been to mass in weeks," Joyce said.

"I have a performance to give," Mrs. Hunnicutt said. "David Merrick will hear about this."

"What about Prokosh?" Rex said. "Does he know?"

"I'm sure he doesn't," Joyce said. "I *know* he wouldn't allow it."

Rex walked slowly back to his room. Evidently there were certain things that needed to be reported. Certain things Prokosh didn't know: that Sandra was afraid of her husband and Mrs. Schiller was being pushed down further and further into her Inferno; and that Terence would not put down his can except for a Latin book. Rex sat down slowly on the edge of his bed but this time he did not stare at the wall. Instead he took out his notebook and fingered the pages. Then he bent his head and began to write.

That night he lay with his sedative under his tongue and his eyes open for a long time. He heard the springs of a bed next door and knew that Bigelow had flung his arms up ready for a forward pass. Occasionally, Mr. Nuffield passed the door in his pajamas with his invisible pack on his back. And across the hall Rex heard Joyce get up and saw the flicker of a candle. And he knew that Sister Mary Joseph was kneeling before a glorious golden altar with flaming wings that lifted her high above the walls of Farnsbee South. To where her Lord was waiting with His eyes turned, at last, on her.

Down the hall, behind the desk at the nurses' station, Dr.

Sourette sat alone writing. At midnight he lifted his head and made a cross on the desk calendar.

In her room in the nurses' home, Miss Catherine Reed looked up from the pages of *The Queen's Necklace* and was reminded of Alicia Hunnicutt. For Miss Reed thought of her patients often —even off duty. Sometimes she even envied them. Especially Mrs. Hunnicutt, who had several necklaces and several names and several kinds of hair. She was a difficult patient in spite of three husbands and an exciting career. Miss Reed, who for fifty years had had only one name and one role, whose whole world had been one room and the halls of an institution, put her feet up and sighed. She had never worn anyone else's hair or spoken anyone else's lines. No illusions ever invaded her stiff white cap. Supported by a starched uniform, she had never broken down. But looking around her room now, these thoughts gave her no comfort. It was a small room in which she was stored each night like a hat in a box, kept fresh and ready for use the next day. But her brim was getting frayed. She closed her book and lay down between the sheets. She kept her reading light on for a long time, staring at the shadows on the wall.

Upstairs in the tower suite, Dr. Arnold Prokosh felt the tension begin to rise and imagined his patients chewing up the days of the week. To spit the pieces, eventually, all over him.

CHAPTER FOUR

Outside it was Halloween and Indian summer and the sanitation workers' strike. But in the ward it was almost always after lunch, with the walls holding up the long afternoon. Miss Reed's cap kept its precarious poise and Dr. Sourette maintained a patina of brown between him and the ward and the wind that blew off the river. Except that the tip of his nose felt exposed. Dr. Prokosh remained secluded, exhaling remotely, invisibly, over the ward. Rex felt the doctor's cool breath on his cheek.

Some of the old patients left and a few new ones arrived, jostling the others, pitching them closer to the edge. The junior from Hunter was taken away, still convinced of her need for a heart transplant, leaving fifty-two begging letters beneath her bed. Rex wondered if she would find a new heart at the County Center. Benson came, a slim blind black boy who had seen nothing but the inside of his own skull since birth. He sat at one end of the couch with his eyes closed. There was, Rex reminded himself, no reason for him to open them. Occasionally he nodded or smiled. How had he learned to smile? Rex wondered. And at what? What are the hallucinations of the congenitally blind? Out of what materials do they create their dreams, men who inhabit their bodies as a tramp inhabits a park bench, stretched out in the dark so that all he knows of it is its texture and shape and the ache in his bones? Beside him, Verna sat listening to the Lord, lifting her hand occasionally with the two raised fingers, that silent secret message to Him straddling the planets and perched on a corner of the ceiling. She did not even talk to Benson, who sometimes carried on conversations with his own private visitors—Nat Turner and Emperor Jones and Marcus Garvey—agreeing with a piece of the wall, frowning at a section of air.

"Make him stop that," Daphne screamed. "He's driving us all batty." Jealous of a blind boy's visions. But Rex stared at Benson in fascination, aware, sadly, that he could not stare back. Eternally exposed, he merely sat there with a white stick between his legs, a stick he rarely used, as if he could smell the chairs and tables, or hear them. If so, he hardly seemed to hear much else. Even what happened right under his nose.

"Let's see if he's *really* blind," Clay, a freshman from the University of Miami, said. He was a tall restless boy in white shorts and a straw hat. He carried a tan and a Southern accent and a tennis ball, which he bounced steadily. He bounced it under Benson's nose. But Benson sat with his chin raised and his eyes closed, unblinking. Yet he knew when to remind Rex to take his medication and where Beverly Ann had hidden Mrs. Schiller's Dante. "Give it back," he would say gently.

"How come you know so much?" Beverly Ann demanded. "You're supposed to be *blind*. How come you know all that without seeing? You a phony or something? You putting us on?"

"I see," Benson said softly. "But not as others see. They see only the corporeal, the physical. But I see the spirit, the essence.

The real you. I see you crouched down in one little corner of your body because you are afraid to live in the whole house. Only in one dark section of it. And you are always ready to pounce, with long nails and a long neck and black hair thick on your forehead. Because you are the spiritual descendant of the Whore of Alexandria, who enjoyed sticking gold pins into her slave girls' breasts."

"Jesus God," Beverly Ann shouted. "Who you calling a whore? Maybe I oughtta stick a few pins in you." She reached out and scratched Benson's left cheek, leaving a long red smear.

"Your soul is a cluster of thorns," Benson continued softly, "and your heart is a stagnant well."

"And you shut up," Beverly Ann screamed. "You goddamn well shut up." She reached for him again but Rex jumped up and caught her hands. Benson sat perfectly still, waiting for the next attack. Until Miss Reed and a student nurse took Beverly Ann away and Dr. Sourette came to examine Benson's wound. Rex felt the sting on his own cheek. Interacting evidently meant preventing one nut from cracking open another. My God, he wanted none of it, preferred the wall with its past and silent horrors.

"You must begin to go out," Dr. Fensterer told him. "It's time you put in for a pass."

"No," Rex said. Beneath the hospital the streets lay like snakes, waiting to bite.

One day Benson discovered the piano in the therapy room. After that he played it constantly, but always the same thing over and over, a slice of Rachmaninoff's Second Piano Concerto, until the opening chords seemed like some dire prediction to the residents of Farnsbee South. As soon as it began, Rex felt his skin tighten and his body became a drum upon which Benson beat unmercifully. And Rex would remember the rolling of the drums in the prison yard in Port-au-Prince just before an execution. He would dash to his room and curl up on his bed with his arms over his ears. The other patients groaned or jeered and yelled at Benson to change the record. Only Mrs. Hunnicutt, moaning to shut off those damned sound effects, seemed really upset.

But Miss Wanda, who arrived soon after Benson, terrified them all. An enormous fierce-eyed woman with her red hair on fire, she wandered through the ward and out to the elevators in search of her kidnaped child. "Do you know who took my baby?" she would ask each patient in turn. "I left her on the counter for just a moment while sorting my change. I think they must have sold her again for new. She was hardly used at all. Completely undamaged, in fact. I'm offering a reward for information." She patted the little muslin bag that hung from her wrist. It was full of jacks and pacifiers and gumdrops and shells.

"We don't know anything about your baby, dear," Joyce said. "Why don't you ask *Him,* the Good Shepherd? He'll find your lamb if only you'll ask."

Miss Wanda shook her head sadly. "She's not a lamb, you see. Only two feet and no wool at all." She turned to Beverly Ann. "You'll tell me where they hid my baby, won't you? Everyone else pretends I never had a baby. But you'll tell me the truth, won't you? You have such pretty frontal lobes. Just like my baby. They wanted to cut hers out but I wouldn't let them. That's why they stole her. To cut out her frontal lobes. But you'll tell me where I can find her, won't you?"

"Sure," Beverly Ann said, looking up from her bridge hand. "Try under her bed." She pointed to Mrs. Schiller lost in the *Inferno* across the room. "Third door on the left. Her bed's next to the window. She hides everything there."

Mrs. Schiller raised her head. *"Ach,* no," she said. "It's not true. Why would I do such a thing? She only persecutes me like always." She looked at Rex across the room. "Cannot you help me, please? Tell your paper it should make an investigation. She is a Nazi spy, that one. She sends reports out twice a week. I've seen her. Through her boyfriend. The one with the paper bags. Why always so many paper bags, please?"

"C'mon, I'll show you," Beverly Ann said, laying down her cards. "I've just made a grand slam anyway." She jumped up and led Miss Wanda down the hall. Mrs. Schiller began to cry.

Rex, unwilling to move, unwilling to do a thing but go on reading Shakespeare's *Tragedies,* read on: "Bless thy sweet eyes, they bleed," he read. And closed his book on Gloucester's bleeding eyes. "Come on, Elsa," he said. "Let's go sit on the balcony for a while. I'll fix it with Miss Reed."

He led her outside and lit her cigarette and blew smoke rings at the full moon peering up behind one corner of the pediatrics wing. But Mrs. Schiller had no use for the moon, the placid selfish moon with its face round and fat as Frau Mendel's, who had sat out the Nazi regime at her third-story window, her bosom resting on her folded arms and her face bent to whatever passed in the street below. She had barely moved even to avoid being spattered by Mrs. Schiller's brother, Rheinhold, who had jumped out of the fifth-floor window at 8:36 P.M. after eating an enormous dinner and kissing his wife good-bye. "Do you think he needed to feel full of something?" Mrs. Schiller asked Rex. "Or just to make sure he dropped quickly?" For Rheinhold was a painter and quite possibly not up on Galileo's law. Like Mrs. Schiller, who on the anniversary of her husband's death had cooked and eaten a huge helping of boiled beef and horseradish, Theo's favorite, and doped herself in the bathtub. She had, out of consideration and a sense of dignity, bought a bathing suit for the occasion. She should be lying beside Theo right now, explaining that she *had* to come, that Frau Schiller and Gerda had each other while he, Theo, had no one. But Gerda had, for the only time in her life, cut an evening class in favor of an early bath.

Rex shook his head silently and went on observing the moon. But Mrs. Schiller turned her chair from that pale, staring, prying face, forever watching, forever following her about. Even here, at the hospital, she was not safe. "The moon is a spy," she whispered. It was always there, like the Gestapo. Above her house, outside her window. And now it had followed her to Farnsbee South, telling the nurses and Dr. Fensterer and the terrible teen-agers where she was. And if she were to escape now, jump the balcony and run home, it would follow her down the streets, a silent siren screaming across the sky. She gripped the arms of her chair more tightly. Rex leaned forward and patted her hand.

"It's all right, you know," he said. "And you're all right. You're in good hands. The best. Dr. Arnold Prokosh and the staff of Farnsbee South. Like having Picasso paint your kitchen. So just be patient and let yourself be a patient for a while. They'll fix you up. And some morning when you sit down to breakfast, the fried egg on your plate will be just that. Just a fried egg. Not an open staring eye with fuzzy edges, watching you."

Mrs. Schiller smiled. Someone else, at last, understood the terrors that lay waiting for her each morning. Her hands relaxed and she began to rock back and forth gently beside Rex while the moon rose slowly, harmless and shiny as Theo's watch case, covering up the fact that, once again, she had misjudged the time.

Of course she'll be all right, Rex thought. Dr. Prokosh will fix her up. Rex was sure he would fix them all up. But where was he, their doctor, their leader, their savior? Holed up in the moon, waiting for the astronauts to arrive? But who would rescue *him,* Rex Bannister, holed up in Farnsbee South, a reporter with no specific assignment but a whole ward full of stories to file? Mrs. Schiller's, for one. How else could she dump that hideous load, that unusable past with its claws still stuck in her back? She turned to him now and smiled again and offered to lend him her Dante.

Walking back to the solarium, Rex met Dr. Prokosh. One of the doctor's rare trips to earth, Rex thought, as if he knew Rex needed to see him. About Mrs. Schiller.

"Could I come and talk to you for a minute?" Rex said, taking his notebook out of his pocket.

Dr. Prokosh smiled faintly. "Of course. Though not for an

interview, I hope. I am always available to my patients. But off the record."

"Now?" Rex said. Dr. Prokosh removed his smile. To save it for another occasion, no doubt. There were so many demands on his smile. And his time.

"Ah, I'm afraid that's impossible," Dr. Prokosh said. "Right now I'm on my way to a staff meeting. Tomorrow, perhaps? Make an appointment with Miss Reed."

Rex put his notebook back in his breast pocket and stepped aside for the mentally sound. We who are sick salute you, he thought. But for us tomorrow is too many nightmares away. Besides, Dr. Prokosh's pockets were flat. He had no need of Rex's notes. They would only spoil the hip line.

In the solarium he heard the piano and Rachmaninoff's opening chords.

"That's enough," Mrs. Hunnicutt shouted hoarsely. "That's all that's necessary. Just those solemn opening bars. Just for the curtain to rise." But the piano continued to play and Rex wondered, as he had before, whether Benson was deaf as well as blind. Or was he listening only to the voices inside his own head?

"That Moor will be the death of me yet," Mrs. Hunnicutt moaned, hurrying, white-faced, to her room. Her husband walked close behind her, carrying her makeup kit and her script and her third-act wig. And behind him Miss Reed carried the sedative and an enormous supply of unused sympathy. Even after twenty years. The sedative was for Mrs. Hunnicutt but the sympathy was for her husband in his tan suit, carrying his wife's extra wig as if he held her head in his arms.

Dr. Sourette hurried by and turned into the therapy room. The piano stopped abruptly. Does Benson know he's black? Rex wondered. And that Sourette is? And what could that possibly mean to him? To be black in a country of perpetual darkness. Where, eventually, his hearing would fade and his touch grow blunt and he would be completely corked up inside himself. Like Rex in Farnsbee South.

"Time you started getting out a bit," Dr. Fensterer told him again. "Otherwise, it will get harder and harder."

"I'm not ready yet," Rex said.

"You never will be until you're ready to stick your neck out. Even in the ward you need to get involved more. Interact."

"I'm here to get uninvolved," Rex said. "I've been overinvolved all my life. That's why I'm here. Detachment is what's indicated now."

"And balance, perhaps," Dr. Fensterer said. "The medication should help. But you'll have to cooperate too. Try for moderation. Try to avoid overreacting. At either extreme. In which case you should be able to function quite normally again."

I shall function best as a corpse, Rex thought. When I no longer react even to a worm yanked from my grave. Or to the sound of someone else dumped down beside me, not caring who lies on my right through eternity. Insensitive at last, with my eyes at rest in their sockets and my ears folded over. And my glands perfectly still.

"Do you know how they bury dead people?" Joyce had asked him one day at lunch. "They just cover up the front. That's only *half* a suit or dress you're seeing. Seems awful, somehow, burying them half-naked like that, doesn't it? Even if it *is* more economical. And, of course, it's not as if anyone will ever see their bottoms again. But I keep thinking of Mr. Einbinder at the secretarial school. He looked so nice all laid out in his tuxedo with his Kiwanis pin on his lapel and his nails so pink and more hair than he ever had before. But now all I can think of is how he'd look from behind. And my grandfather and my aunt and even Father Ferruggi. Spoils it all, somehow, doesn't it? I wish Beverly Ann'd never told me." Her own death, Rex knew, was ruined forever for her now, haunted as she was by the thought of meeting her Maker with her buttocks bare. What gland, he wanted to ask Dr. Fensterer, was responsible for *that* obsession?

But Dr. Fensterer was a busy man. He stood up.

So am I, Rex thought, standing up too.

"I want you to apply for a pass," Dr. Fensterer said.

"No."

"If you're afraid of walking the streets, just go to dinner with your wife."

"No. She's hardly my wife anymore."

Dr. Fensterer sighed, remembering Rosalie, his fiancée, a girl with an enormous watch always strapped to her wrist, forever waiting for him under a clock. She was waiting for him right now, he knew, under some damn clock: the Biltmore, the Commodore, even as far up as the Plaza. Somewhere with an expensive restaurant nearby. "Parents? Relatives?" he said.

Rex shook his head.

"No one?" And might have added, "Lucky bastard." Dr. Fensterer could hardly remember a time when there had been no Rosalie breathing down his neck, pushing from behind, making the seconds and the minutes jump, turning his intestines into a length of tatting.

"Then try going out on the buddy system for an hour or two," he said. "I'll tell the group I think you're ready. We must help you take the first step." But he sounded almost sad as he said it. As if he wished he had never allowed himself to take that first step—in the wrong direction, leading so clearly to the wrong exit. He was standing behind the desk with his back to the window, and for a moment Rex imagined he was wearing only half of that long white coat; that from behind he was completely bare. Or nonexistent. Dr. Fensterer, he suspected, was not a whole man. Was not completely committed to his work. He thought of Audrey's back going down the hospital hall, not bare at all but well covered in powder blue with the little fox hanging down behind and a shopping bag at her side.

Outside Dr. Fensterer's office he saw Garrick Troy leaning against the wall, writing with his left hand. "I've got to get out of here," he said. He had a long thin face with dark sunken eyes like something in the bottom of a martini glass. When he wasn't writing he wore an expression suggesting silent prayer. Actually, he was merely reciting poetry to himself. He had reams of the best poetry in the English language wound up in his head. He could unwind it at will. "I've got to get out of here. Quick."

"You too? The chronic complaint. Everyone but me. Me, I'd like to be a permanent resident—without the meetings and the therapy. Just peace and quiet. But what's so wonderful out there? Screaming sirens and screaming headlines and Mrs. G. Patterson Slade lunching at the Colony?"

"Normally, I'd agree," Garrick said. "Usually I aim for at least four to six months in residence. Which is about as long as they want to keep you anyway."

"Normally?" Rex said.

Garrick nodded. "For writing poetry, you know." Which could not be written in a world where even the space came in unequal chunks. He solved it by inhabiting the cracks and moving, if at all, counterclockwise. And hiding in the institutions of the city. There he wrote all night while the others slept and the snow fell silently, gently, in his head, forming a private curtain of flakes between him and the seasons outside. Until the landscape of his mind was cold and covered and the curtain had disappeared. Then he packed his bag and went back into the city to sleep and deliver his poems to his publisher under a new alias.

"How long have you been in this time?" Rex asked.

"Two odes and a sonnet's worth. Shorter than usual. But this time it's different." This time Grant, his twin, was in trouble. He knew because his right arm was paralyzed. Which was why he was writing with his left. But it slowed him down considerably. "I've got to get out," he said. "Grant may need me."

"Does Prokosh know?"

"Who knows what Prokosh knows? Except Prokosh."

"I'll see what I can do," Rex said. Dr. Prokosh, it was clear, must be informed. Rex reached for his pocket, feeling for his press card. It had won him interviews with kings and presidents and movie stars. Surely it could win him a word with Dr. Prokosh. But his pockets were empty. His press card—his credentials, his profession, his identity—was in his wallet locked up with his past.

"Never mind," Garrick said. "I'll manage. I'll get to him somehow."

"Dr. Fensterer will see you now, Garrick," Miss Reed said, coming down the hall.

"He needs to see his brother, not a shrink," Rex said.

"Right now he has an appointment with Dr. Fensterer."

"Which isn't, at all, the same thing." Rex longed to rush back to his room and sit on his bed and hide behind the wall. But Miss Reed was watching. He walked slowly into the solarium and sat down beside Verna. She, at least, would not tell him her troubles to be released in the morning press. She would, he suspected, someday proclaim her own bulletins herself: "Behold, I am bringing such evil upon Jerusalem and Judah that whosoever heareth of it, both his ears shall tingle."

A nice boy, Miss Reed thought, watching Rex. But impatient. She was never impatient. Middle-aged but still pretty with pink cheeks and white hair, pushed by the days and bumped by the darkness, she submitted. At night, alone, she removed her pillow and lay absolutely flat, adjusting to the shape of the future, a future trimmed like the past to fit still another institution: orphanage to dormitory to the final home for the aged, taking with her her uniforms and the complete works of Alexandre Dumas. Not until Farnsbee South and old Mr. Nuffield had she found anyone as alone as she. Even Mrs. Hunnicutt, a woman with a tiny talent and an enormous temperament, had someone. Her husband was sitting in the solarium beside her right now, nodding steadily while she complained about the food and the other patients and the latest pair of stockings he had brought. He merely nodded and held her hands as if trying to pull her back to sanity by sheer physical force. Miss Reed smiled at Mr. Hunnicutt and pretended she did not hear his wife.

But Rex wondered how much longer the poor man could possibly refrain from playing Othello to his wife's Desdemona. Rex was beginning to wish the day of the padded cell had not gone forever. Or that, like Sandra, he could retreat at will, curling up inside his own Eustachian tubes, making it impossible to hear. Which was what she seemed to do whenever her husband came, a large man with a small head like one of those chapels perched high on a mountaintop to which, surely, few worshipers ever go. His features looked crowded, probably nestling together for comfort, frightened at finding themselves so high up. He sat silently beside his wife, breathing heavily as if hoping to thaw her into life. Why was she so afraid of him? Rex wondered. When he's afraid too. Scared to death. His very size made him vulnerable, so clearly visible even in a crowd, to mishaps and catastrophes and minor annoyances. And death, who might easily, at the sight of Marcus, decide to take time off, leaning for comfort against that great bulk. Before filling, in one stroke, his quota for the week. Marcus, supporting death on his left side. No wonder he looked scared. But Rex refused to get involved. The last time Marcus came, Sandra had been off the ward for a psychological test.

"Have you seen my wife, Sandra Mishkin?" he asked Rex.

"I'm new here myself," Rex said.

Marcus sat down to wait with his hat on his lap. One of those large men who always wear hats as if in a belated attempt to contain themselves. He had sat there for two hours, shifting his feet uneasily from time to time, adjusting his equilibrium.

But Sandra could remain rigid while the earth turned and the last train for Pleasantville disappeared into the nearest tunnel. And Clay, the tall restless boy from Miami University, wandered up.

"How about a cozy little game of ping-pong, baby doll?"

She went on sitting absolutely still beside Benson and stared.

"You're too purty to waste your time with a blind man," the

boy said. "And a black one at that."

"She said no thanks," Rex said.

"Well, bless mah fuckin' mammy. If it ain't the gentleman of the press. Interpreting the news. Funny, Mr. UP, suh, I didn't hear her say a damn thing."

"Your hearing's bad."

"And your fuckin' mouth's too big. What do *you* say, chicken? I don't ask twice."

"No thanks," Sandra said.

"Aw, come on, little girl. Don't listen to this shithead. We can skip the ping-pong if there's somethin' else you'd rather do. Me too. Only let's split this scene. Get away from the mass medium." He took her hand and began to pull her up.

"Leave her alone," Rex said.

"Yes. Leave her alone," Bigelow and Terence said, coming up from behind.

The boy dropped Sandra's hand and turned. "Well, if it ain't the faggoty little professor with his faggoty little can for his faggoty spit." He grabbed Terence's can. "Always wanted to see what faggoty juices looked like. Pastel, I reckon. Pink and puce and baby blue, I reckon."

"Give it back," Rex said.

"When I'm ready."

"Now."

"Your hearing's bad, Mr. AP, suh. I said when I'm ready."

Rex looked at him, a bully in white shorts and a straw hat, bouncing a ball for emphasis. He was bouncing it now under Rex's nose and holding Terence's can. And grinning. Like that legislator from Mississippi. Watching the smile slide across his face was like watching the other team steal across home plate. Rex jumped up. *"Now,"* he said. "You heard me. I said *now,* damn you." And swung.

The boy fell and his ball rolled across the room to meet Dr. Fensterer at the door.

"He socked me," the boy shouted. "The fuckin' maniac up and socked me."

"What about it, Rex?" Dr. Fensterer said.

But Rex refused to say a word. Except to demand to see Dr. Prokosh. And Sandra and Terence followed suit. Back in his room, Rex pulled out his notebook. He must see Prokosh about Sandra.

The next day, in his office, Dr. Fensterer tried again. "You'll have to learn to cooperate," he said to Rex. "And, of course, all your privileges are automatically suspended." But he rubbed his cheek in dismay. How deny privileges to a man who wanted none? What is a privilege? Why board up the world against a man who has already rejected it? This was clearly a problem for Prokosh.

One night, Miss Wanda disappeared from the ward. "Gone back to her family in Idaho," was Dr. Fensterer's official explanation. But most of the patients knew better. They knew she had been carted away to have her frontal lobes removed like her baby. And that she would be back soon. They wandered up and down the halls restlessly, as though they feared their own frontal lobes were in danger. The ward door was kept permanently locked. Only Mrs. Schiller, sitting on her bed with her Dante open on her lap, did not believe it. She knew that Miss Wanda, a brave woman and a good mother, had gone off to find her baby. While she, Elsa Schiller, sat taking her ease, reading Dante and tending her body chemistry, deserting Theo's mother and daughter. The group had voted down her weekend pass for the third time that afternoon. "But I must go," she pleaded. "My mother-in-law is eighty-five with a virus infection. My daughter must go to a conference in Washington. I *must* go." She sat on her bed with her eyes on the ward door. Miss Wanda, she was certain, would never be back.

Sure enough, Miss Wanda did not come back and the ward

door was unlocked again as usual. And one morning Mrs. Schiller, on her way to the bathroom, slipped out with a coat over her nightgown and her hair in a skinny braid. She went straight to the nearest Catholic church and spent an hour on her knees to a God she did not accept in order to take twenty cents from the collection box. "He owes me that," she told the priest at the door. "He can spare me twenty cents for the subway." Privileges were suspended again and the ward door locked.

"My God," Terence said. "Everyone gets out but me." He spat into his can.

"Why do you all want out?" Rex said. "To go where? Do what?" In a world where even the trees were diseased and colonies of parasites clung like tumors to the trunks of the palms. But Terence's face was pale, as if he'd been spitting blood as well as saliva into his can.

"To walk the streets and have a beer and teach Latin, to begin with. Instead of being stuck here." Moving from one chair to another, from one chemical reaction to another, stacking up the days like plates. Because of an analyst who sat behind his desk while he, Terence, stripped to his *id* on the couch. "I thought I would get help with Marlene, my wife," he told Rex. But the analyst hadn't seemed interested in Marlene. Instead, they talked about Terence and teaching. After the second session Terence felt teaching was, in itself, a form of escape and teaching Latin was an aberration, a "retreat to the past." He taught in a small boys' school where he also coached dramatics and soccer and ran the Boy Scouts. Until he made the mistake of getting married. Marlene was pretty but dull. And expensive. She liked "nice things." And now there was a baby coming. Bassinets and layettes and two dozen receiving blankets. He had begun to hate his wife. Which was why he had gone to the analyst. She could not understand why he could not work from nine to five like everyone else and never on weekends and Columbus Day.

"And you prefer the boys' company to hers?"

"It's my job."

Terence was beginning to hate the analyst too, a large man who spread himself all over Terence's unconscious but remained silent and noncommittal. Like a hearing aid, Terence thought. Except for an occasional question.

"She wants me to give up teaching," Terence said.

"Teaching in general or just teaching boys?"

Terence's head jerked on the pillow. He liked teaching. And he liked teaching boys. He was good at it. "That's all I want to do, you know. Just *teach* them."

But he faded and weakened during those months on the couch while the doctor sat calm and silent behind his desk with his huge feet wide and flat on the floor, holding things steady, stamping out defenses. After six months Terence gave up teaching Latin in the small boys' school, which he loved, to teach civics in a huge coed public high school, which he loathed. When he could stand it no longer, he tried to get his old job back. The headmaster looked embarrassed. A man who had to quit school in the middle of the year and see an analyst did not belong in a boys' school. And Terence knew that every other headmaster in the country would agree. The next morning he poured out a cup of coffee for his wife and a can of Drano for himself.

"The next time that ward door is open, I'm going through. For good," Terence said. "You won't tell, will you?"

Rex shook his head. But why didn't someone tell Prokosh?

After Mrs. Schiller's escape, the door remained locked for a long time. When it opened again, it was for a large white man with a black beard and a black toupee who came for Benson. He claimed to be Benson's uncle by marriage. "Been looking all over LA and the Southwest for him," he said. "Why he's the best damn little medium this side of the Great Divide. Haven't held a single séance since he left. Even the spirits are getting impatient. Not to mention the customers." He smiled quickly, unzipping his beard for a moment. Then he led Benson away to spend his life talking to the spirits of the unknown dead.

The piano remained silent after that, though occasionally Rex, waking in the night or sitting in his room, seemed to hear the opening bars of the Rachmaninoff concerto and thought of Benson bound up inside a double coating of black, sealed off from the world but available, at will, to the spirits of the dead. Rex would get up, then, and look out the window: at the traffic racing along the drive, racing to pounce on some new disaster, at the river lying patiently beneath the bridges and Ward's Island, sinking slowly under its terrible weight of the criminally insane. At night it was always worse, when the earth seemed bare—and he could discern the shape of its skull. Why had Dr. Prokosh allowed it? Why had he let Benson go off to serve the dead and a charlatan in a toupee? With only a white stick to connect him with the living. And why hadn't he, Rex Bannister, ace journalist, reported it? And why were Terence and Garrick and Mrs. Schiller forced to remain shut up, away from the world they required for sanity and normal necessities, while he, Rex, was being slowly pushed out of isolation to bump knees with men lacking feet? He could feel the pressure in the small of his back.

He crawled back to bed and watched Garrick typing silently in the straight-backed chair. Rex fell asleep, at last, to dream that Garrick was playing Rachmaninoff's Second Piano Concerto on his silent typewriter with his left hand. While Dr. Prokosh, in a beard and toupee, nodded with approval and turned the pages of the music with a long white stick.

CHAPTER FIVE

Some nights Rex dreamed of his father and the country across the border and the mayonnaise jar with the vital organs suspended in solution. Waking, he remembered the inhabitants of Farnsbee South, their parts twisted and loose, for whom there was, very likely, no solution. Yet he felt an impulse to reach for the light, to hold it steady while someone, Dr. Prokosh, perhaps, went to work. Quickly, before the sun came up, before the daylight turned the gray fields of dawn into ordinary grass and paths and macadam roads. So that the traveler passing by would never stop or even turn his head, ignorant of what lay buried beneath the sun. And Rex would long to jump up and rummage through his bag for the old flashlight lost long ago; to turn its steady beam on Terence and Garrick and Sandra and Joyce, his left hand covering the lip of the horizon, restraining the sun. Not like his father, a doctor, who made no attempt to heal the day but worked quickly in the dark, exposing only to cover up again with dirt and daylight, compounding evil with knowledge. Making the sun an accomplice.

Waking from the old nightmare, Rex lay still and watched Garrick and his typewriter while dawn came, turning the corner into Farnsbee South. Until Garrick, suddenly aware, closed his typewriter and slipped between the folds of a new day. Rex, with his dream still loose around him, pulled out his pad and began to write, slowly at first, then more quickly, of the inhabitants of Farnsbee South whose vital organs had been reduced to a cross or a poem or a pose from the past. And of these surely Terence Drew, who had only a can, was the saddest.

He heard a shuffling movement and, glancing up, saw Terence bending over the bureau. He looked different, somehow, Rex thought, until he realized Terence was not holding his can.

"Want a light?" Rex asked. He looked around. Garrick had fallen face down on his pillow like a man with his head on the block. Hartley, with his arms covered, played onehanded baseball in his sleep and smiled. "No one around here will mind," Rex said.

"Good God, no," Terence said. "No light. What I want is a little privacy. Hopeless in this institution. Doesn't anyone in this damned heaped-up room sleep through?"

"Take your privacy," Rex said. "Don't mind me." He turned back to his report. But Terence continued to stare at him.

"Are you planning to expose me?"

"Hell, no. What's there to expose?"

Terence shook his head and went on staring. Rex's hair, he noted, lay in a low bang on his forehead like one of those Roman generals in his high-school Latin grammar. And Rex's voice, heard in the semidarkness, reminded Terence of another voice he had heard when he first came to the hospital.

He had not gone directly to Farnsbee South then, but to another wing where the patients were mostly old men who spent their days in bed. Except for a few who sometimes walked slowly by in gray bathrobes with skinny yellow ankles, their feet dragging as if they were being pulled, their heads to one side. Terence had never seen such old people before. And so many of them. He wondered if all the old men of the city had been shut up in the Mayflower Memorial. At night there were strange noises and the orderlies shouting and the sound of scuffles. Then silence. He would fall into a restless sleep, dreaming that the old men had been dragged away and hung up on hooks, like empty robes, at the other end of the ward.

The bed next to his had its curtains permanently closed. He never saw who lay there. Occasionally a nurse, carrying something covered with a towel, would disappear behind the curtain and a man's voice, clear and beautifully accented, would say: "Would you be good enough to call the medical director, please? I wish to lodge a complaint." But as far as Terence knew, the medical director never came. And one morning the curtains were drawn back on an empty bed. Had the patient, tired of waiting, finally gone to lodge the complaint himself? Or had he been dragged off in the middle of the night to avoid just that, and been hung up on a hook at the far end of the ward to complain to the ceiling? Like the old men who shuffled by his bed with their necks on one side, as if they had just been cut down.

Terence still thought of them sometimes at night, imagined them hanging from their huge hooks with their yellow legs dangling and their heads askew. And there were times when he wished he had been in that bed with the drawn curtains, to disappear one day, leaving only his can behind.

He looked down at Rex now, writing quickly, and realized he felt strangely pleased that Rex was there, in the next bed, not whisked away in the night like his neighbor in the other ward.

"I'll tell you something if you promise not to put it in that damned dossier," he whispered. Rex nodded. "I'm checking out of here."

"They letting you go?"

"Nope."

"Then how . . . ?"

"On two legs. Which, thank God, I've still got."

"When?"

"First chance I get. At mealtime probably. They're less likely to miss me then since I never eat with the others."

"And if they catch you?"

"Parole refused. Privileges canceled. Sentence extended. For God knows how long. It's worth the risk though."

"But why?"

"Because spitting into a can is no occupation for a grown man. Even a crazy one."

"You're not crazy," Rex said.

"Say it again." He picked up his can and held it out. "Say it in here. So I can have something to aim at."

"Wait," Rex said.

"For what?"

"They must be getting ready to let you out soon. All those job appointments."

"Soon? How soon? Two months? Two weeks? Even if it's two days, I can't wait. In another two days I won't be able to lift the can."

"Good God, what's the matter? Getting weak on that liquid diet?"

"No. But the can's getting heavy. I feel as if everything I ever thought or felt or said is stored in that can. I can't swallow it or incorporate it like everyone else. I have to carry it around. Outside me. Like that damn hideous little tube."

"Not a bad way to handle it," Rex said. "Spit it all out, then throw it away."

"But I can't. Not in here. That's why I'm getting out. Out of here. Where I can dump it. And start teaching again. Maybe then I can begin to feel human again. Learn to swallow again." He tried to remember what it had been like before Farnsbee South, before Marlene and the baby and the matching "lounge chairs," when he marched boldly with Caesar and the second-form boys by day and read Horace and Virgil at night: *"Tacitaie per amica silentia lunae."* "Besides," he said, "I can't afford it here any more. These are pretty damned expensive accommodations, you know. For an unemployed schoolteacher."

"Have you told Prokosh?"

"Fensterer. He said it was part of the therapy, to make you pay. Make you face up to your responsibilities. Cooperate in your own cure."

Fensterer had blushed as he said it. And wished he were out in the field with the sun on his back and a firm foundation of rock beneath his feet. There were times when he felt completely inadequate, even to carry out Dr. Prokosh's instructions. "Maybe you could take it up with Dr. Prokosh," he had said. Otherwise Terence would have to face the state mental hospital.

But Terence was afraid of Prokosh, who reminded him of that other analyst who sat behind a desk and had, with a few crossed questions, laid a fire. The day Prokosh appeared in the ward, Terence felt his insides begin to burn all over again. And he felt he would never be well again, would live out his life in a hospital ward carrying his can and the illusion that his throat was permanently scalded. For even after it began to heal, he felt the old pain and was afraid to swallow. He would never feel clean again, in spite of having been scoured by a can of Drano. It had burned away part of his body but had not succeeded in purging his mind. So, though Dr. Fensterer and Dr. Sourette and even Dr. Prokosh himself told him his throat was healed, he could not drop the can. Just as he could not go back to Marlene and the new settee. But he could not stay in Farnsbee South either. And the thought of the state mental hospital made him burn all over again, right down to his knees.

"So you see," he told Rex, "I've got to get out."

"Go on. I'll cover for you any way I can."

"Thanks," Terence said. And turned back to the bureau. Rex, bending over his report, felt the sun on his back and knew it had popped up suddenly as if he had withdrawn his hand, at last, from the horizon. And became aware of the burn on his palm.

"I think Terence should come to meals regular," Beverly Ann said at Group Therapy. "Even if he can't eat. He's supposed to interact. After all."

"Right," Daphne said. "There's not nearly enough men as it is. And one of them's Nuffield, don't forget."

"What about it, Terence?" Dr. Fensterer said.

"I prefer not to," Terence said.

"No one gives a damn what you prefer," Clay from Miami U. said, stressing his Southern accent.

"I thought it was one of the rules," Daphne said. "'Communal dining.' Part of the therapy. Anyway, I don't see why if the rest of us have to. . . ."

"OK, OK," Terence said. What else could he do? Escape would be more difficult if he had to sit with the others at meals. Otherwise, it didn't matter *where* he did his spitting. But he wondered about Beverly Ann, who knew everyone's most vulnerable spot and probed it. Was it part of her sickness to be cruel and nasty round the clock, like a boil or a fever? Especially toward the weak. As if they had some secret weapon she did not understand so that she must always attack first. Like Biswanger, the fourth former, an ugly boy with an enormous chin who knew he was unappealing and went around punching people so they would have a reason for hating him—a reason he could tolerate. Terence found him in the latrine one day after school, staring into the mirror, punching his enormous jaw while the tears ran down his face and his knuckles bled. But Beverly Ann was not deformed. Just sick. Then why had she chosen this way to be sick, so different from Rex or Garrick or Mrs. Schiller? Was it simply the difference between measles and whooping cough, one chemical and another? And, if so, what was *he* now that he no longer swallowed his own saliva and consumed only what could be contained in a dropper and entered through a tube? He had had nothing by mouth for months, could hardly remember any taste but Drano. He must certainly be different from the man who once swallowed his own spit and ate meat and potatoes twice a day; a man who had wooed and won Marlene Seitz with the beaux three-deep around her; a man who had gold in his hair instead of his pockets, who had worked hard as a tutor and exterminator and billboard painter to buy the necessary rings and the new bedroom suite. For Marlene liked to have things "nice" and felt nothing but horror for a husband who could drink Drano right from the can. Thank God she couldn't see his meals now. He still faced them with disgust and that tube like a second obscene little mouth protruding from his middle. He was a freak even in Farnsbee South. And now, thanks to Beverly Ann, he would go on being that indefinitely.

At one end of the table, Dr. Sourette wondered why he was sitting there, encouraging the patients to claw each other while at home the wounds were already open and waiting for treatment. Why should he prescribe drugs for Joyce instead of the penance she craved, or insist on "treatment" for Garrick, who needed nothing but to be left alone to write his poems? Why was he, a Haitian, sitting down in the presence of white men's illusions when he should have been up on his feet healing black men's bodies? He had forgotten the taste of *malangan,* could hardly remember the sound of a rooster or a drum.

"'The coffins of the poor are light,'" his father used to say. And Dr. Sourette knew that all over Haiti coffins were being lowered, featherlight, despite the combs and the soap and the rosaries that accompanied the corpse. While he grew heavier and heavier on hamburgers and buns, covered with mustard and relish and ketchup and onions. In ten years he had learned to pile the condiments high. And carry a heavy tray. But he knew that terror and hunger and malaria and dysentery still raged through the villages of Haiti while he pushed his tray down the long counter, past yards of "Hot Foods" and "Salads" and "Beverages" and "Pies." He should have gone back last year when he had his medical certificate in his pocket and a year of internship for ballast. But that was before the strange white doctor in the black suit sat down opposite him at lunch. Like one of the Divine Horsemen who had ridden him, against his will, into Farnsbee South. Verna, he noted, was sitting off by herself as always. She, at least, had the courage to follow her own god in her own way. She was sitting with her head bent now, as if the Lord had laid His heavy hand upon her in a long silent benediction.

"Actually," Beverly Ann was saying, "there are just too damn many people in this community who don't interact at all. It's a lousy community. In fact, it's hardly a community at all. When I was at Greenwoods, *everyone had* to participate. If not, *out.* And here we've got Verna, who thinks she's in heaven already and won't interact with anyone but God. And Garrick, who is so goddamn superior he won't interact with anyone at all."

"What about it, Garrick?" Dr. Fensterer said.

Garrick looked up.

"You've never really told us what it is you're hiding from," Joyce said gently. "Never really had a chance, I guess. What *are* you afraid of, Garrick?"

"The world," Garrick said softly.

"Hell, that's too easy. We're *all* afraid of that," Beverly Ann said. "Even the people out there. Anyone in his right mind *has* to be."

"Only they don't go around writing all the time. And writing *poetry* of all things," Daphne said. "Why do you?"

"Because I'm a poet. That's what poets do."

"But how do we know it's poetry? You never let anyone see it."

"Besides, no one writes poetry *all* the time. Unless he's using it.

To hide behind or something. So what are you hiding from?"

"Nosy adolescents," Garrick said.

"Yourself, obviously," Beverly Ann said. "Something you've done or something you're afraid you *might* do. If you let yourself think about it. Like kill your precious twin brother. Maybe you don't really like him at all. Maybe you hate him. Maybe that's why you won't let him come to see you. Not to protect *him*. But to protect *yourself* from doing something terrible."

"And won't ever let anyone see your poetry," Daphne said. "Like maybe it isn't poetry at all. Maybe it's letters to the FBI. Denouncing him. Maybe you're trying to make him lose his job or something."

"Yeah, maybe you're mad 'cause he isn't in the bughouse too," the boy from Miami said. "Like my sister-in-law. Got mad at my brother for locking up the booze so she told his boss he was a faggot. Got him fired and now she's starving to death. No one will hire him *or* her. Not in Maybelle, Alabama. Figured she must be a faggot too if she married one." He laughed but stopped when he realized that no one was laughing with him.

Garrick was not even listening. He had his head down and was writing furiously. With his left hand.

"Don't be stupid," Daphne said. "He wouldn't say that about his *twin*, after all."

"Why not? Could be they're not identical."

"How about it, Garrick? You *identical* twins?" But Garrick was still writing. When the session ended, he moved to one corner of the lounge and continued to write.

Sandra sat down beside him. She had her hair pinned up and had forgotten all about trying to find a pose. She was watching Garrick write in his tiny tortured script.

"Will you let me read your poetry sometime?" she said.

He looked up in amazement. It was, surely, the first time in the history of the ward that Sandra had been known to initiate a conversation.

"I'll read it to you," Clay said. "Any time you like, baby. I'll be glad to read it to you."

"It's not yours to read," Rex said.

"Then let *him* read it," Beverly Ann said. "Shut up, everyone. Garrick's gonna give a public reading."

"Will you?" Sandra said.

"No. Sorry. My poetry isn't meant for public performance. It's very private."

"Then let her read it to herself," a bearded boy said.

"Yeah. Let's all read it to ourselves," Beverly Ann said.

"Great!"

"Groovy!"

"Sorry. You'll have to make do with Pound and Keats and Blake and Yeats," Garrick said. "And several hundred others."

"Oh, no we don't," Beverly said, grabbing his pad. "Here, Clay. Catch."

"That's shitty," Bigelow yelled. "Give it back." He grabbed it and tossed it to Garrick. But it was intercepted by Daphne, who raced to the door and stationed herself on the threshold. She took a deep breath and held up the pad. "OK. Shut up, everyone. Here goes." Garrick, his cap pulled down, turned his face to the wall. For a moment there was complete silence.

"Nein," Mrs. Schiller called.

"Please don't," Sandra said.

"You bitch," roared Bigelow, and prepared to charge.

Rex put a hand on his arm. "Don't," he said. "Go ahead, Daphne. You want to read, read. Your audience is waiting."

Again there was complete silence. Daphne held up the pad, frowning. "But I can't," she said. "I can't." She began to giggle. "It isn't writing at all. Unless it's Egyptian. Just wiggles. Like he didn't know how. Would you believe it, like he didn't know how to write at all."

"Or maybe you just can't read," Rex said. "In which case you might as well give it back."

"No," Daphne said. "We need the pad for hearts. He can do his squiggles on TP."

"It belongs to Garrick. You can do your hearts on TP." He yanked the pad from her.

"No," Daphne screamed, clawing his face. But Rex, with a long red scratch on his cheek, handed the pad to Garrick.

The rest of the ward broke into pandemonium. People hooted or cheered, called Daphne a moron and Garrick a genius. Or the other way around. Until Dr. Fensterer and Miss Reed appeared in the doorway with two male nurses.

"What happened?" Dr. Fensterer said when the patients were all seated in rows before him. He wished he'd been given a better script. "What happened?" he asked Rex, pointing to the long red scratch on his cheek.

Rex shook his head.

Dr. Fensterer sighed. "You know we talk things out here," he said. "That's the whole point."

But Rex shook his head again. "This is a mental ward. Not a CIA briefing. You want spies, go hire them." He folded his arms. Dr. Fensterer looked up and down the rows. But the other patients were all sitting perfectly still with their lips tightly shut and their arms folded. Except for Garrick Troy, who was writing lightly what only he could read.

"That means, of course," Dr. Fensterer said, "that all passes will be canceled. As usual."

Terence's head drooped over his can and Garrick looked up from his pad.

"And Dr. Prokosh knows nothing about it," Rex said. "As usual."

"Of course he doesn't," Joyce said. "He'd never allow it."

"Well, he's going to know right now," Rex said, getting up. The authorities *must* be advised. Prokosh must be informed. Passes must not be canceled *en masse*. Collective guilt is an obscenity. In a just society the innocent are not punished with the guilty. In an egalitarian society the weak must be protected from the strong. Sandra must be saved from the world and Terence from the state mental hospital; Garrick must be protected from the illiterate and the cruel and Mrs. Schiller from the heedless young. "Lest the lion devour the lamb and the mountains trample the hills."

"Don't worry," he said, hurrying out. "I think I can promise you that this is the last time they'll cancel our passes." And slapped his breast pocket. Up and down the rows, heads turned toward Rex.

"I want to see Dr. Prokosh," he told Miss Reed at the nurses' station.

"Try him now," Miss Reed said. "Before he begins rounds. And try to remember. . . ." But Rex was already down the hall, knocking on Prokosh's door. He heard the sounds of shuffling and shutting, of brilliant diagnoses being laid away and the doctor telling him to come in.

It was a bare little office with a desk and a blotter and a tape recorder in the corner. And the lights always burning. For Dr. Prokosh was always on duty. There was a chair for the patients, a straight hard chair for resting the rump while the doctor examined the mind. Without so much as a swab or a tongue depressor.

"Ah, Rex," Dr. Prokosh said. "Sit down." He had his elbows propped on the desk and his huge watch strapped on the inside of his wrist so that its bold face stared directly at Rex, exhibiting the time, the doctor's time, which he, Rex, was wasting. "What can I do for you?"

"I want to talk to you about Garrick."

"About *Garrick?* I was hoping you wanted to talk about *Rex.*"

"Garrick needs to see his brother."

"I'm afraid that's not possible."

"But it's necessary. I don't think you understand ***how*** necessary."

"And *you* don't understand how impossible it is."

"But my God, why?"

"I'm afraid you'll just have to take my word for it. You know I can't discuss the other patients with you. That's one of our most fundamental rules. Unless you want to talk about Garrick's poetry."

"You've *read* it?" Rex remembered that illegible scrawl.

"Of course. Just as I've read all the news reports published by one Rex Bannister."

"You have? Christ, why? A special interest in underdeveloped countries?"

"No. Obviously. A special interest in Rex Bannister."

"From my *reports?*"

"Yes."

"Why not from *me?*"

"That too."

"But this is the first time I've talked to you since I got here. Over a month now."

"I have my methods."

"Why not learn about me from *me?*"

"Because you are Dr. Fensterer's patient. You must have realized by now that I do not treat patients. For reasons of my own. But believe me, I know a great deal about you."

"And Sandra and Terence and Mrs. Hunnicutt too?"

"About *all* of you."

"From reading *Othello* and Dante and visiting art galleries?"

Dr. Prokosh smiled. "I have, indeed, become quite an expert on the *Inferno* and Desdemona and a certain brand of contemporary art." For a moment, Rex had an odd picture of Dr. Prokosh wandering around the galleries of Manhattan with slides and a microscope, examining Sandra's bare thighs. "I've even brushed up on my Latin," Dr. Prokosh went on. "And now, unless you have something to tell me about Rex Bannister, I must go. I am already late for rounds." The big hand on Dr.

Prokosh's watch was pointing straight at Rex. He stood up.

Outside the office, Rex watched the doctor hurry away. Amazing man, he thought. An expert, not only of the mind but of all the various and intricate by-products thereof. From Latin to Verna's manufactured voices.

"Don't worry," he told the other patients. "I've just checked it out. Dr. Prokosh is well briefed. Completely briefed. Just be patient. Give him a little more time."

"I can't wait another minute," Mrs. Hunnicutt screamed, jumping up. "I have a public to consider. Now. Right now. This afternoon. Nothing and no one will make me miss another performance. Ever. I'm going to my dressing room to rest. And I warn all of you to stay away from me. My nerves won't stand any more." She nodded at them, a tall bedraggled woman in a worn dressing gown with her wig slightly askew, and walked with grace and dignity out of the room and down the hall. She smiled graciously at Mr. Nuffield and told him to please slip any messages or cables under her door. Her maid would take care of the flowers. "See that I'm not disturbed, won't you, darling? I've just been clawed to death by the gentlemen of the press. My nerves won't stand any more. I must rest." She disappeared down the hall.

She walked slowly, her hands slightly raised, ready to push back the walls. They were leaning dangerously close, trying to read her thoughts. Or steal her lines. But she maintained her slow dignified pace though the doors closed automatically as she passed and strange little cries came curling out at her through the keyholes. At the nurses' station the charts whispered together.

"Alicia Hunnicutt. Age: 52."

"42," Mrs. Hunnicutt said.

"Weight: 130."

"110," Mrs. Hunnicutt said.

"Hair: Gray."

"Blonde," Mrs. Hunnicutt said.

"Married or single?"

"Actress," Mrs. Hunnicutt said.

"Diagnosis. . . ."

Mrs. Hunnicutt hurried past. At the utility room she turned the taps on full force to drown out the sound. The little carts, lined up for four-o'clock temps and medications, rattled in sympathy.

In her room she walked slowly toward her bed. It was a large room, she noted, larger than any she'd had on tour before. Recognition was coming at last, though she would have wept at its tardiness had it not been for the dresser waiting. " 'Prithee, unpin me,' " Mrs. Hunnicutt murmured, standing straight and tall, ignoring the insolent years mocking from the wings. She moved with assurance, sustained for almost thirty years on brandy and black coffee. And the scattered applause that rode the drafts across the footlights, stirring her flimsy fifth-act costume. And Orin waiting in the dressing room to rub her chilled hands and feet and tell her she was adorable. Warming his own hands and feet, really, at the fire of her art, which she had so prodigally bestowed upon the nation, igniting it in Atlanta and Akron and Detroit. With the portrait of Will Shakespeare between her lingerie. It was hanging over her bed now.

How quiet the house was tonight. And how tired she was. He demanded too much, the silent bearded man watching, at an angle, from above her bed. A hard man for all his sweet words and the soft ruff at his neck. " 'Sing willow, willow, willow;/Her salt tears fell from her, and softened the stones.' " But had she ever softened *him,* in thirty years of moaning and suffering and dying on the hard planks of improvised beds? With Othello, smelling of mediocrity and mentholated cough drops, heavy upon her. Leaving her full of frustration and anger and splinters in the seat. To rise stiff-necked and brokenhearted for the final curtain call.

How quiet the house was tonight. Was anyone there? The

ultimate horror, five acts to an empty house. "'Good faith! How foolish are our minds!'" Still, she could rise above even that, if necessary. Would play it all through just for *him*. Five acts with her back to the pit. And no supporting cast at all. Alicia Hunnicutt making theatrical history in Farnsbee, New York. For the rest of the company had, of course, gone on to Providence, where the sales were better: Emelia and Othello and even Orin, waiting outside an empty dressing room. Poor Orin, doomed to play only one role all his life. "'Prithee, dispatch.'" She waved a hand and sat down on the bed, her eyes on the portrait of Shakespeare.

"'O! These men, these men!'" They were cruel, all cruel, even Will, dooming her nightly to a guiltless death. She fumbled with the zipper of her dressing gown. "'Unpin me now,'" but kept her eyes on Will, wise, compassionate, tolerant Will, with a thousand hearts beating inside his breast. "'And yet I fear you; for you are fatal then/when your eyes roll so. Why I should fear I know not,/ since guiltiness I know not; but yet I feel I fear.'" She took off her dressing gown and lay down, back flat, face up. She could hear him breathing above her. Everything else was so still. Only *he* dared to make his presence known, waiting. Though he knew Othello would not come tonight and the house lights would not go up or down but would remain neutral, and she would have to play it all without spots or shadows. And all alone. Would have to embody, slight as she was, murderer and victim and the entire supporting cast, including attendants armed. A woman with a low voice and a large iron deficiency. Still, he was waiting, bending low now, even smiling slightly. She felt her head raised for a moment, then laid flat, while the pillow gently covered her face, warm, soft, pressing down, flattening nose and cheeks and eyelids, squeezing air out and darkness in until she lay heavy and still, closed to the world with the darkness sealed up inside her. Except for some tiny pinpoint through which she heard a distant voice: "'Who hath done this deed?'" And answered feebly through the black: "'Nobody; I myself; farewell.'" Above her, the portrait of Shakespeare, slightly lopsided, waited.

When they found her, Daphne had to be kept sedated for forty-eight hours and the ward door locked for a week. Miss Reed packed the wigs carefully in their boxes and took down the crooked picture of Shakespeare. The dead woman's roommates were moved, temporarily, to other quarters.

Across the hall that night, Rex heard the stretcher come and go and knew that Mrs. Hunnicutt was making her last exit—off stage and into the wings. His report, thick as it was, would do her no good now. She had gone while he was talking to Prokosh about *Garrick*. Rex had covered the wrong story, a crime not only against his profession but against humanity, especially Mrs. Hunnicutt and the inmates of Farnsbee South. He had even forgotten to give Prokosh his dossier.

Beside him, Garrick, unable to type, was moaning in his sleep to his twin brother, his *Doppelgänger,* that extension of himself who walked the streets of the world outside while he, Garrick, huddled behind the walls of an institution. Garrick was talking to him now, warning him to be careful, to take the stairs one at a time, to hide his pillow under the mattress and avoid walking under helicopters. Terence was tossing and mumbling something in his sleep that might have been Latin. Today Mrs. Hunnicutt. Tomorrow?

Rex got out of bed. He must try to communicate with Dr. Prokosh, to tell him about Terence. But Dr. Prokosh was not in his office. Rex would have to phone, wire, anything. They caught him at the nurses' station, reaching for the dial. "Let me get through," he shouted. "Otherwise I'll spill it all. A full exposure. To *The New York Times*. And the UP and AP and Reuters too." He broke away and began to bang on the door of Prokosh's office. Until he was led away to a hypodermic and the blank wall beside his bed. So that when Dr. Prokosh finally came down, at last, Rex was fast asleep.

But in the tiny office beside the utility room, the staff waited.

Dr. Sourette kept his dark face still above the white coat, a token of respect for the dead, an elementary gesture, appropriate surely in any culture. To the general condition. The particular, in this case, hardly merited more. An aging female, Caucasian, schizophrenic and selfish. At home they thought nothing of burying whole villages in a week. Except for the problem of finding enough gravediggers. Though most of the graves were half-size. And there was always the river. And how many lives might he be saving, right now, he wondered, while he waited for Dr. Prokosh, to discuss a dead woman?

Dr. Fensterer glanced surreptitiously at his watch. Rosalie was waiting. Rosalie, he thought, was always waiting. When she wasn't complaining. "Late again," she would say. "The sacrifices I make for your profession." But if he suggested that it might not, after all, *be* his profession, she would respond as if to treachery. "You wanna be a *geologist?*" she would say. "Now that you're practically a full-fledged M.D.? A *psychiatrist,* even? You wanna start all over again? Like go back to school? Like *pay* money instead of *making* it? And spend your life in a tent, drinking water out of rusty old canteens? You *afraid* to be comfortable or something?" She would tell him he didn't really love her and Dr. Fensterer, who suspected this was true, would feel ashamed. So now he fidgeted, waiting for Dr. Prokosh, thinking of Rosalie waiting outside the Little Carnegie. Mrs. Hunnicutt's death would become merely the occasion for another quarrel with Rosalie. Mr. Hunnicutt, he considered, was not, perhaps, entirely to be pitied.

Miss Reed wondered. Would Mr. Hunnicutt be happier now, free to walk in the park instead of to Macy's and a hospital ward? Free to hold a book or a theater ticket or even a suitcase for a weekend at Montauk instead of his wife's clutching hands? Miss Reed sighed and shook her head but could not shift the pattern of her thoughts. Unless it was to wonder whether he might actually grieve for the wife who had brought him drama and a constant seat in the ward. Where would he spend his free time now? And what would he think of her in her starched white cap, entertaining such unprofessional thoughts? Her uniform would surely turn some hideous spotted yellow. If that was the color of shame.

Across the hall someone was closing Mrs. Hunnicutt's door very slowly and softly, as if not to disturb her. And the three staff members waiting in the tiny office remembered, suddenly, why they were there. For a moment they looked at each other over the low wire mesh of their own thoughts. And saw the flecks of guilt trembling on each other's lashes.

CHAPTER SIX

At Family Meeting the patients sat at the big table with friends and relations around the side. Like one of their terrible Thanksgiving dinners, Mrs. Schiller thought, except for the absence of knives. "That's her," she heard a girl say to the young man beside her. "That's Lolly. Looks normal as rice pudding, don't she? And all of a sudden she's crackers. Sitting on the bus to Asbury Park with her baby squawking its head off at home and her husband screaming it was his night for poker. Said she just wanted to smell salt water. For once in her life."

Mrs. Schiller had no one. She would not allow her daughter or her mother-in-law to watch them peck at her pieces on the table. She sat next to Rex and kept herself intact between the arms of her chair. He had no one either. Perhaps because his wife was too tired from shopping all day. Mrs. Schiller had seen her once or twice during visiting hours. She always carried a shopping bag and walked as if her feet hurt. Mrs. Schiller wondered what she needed from the stores all the time with only seven days to the week and her husband in the hospital. Rex, she could see, needed so much: buttons on his shirt and his socks mended and a wife sitting down to listen. For Rex's conscience, she knew, was forever hanging by a thread, ready to fall off and go rolling, wantonly, down the streets. He sat quietly during Family Meeting and stared at the walls or watched Mr. Nuffield walk up and down, carrying the mail right through the evening. Mr. Nuffield never sat still.

"Your wife will be expected to attend Family Meeting regularly," Dr. Fensterer had said.

"No," Rex said. "She's very young. It would only upset her."

"Can you get a substitute?"

"For my wife?"

"For Family Meeting."

"I'll be my own family," Rex said. And he was. But it left him looking exhausted and sensitive to Mrs. Schiller's heavy breathing. As if she were creating, out of air and energy, the necessary kin.

But there were others, Rex noted, who had no one to sit down with them through Family Meeting, picking at their hangnails while wife or brother or sister or son tore off whole layers of skin. Mr. Nuffield and Joyce, for instance, who might have claimed the United States Post Office and the hosts of heaven, respectively, as their constant attendants. And Terence, whose wife was home with a new baby and who had only his can for comfort. And Garrick Troy, with his back to the visitors and his cap pulled down and a pad and pencil under the table. Rex wondered about his twin brother. He never came.

"He's much too busy," Garrick insisted. Grant, Garrick had told him, was a social worker who sat in one of those storefront offices in East Harlem behind a plate-glass window, surrounded by green walls and black faces and a ring of problems eight feet deep. He did enough for two men to improve the world, carrying

Garrick's share too, who could not tolerate it for more than a few months at a time. Which left Garrick free to find a haven for his poems. Thanks to Grant, he could withdraw into the various "homes" of the area: for convalescents and incurables and alcoholics; for the aged and the addicted and the mentally ill. He was all of these and these were the only homes he knew. He wrote in institutions where there was order and regularity and a rationale to the day. Emerging only intermittently to catch a falling metaphor and pluck a few rhymes from the sea. But he felt no guilt. The world was well left to Grant. For if Garrick was less than whole, he and Grant together made up more than the normal sum. But it left Grant far too busy for anything but his own cases. "Besides, he knows I'm busy too," Garrick said. He had a new volume of verse coming out in the fall. Under a new alias.

"What is it with Sandra's hair?" Daphne was saying now. Her own hair was held back by a velvet band and her huge topaz eyes gave the impression of tears held back too, tears for something she hadn't done. "Her hair keeps going up and down all the time. Up most of the time but down for visiting hours."

"Loss of identity, probably," Beverly Ann said. "Role confusion. Now that she's not a model any more, she doesn't know what the hell she is."

"Maybe she puts it up for her husband," Joyce said. "Maybe he likes it that way."

Sandra, with her back to the visitors, smiled. Joyce was her friend and down the table Bigelow tossed her a tiny forward pass. She thought of Rex's sketch of her still hanging above the bureau. For the first time in her life, she had friends. Her hair, pinned up into the large flat disk, revolved slowly, repeating over and over: "I like it here. I like it here." She was content to let Joyce brush her hair and Bigelow take her hand and let the days glide by, crowded with meals and meetings and movies and lectures and even dances. And, lately, there were afternoon walks in

Gracie Park with a "buddy" beside her and the mayor's mansion just beyond, where the mayor himself might be peeping through the curtain, enjoying the view of the river and the trees and the citizens exercising their rights to the sun and the grass and an empty hour. It was a world she had never known before, a world that did not smell of clay or paint or bourbon, a world not for copy or sale.

"Don't be silly," Daphne said. "Of course she doesn't put it up for her *husband*. She takes it *down* for him."

Rex became aware of Marcus sitting far behind Sandra. He had, Rex thought, the chronically anxious look of an only child, a child aged early on long afternoons filled with fingerwaves and fittings and the funerals of distant relations. Not so much a man as a small boy grown big who has not yet taken his own measure, despite the perpetual glasses which he had probably been wearing since he was seven. Even now, he kept his suits pressed and his shoes shined and his hair always at the same trim length. Suggesting the voice of his parents, alive and still complaining, in Queens. Or an attempt to escape notice by avoiding change. But why, Rex wondered, was Sandra so afraid of him? Did he insist on hand-knitted socks and homemade bread and a man child every nine months?

Marcus, staring at the back of his wife's head, tried to get used to that big flat bun. He had never seen the back of her neck before but she was exposing it constantly now, to the patients and staff of Farnsbee South.

"She's much better," Dr. Sourette had told him. "She's coming along. Interacting more. Less frightened, less withdrawn." He said it slowly, giving it the full weight of the staff's collective opinion. Though he knew she was still frightened, would always be. And withdrawn, having hidden away whatever tiny fragments of Sandra Mishkin still remained after a lifetime of constant exposure. In a society of one-way screens and complete television coverage. A girl whose very pubic hair had been a matter of public interest. In a society where staring was considered rude and voyeurism a booming business. "Oh, yes," he said again, looking past Marcus at a straining tug leaving black smudges all over a clean blue sky. "She's interacting much more."

But not with me, Marcus thought. Not with me. The flat bun on top of her head made her look entirely different, like any young woman one might see, pushing a grocery cart or a baby carriage. But he could not imagine taking her home with him, this strange new Sandra with the self-assured bun.

She was no longer the Sandra of Millicent Carr's living room, perfection beside the tea tray. Until the day Millicent Carr had invited him home and given him her daughter, complete with pedestal, his life had been calm and monotonous and safe. He lived all alone in a small apartment off First, with his shoes in a bag and seven ties hanging over the bedstead. At night he sat up late reading sea stories—Melville and Conrad and *The True Adventures of Captain Cook*. His desk at the office was piled high with ledgers but his walls at home were covered with maps, which he studied with care before turning out the light. And he climbed into bed with the sense that he was boarding a ship.

When Millicent Carr presented her daughter like a sheet of returns to be gone over, he had simply stared, a big bulky man who sat with his cup in his hand and his huge feet headed for the door. For Sandra was white-skinned and dainty in a blue dress, with long fair hair that would glimmer in the sun and blow in the wind, a perfect figurehead for the ship he sailed each night. Was that what Millicent Carr had had in mind? For them to lie side by side on some high deck, riding the same waves, stretched out under the same length of sky?

That night he did not go to bed at all but strolled beside the river, feeling light enough to walk the waters with his head above the skyscrapers, singing sea chanties to the moon, jingling the stars in his pockets. He would marry Sandra and bring her home and they would voyage through the oceans of the night together.

But Sandra remained a mere figurehead. She heated his soup and poured his water and said "Yes" and "No" and "If you like." She never used his name, never called him anything at all. She remained a figurehead, beautiful and wooden, to be attached to whatever he desired: his table at dinner, his couch in the evening, his bed at night. Her face looked paler than ever, with a whiteness that no longer seemed delicate but lifeless, as if her mother had drained off her daughter's blood to wet her clay. He began to bring work home so that he could spend the evenings at his desk with his back to her. He no longer read sea stories or studied maps. He no longer climbed into bed with the sense of adventure ahead. Instead, he stared at the ceiling with his displaced figurehead rigid beside him and felt himself slowly sink.

When Sandra was first taken to the hospital, he was not allowed to visit her. For three days he walked up and down beside the East River and even over to Ward's Island to stare at the New York State Mental Hospital with its high wire fence and the "No Trespassing" signs. As if anyone would *want* to go in there, to be closed up inside one of those huge thick buildings with people in hospital gowns screaming at the horrors in the hall. And he marveled that there should be so many of them, a whole island full, stuck down in the middle of the river like immigrants waiting to get across. Yet he never saw anyone. Just a few parked cars with no one going in or out and the swings and slides for the children in the apartment houses across the drive. They were always empty and the swings swayed gently in the wind as if only the spirits of dead patients dared venture so far out and up. Sometimes he sat on a bench beneath the trees and watched the barges, dragged like crates across a polished floor. Motorboats roared by and jets moaned overhead and the gulls complained constantly. But always, behind him, the mentally ill remained silent, defined by the high wire fence.

Most of the time he stood staring up at the buildings, waiting for a glimpse of a face at the window, wondering what it was like to be "mentally ill" and why they should be locked up on an island as if they had committed some terrible crime or contracted something contagious. He had always been afraid of hospitals, ever since he was three and had his tonsils removed. His mother had taken him to a big store, as she called it, where they would buy something to fix his sore throat. And then she had disappeared, leaving him surrounded by strange people in white who kept telling him he was a big boy now, such a big boy. He was, of course. Had been since birth. His mother claimed he came out looking ready for a shave and a haircut and a full-scale *bar mitzvah*. At three he was so big that it took four people to hold him down while they forced something bad-smelling over his face. It made a strange whirring noise, like a saw, trying to slice him thin, he was such a big big boy. Death, he imagined later, would be like that, carrying not a scythe but a buzz saw, cutting him down like a tree that had grown too big.

And now Sandra was in a hospital too, a mental hospital. He imagined her sitting barefoot on the floor in a coarse gray gown, with her long hair like knotted ropes, staring at the nightmares between her toes. He had dragged her down with him to be drowned forever and flung, like a piece of dead wood, on the floor of a mental ward. He would go home sadly with the traffic roaring past his right ear and the island moving slowly away behind him until he could no longer see it without walking backward.

At first, the sight of Farnsbee South astonished him: the solarium and the lounge with card tables and television and the sound of rock-and-roll. The patients were mostly young and attractive. They laughed and smoked and wore regular clothes and some of the girls had rollers in their hair, as though getting ready for a date. Even the doctors and nurses were young and nice-looking. Marcus felt awkward around them, and gross, too insensitive to break down, too coarse for Farnsbee South. Sandra wore her blue dress and her hair to her waist, the Sandra of Millicent Carr's living room. But when he sat down beside her, she remained absolutely still with her head turned away, a mere profile, half covered by the long flow of hair, an elusive profile for a phantom ship. He left as soon as Family Meeting was over. He did not want their coffee, which always tasted as if it had been in the pot too long. Rex watched him go. Near the door he stumbled over Garrick's long legs.

One Sunday when Marcus came to visit, Sandra was gone. They've sent her away, he thought, remembering Ward's Island.

Rex saw Marcus' face on its high peak begin to fall. "She's out on pass," he said. He stared at the small head atop the huge frame and the slightly scared expression as if surprised to find itself up so high. He wondered what Sandra saw to frighten her so. "She'll be back soon," he said.

Marcus nodded. He recognized Rex as one of the patients in spite of the white shirt and white pants, suggesting a cruise on the Sound. His name, Marcus knew, was Rex Bannister, a famous free-lance journalist who had covered crises all over the world. What crises, Marcus wondered, had brought him to Farnsbee South. And would he talk like *The New York Times?*

"She's only gone for a walk in the sun," Rex said.

But Marcus could not imagine Sandra walking in the sun. It would be like meeting a runaway image from St. Patrick's on Fifth. "Oh." He wondered what she expected him to do. He knew nothing about her anymore. And she was nothing to him now, not even a figurehead. He was relieved that she was gone, that he would not have to spend the next half-hour sitting silently beside that wooden figure of his wife, who had, in reality, gone down with his ship and his soul on their wedding day. But he was ashamed. He peered down at Rex like a man looking timidly over the top of a high wall. "I wonder what she wants me to do," he said.

Christ, *he's* afraid of *her,* Rex thought. "You can come and wait in here," he said. Anything to keep that head steady. The sight of fear moved him even more than grief; fear that could swivel and swirl and reduce a man to his discrete and elementary parts. He did not want Marcus spinning about the ward. He turned and led the way out of the noisy solarium with the TV roaring and the patients watching each other and him.

Marcus followed Rex down the hall and into his room, where he offered Marcus the only chair, a small straight chair, no doubt the sole survivor of some dining-room set, come to have its final breakdown in Farnsbee South. "Take it," Rex said. "I can't sit still very long anyway. It's the drugs. They make me restless." He smoked steadily and paced the room and rubbed the back of his neck as if he were being constantly hit from behind. He sat down on the bed at last, giving Marcus his full face. Marcus coughed and rattled the coins in his pocket. He was a big man but had no small talk. Only numbers with which he could do many things. But he could not talk about them. Certainly not to a stranger who had encompassed the world and was now trapped in the middle of a bed in a mental ward and would need a "buddy" and a "pass" just for a walk around the block; a journalist who could analyze international affairs while he, Marcus, was merely an accountant limited to analyzing other people's incomes. Staring around the room at the bed and the bureau and the mirror waiting for a face, he might have remembered that they had much in common. Rex was staring at the wall.

"How much longer will you be here?" Marcus asked at last.

"You mean when will they let me out? Release me?" Rex smiled. "I've no idea. Never, as far as I'm concerned. I'd rather stay." Twirling the years on his fingers with the world somewhere out behind the keyhole and the key always in the lock.

Marcus, embarrassed, looked at his feet, those big clumsy feet which had led him into such narrow and private paths. Rex continued to stare at the wall, a blank wall, dividing space, supporting a ceiling, shutting out everything but time, which in Farnsbee South came in convenient doses. Taken easily with a little water. And no bloodletting except his own, sucked up for medical purposes by an earnest lab technician in a white coat, while he sat quietly, arm extended. Might even close his eyes if he liked. Which he did. He had spent so much time in planes, had taken in whole towns at a glance, even seen across borders. From now on he would be satisfied with the view through a keyhole. Not like Marcus, who was big enough to concentrate on himself, wherever he was. He was staring at his feet now, huge feet, allowing him to take a firm stand. But his face, so far away, was pale and small as if he had grown from the bottom up and run out of supplies too soon.

"Of course, in my case," Rex went on, to help him out, "it should be easier to stay. There's no one to release me *to*." The chain merely lengthened and handed over. For he was no longer a whole person. Just a collection of glands which were unreliable. Not like Audrey, so neatly contained in a blue suit, who watched the world with the eyes of the little fox and kept a shopping bag handy for what could not be consumed on the premises.

"No wife?" Marcus asked.

"No," Rex said. "Not anymore." Just a girl with her initials on everything and a color photograph of herself on the piano.

"Parents?"

"No." He thought of his father the night he died, with his hat on the bedpost and his old burlap bag on the floor as if ready to move on in the morning. "Take me home, boy," he had said. "This country isn't safe. Not even for the dead." Afraid they might, perhaps, dig *him* up one day and fit *him* into a mayonnaise jar. "I delivered you, boy. Sweated over you for seventeen hours. Now you can bury me. It won't take anywheres near as long. But don't tell the others. Not till I'm safely stowed away. Then you can contact Uncle Joe. Promise to take me home, boy. You promise."

Rex had promised, though he had no idea where "home" was and certainly no money to get there. They had lived in so many places, all up and down the Pacific coast. Home was where his father could do a bit of doctoring and a lot of drinking. So, in the end, Rex had pushed him over the border in a wheelbarrow. He dug the grave himself, with the burlap bag over the coffin and the bedstead for a tombstone, still holding the hat. Rex could not even remember the place now. Only that it was this side of the border, a border his father had not dared recross until he was dead, leaving his only son to push him over.

"I was *born* an orphan," Rex said. "And an only child. I had an Uncle Joe once. In Canterbury, England. But he's dead too." A saintly man, a preacher to the deaf and dumb who made the words of the Lord visible with fist and finger. Until he grew deaf himself and the voices of the saints rose in his ears, drowning out the siren the night the bombs fell. He had died in his pulpit with his flock around him and the letters JC in his hands. Rex smiled at Marcus. "So you see, there's no one."

"Doesn't seem possible," Marcus said. Even he, Marcus Mishkin, built for outer space and the fun rides at Coney, could, if necessary, be stapled down by his parents in Queens, who expected him for *mah-jongg* every Saturday night. Yet there was Rex, who had talked to kings and presidents and movie stars and champs, with no one to sign his chit. Marcus wondered if anyone would ever print his stories again, would ever trust a madman to report on a mad world. "Doesn't seem possible," he said again.

"But that's how it is. It happens." Rex was sitting far back on the bed now, leaning against the wall, his arms stretched out, palms up, as though they'd been dropped there after the rest of him and he had not yet picked them up. He looked very tired. He had covered riots and revolutions and earthquakes and floods. He had seen death and disaster and a man sliced in two by a motorboat in Wellfleet. No wonder he was tired. His chin was on his chest and his eyes on the opposite wall.

"But I only watched," he said. "I stood there and *watched.* And then I wrote it all down for the world to enjoy. That's my sickness, though Fensterer wants to blame my poor glands. I never *did* anything. I just watched." Unless you could call deserting Jacques and kicking the soldiers of Haiti *doing* something. "And now I'm forced to sit here and watch it all over again." But that was better than going out into it and smelling and tasting and bumping it again. His arms jerked up for a moment, then dropped.

"Visiting hours are over," Beverly Ann, the monitor for the day, announced, sticking her head in the door with her hair teased up beyond all reason. "Take over for a minute, willya, Rex? I wanna kiss Al good-bye. He's off down Route 1, lucky bastard."

"Aber nein, nein," Mrs. Schiller said, appearing suddenly beside her. "She wants to smuggle him out my Dante, my *Paradiso*. My *Inferno* she does not want. Because that I do not need. That I have in my head, always. And in my ears and eyes and heart. That I live. But my *Paradiso*. *Ach,* that I need."

"Why you old bitch," Beverly Ann said. "Who you calling a smuggler? Say that again and I'll tell Prokosh what you've got under your bed. Buttons and old Band-Aids and used stamps and dirty dental floss. And pieces of toenail too, I wouldn't be surprised. And probably, holy God, some of her own private shit. Scared to death she might be giving something away. And now, sweet Mother Cabrini, would you believe it, accusing me of smuggling out her crummy books. In *German!* And *paperback!"*

"Ach, no," Mrs. Schiller said. "No. It's not true. Not one word." She sank down on Terence's bed with her head in her hands. She rocked back and forth, her face covered. She would never raise it again. Not in this world. It was spattered and smeared beyond recognition. She had escaped from the Nazis and the nightmares of Germany to run straight into Beverly Ann Grumm, waste product of the American industrial system. Mrs. Schiller began to scratch her face, the face that had made people say: "But you don't look the least bit Jewish." The face that had trapped Theo before he realized that life with Elsa Grossbach,

handsome and intelligent as she was, would mean exile and alienation and death. A pitiful death from the heart. Most Americans, she knew, had heart trouble and it was undoubtedly catching. A death preceded by a terrible "stroke," as if God, with a forefinger, had casually crossed out all Theo's faculties—speech and memory and motor control—leaving only his sight, toughened, no doubt, by daily confrontation with the American scene. But he had used it, those last few days, to look at her as though he were not speechless but merely waiting—waiting for her to give it all back to him: his country and his colleagues and his native language. His tongue could no longer wrestle with the strident sloppy American sounds. His muscles would not take him to his classes or his colleagues; to the arrogant lazy-looking boys who carried combs in their hip pockets and walked six abreast, forcing him into the gutter; to his colleagues, small quick Jews whose knowledge, like Talmudic scholars', seemed deep because it was so narrow. He did nothing but stare at his wife. And she knew that it was only a hollow man lying there, waiting for his eyes to close. The rest of him was still in Germany. He had never had a life here—nor a proper death either. Only a meager funeral and "memorial services" four months later with half a dozen strangers in some old lecture hall with the formulas still on the board. At home there would have been a procession of *Direktoren* and *Professoren* and *Dozenten* and, possibly, Herr President himself, with four younger brothers to carry the coffin and a whole town to mourn. Here there were only three weak women who could barely support their heads against the harsh sea wind.

"Ach," she moaned, raking her face. How could she have done it? How could she have brought Theo to this strange place, leaving her parents and her sister and brother to line up without her, pressing closer to fill her space? *"Aber Liebchen,"* Theo had told her over and over again, "you couldn't have saved them. And I could not have lived in Nazi Germany. Not if I had married Brunhilde herself. How could you think it? I did not leave be-

cause of you only. But for me also." But she never believed him.

For months after he died she sat alone at the big dining-room table long after the others had gone to bed. But she was never alone for long. Soon silent figures filled the empty chairs. Sometimes they were skinny with naked arms; sometimes they were fat with yellow skin like bananas. But they all had helmets like chamber pots over their heads and she could not see their faces. They came as a group, some nights the fat ones, other nights the skinny ones. But they left alone. She sat rigidly watching as, one by one, each got up, pushed in his chair, and bowed ceremoniously to her. She could not tell which group scared her more, the fat or the skinny.

"Guilt can, of course, be frightening," Dr. Fensterer had said in Group Therapy one day when she had been tricked into talking. "Very."

"It's your guilt, your guilt," the other patients had shouted.

"You want to punish yourself for being alive when the rest of your family, and even your husband, is dead," Terence said. He made it sound so easy. And spat to show he had something far worse to absorb.

"Bullshit," Beverly Ann said. "She *wanted* them, all those hideous men. With bananas for arms. Get *that!* She wanted them to come and sit at her table instead of her boring daughter and her drag of a mother-in-law. She *willed* them there."

"No bananas," Mrs. Schiller said. "Only yellow *like* bananas. And I did not say they were men."

"Of course not. Because you're too ashamed. You've got dirty shitty thoughts so you think you have to punish yourself. Like pretending someone's always following you, spying on you. That's why you go around accusing perfectly innocent people. . . ."

"Ach," Mrs. Schiller broke in. "Innocent. She steals my books and spies on my mail and tells lies to the doctors."

"Why you old bitch. Just goes to show how crazy crappy nuts you are."

"My grandmother was like that, God rest her soul," Joyce said softly. "Just like that. She counted the chocolates in her Whitman Sampler every night."

"Holy Christ," Beverly Ann said. "Don't you know the difference between gluttony and paranoia *yet?* Do we have to have morons at these sessions, Dr. Fensterer? Aren't just plain everyday nuts enough?"

"Who you calling nuts?" Bigelow said. "Look, Dr. Fensterer, I thought we were supposed to be *helping* each other here. Not *insulting* each other." He stood up.

"We are," Rex said. "And right now we're supposed to be helping Elsa. So sit down."

Bigelow sat down.

"How do you explain it, Elsa?" Rex said.

"I don't know. It was so strange. I was not so much afraid. Only sad. And one night I followed them. After the last one left, a skinny one with such skinny arms like my brother Rheinhold, who jumped out of the window just before the Nazis came. A painter and always so skinny. So when he sat in the dining room with his head on one side like always, to get the perspective right, I recognized him. And I followed him right out of the door and into the street. But he disappeared into the garbage can and I tried to get in with him. I thought it would be safer in there with a big cover over the top. But a policeman came." She had banged him on the head with the lid, screaming to let her alone, she must follow Rheinhold. He had taken her home to Gerda and Dr. Schlosser. And the next night she had doped herself in the bathtub.

"*Ach,* of course they think I'm crazy," she said now, the tears running down her cheeks. "And they keep me here. But what good can they do me here? Even if I am crazy. Rheinhold is dead, lying in the street with his head on one side. And Vater and Mutti and Ernst and Giesele, burned up like garbage in an incinerator. And Theo stuffed into a box in the ground. So why shouldn't I go into the trash can? What does it matter if I'm crazy? It's true, isn't it? All of it? Isn't it?" She rocked back and forth on Terence's bed. She might have filled one of his cans with her tears.

Rex knelt beside her and took her hands. She raised her head. "*Ach,* I am a crazy old woman. Pay no attention."

"So are we all," Rex muttered. "All quite mad. And why not?"

"Exactly," Terence said from the door, with Hartley beside him. And mumbled something in Latin. He raised his voice. "Spit it out whenever you like, Elsa," he said, extending his can. "To hell with the rest of them." Hartley nodded vigorously and jerked his crippled arm and said something that no one understood.

"OK, Beverly Ann," Rex said. "Go kiss your Al. You're damn lucky you've got *someone* to kiss. Even Al."

"I've got dozens," Beverly Ann said, whirling on her heel. "Dozens. And if the time ever comes when I don't, I'll climb into a garbage can too. And no damn cop will stop me."

"It *will* come," Rex said. "But you won't." But Beverly Ann was gone down the hall, and there was only poor Mrs. Schiller to stiffen in fear and shame at her failure. She had been unable to dispose of herself—twice.

"Does anyone ever get well here?" Rex asked Miss Reed, passing the door. "Some people have been removed and some have removed themselves. But no one has been discharged with honor since I came."

"You haven't been here very long," Miss Reed said.

Which was true. It had taken years to break them all down. He could hardly expect them to be put back together again in a matter of months.

There was a sudden commotion from the lounge. Rex, hurrying down the hall, heard a muffled voice shouting: "No! No! Go away. I'm afraid of you."

In the lounge the others had frozen: Sandra, standing at the ping-pong table with Bigelow and two boys from NYU; Beverly

Ann on the couch with Clay and her latest male cousin. The others were scattered in groups of two and three, staring in the direction of the voice.

"It's that nitwit, Daphne," Beverly Ann said.

They could hear her still screaming from somewhere out of sight. "Go away," she was shouting. "Go away. You're dead. You're dead. Go away."

"Oh, for Christ's sake," Beverly Ann said. She got up, strode across the room, and pulled open a cupboard door, revealing Daphne crouched beneath the shelves.

"Tell her to go away," Daphne sobbed.

"Oh, stuff it," Beverly Ann said. She reached down, grabbed Daphne's arm, and yanked her out. "OK," she said. "Third-act curtain. You can go back to your dressing room now."

But Daphne kept on crying, wordlessly now, until she spotted Miss Reed. "It's Mrs. Hunnicutt," she said. "She keeps coming back and threatening me. Benson brought her. He said she wanted to come to warn me to stay away from the stage. Because she's crazy jealous. She knows I'm going to be a big star someday. On Broadway. Not in rotten little tenth-rate towns like her. But that's no reason to pull my hair and scratch my. . . ."

"Jesus Christ, spare us the details," Beverly Ann said. "Go talk to my new cousin instead. Tell him I said it's OK. Holy Mary, every time she thinks she isn't being starred, she pulls something."

Daphne broke into fresh sobs.

"Thanks, Beverly Ann," Miss Reed said, putting her arm around Daphne. "But save the analysis for Group Therapy, OK? I'll take care of her now." She led Daphne, still crying, to her room.

Rex walked through the lounge and past the kitchen and on down the hall. At the door of the therapy room he paused. He could almost hear the sounds of the Rachmaninoff concerto. And remembered it was time for his pill. In a way, Daphne was right.

Benson was still around, still "seeing" to him. Rex nodded his thanks to Benson and hurried on to the nurses' station and his medication. Thus insuring that the privileges he continued to refuse would not be denied him.

Miss Reed sedated Daphne and put her to bed. And remembered what Rex had said. Was anyone ever cured here? How could she know? They came and went. Sometimes they went out far better than they came in. Sometimes not. Sometimes they came back. Sometimes not. Which meant nothing. They might stay outside in the world for weeks, months, years, taking dictation or selling gloves or studying social psychology. Yet suspicious of the dial tone and terrified of the fridge, white and whirring and creating continuous ice. There were times when Miss Reed herself felt the fear, felt it rustling her uniform and brushing her cap, a nameless fear of a future with no form and a time with no purpose.

She had spent her life inside carefully tailored days in firmly shaped institutions constructed for that purpose: to house and mold the Miss Reeds of the world and fit them in where needed. She had inhabited an orphanage, a student dorm, and a nurses' home, moving from one to the other when necessary, taking with her obsolete addresses and the collected works of Alexandre Dumas, given to her volume by volume each Christmas by her only known relative, a maternal uncle who had visited her once a year until he died when she was twelve. After that she allowed herself to become attached to no one but the characters in Dumas. Except once, to Dr. Curran Harte. But who could blame her when he was D'Artagnan and the Duc de Berry and the Vicomte de Bragelonne all rolled into one? And more. A young intern with red hair that lit up the corner where he was and a smile that tilted the ward way over in his direction and sent her sliding to his side. No wonder she forgot herself when he asked her to marry him, leaning across an empty stretcher in the labor room with his stethoscope swinging, like a huge benevolent eye, on his chest. Of course she said yes, and of course he was killed a week later, treating a patient in a burning tenement.

She switched from Maternity to Psychiatry to work with Dr. Prokosh and a new clientele and moved from the second floor of the nurses' home to the tenth, taking the works of Dumas with her. They were all she had, constant and impersonal. Like the patients in the ward, who would always be there and would always be strangers. She walked among them softly, slender and self-contained, corked by the little white cap.

But there were times when she thought she might someday, in desperation, adopt the more direct methods of her patients: invite their more specific fears, their more demanding compulsions. She might, someday, prefer to live in a mental ward, rubbing one spot on the wall or endlessly counting the knives and forks or measuring the width of the blinds. Rather than sit in an old-folks' home doing nothing.

Daphne was asleep. Miss Reed sighed and got up to return to the others, trying not to remember Rex's questions. And met Mr. Hunnicutt, walking down the hall.

He bowed and smiled. "I hope it's all right," he said. "I find I miss it." After that he came regularly, to play ping-pong with Bigelow and discuss Dante with Mrs. Schiller and the deplorable state of modern fiction with Hartley's mother. To admire Daphne's crying act or make a fourth at bridge. When no one else needed him, he walked the halls with Mr. Nuffield, discussing the weather forecasts. He always smiled at Miss Reed and wished her good evening. And she realized that she looked forward to his visits and hated Mondays, when he worked late at the library. Once she had to rescue him from Beverly Ann, who wanted to claim him as an uncle, and once from Dr. Fensterer. "He'll have to be a patient or attached to one," Dr. Fensterer said. "You know Prokosh doesn't allow visitors-at-large."

"Tell him he's my second cousin once removed," Miss Reed

said. "A clinical psychologist from Kansas City, interested in his methods." Her cap wobbled as she said it.

Mr. Hunnicutt smiled and went in search of coffee for Mrs. Schiller. But first he shook hands warmly with Miss Reed.

" 'Go, since I needs must die,/And give the world the lie,' " he murmured.

Which seemed to her a beautiful thing to say.

CHAPTER SEVEN

Upstairs, in the tower suite, Dr. Prokosh considered the atmosphere. It was a week after Mrs. Hunnicutt's suicide and he might, normally, expect the tension to subside. Around him were files and tapes and an array of stout-hearted books. And primitive masks and carvings and rugs. The latter were as much a part of his professional equipment as the former. For his field was human behavior—then and now, here and there. He was fascinated by the primitive, in civilized man and in the savage. And his breadth had won him a reputation. A man of science, of reason, he worked hard to control the irrational. In himself and others. He hated the dark—literally and figuratively. The lamp on his desk, in the tower and in the ward, burned constantly.

"Arnold Prokosh, M.D." hung in small gold letters on his door and "Arnold Prokosh, M.D." was inscribed in all his books, and there were those who suspected that the initials on his watch and his wallet and even his socks and shirts were "A.P.M.D."

For the M.D. was actually the most important part of his name. He lived his profession as, perhaps, only the Pope lives his. His office was his residence and he devoted himself, full time, to the care and cure of his patients. Though he rarely visited the ward, he was aware of it always, far beneath the thick pile of his carpet. And had the sense that, just by laying his palm on the desk, he could feel the vibrations twenty floors below. The day Mrs. Hunnicutt smothered herself, he had noticed a definite turbulence in the atmosphere. But the intercom in the ward had been turned down. By the time he was able to make contact, it was too late. After that he installed a special phone to be used only in emergencies. Known to his staff as "The Upstairs Line."

Though he saw little of his patients, he knew them intimately, for he listened, far into the night, to the voices of Joyce and Terence and Beverly Ann. They related better, he believed, to the younger men, talked more easily to the simpler personalities of Fensterer and Sourette and whatever other interns came and went each year. It allowed him to remain detached, objective, uninvolved; to study the raw data—the voices, the intonations, the symbols of his patients. And left him free to supervise the ward and carry on his research. And to treat hundreds instead of a handful. For he had a vision of a long queue outside his office, a queue stopped only by the rivers, east and west; men and women shivering in the wind with their neuroses by the hand, waiting to see Dr. Prokosh. So he communicated mainly through his staff but kept his fingers and his ear on the pulse and heart of his ward. And noted the new disturbances. The result, evidently, of the presence of Rex Bannister, who wished to remodel the ward as he longed to remake the world. Dr. Prokosh sighed and turned to the tapes of the past, tapes that covered ten to fifteen years of a single life, before the world had grown too big and hurried for a single patient on the couch. When the "hour" had fifty minutes instead of five.

For, unlike his patients, Dr. Prokosh had a past, a past that gave a special tilt to his words, as though he had learned them in some distant province of his youth. Though he was as American as his tape recorder, he had never, until he entered medical school, felt at home. Childhood and youth had been alien territory and his speech retained the formal quality of a man speaking a foreign tongue, a speech cultivated carefully at night behind his father's tailor shop, copied from recordings borrowed from the library. He spent his evenings imitating Gielgud and Olivier and Maurice Evans in clothes taken from his father's stock. By the time he left high school he felt reasonably at home in upper-class clothes and an upper-class accent. His parents cooperated by dying early. He emerged from medical school a self-made man as well as an M.D., ready and able to make over others.

"You have a gift," his math teacher told him. "You should go to the university. Become a scholar, an Einstein." His economics teacher was enthusiastic, his anatomy teacher impressed. He should be a banker, a surgeon, have a brilliant career. He thanked them and opened an office for psychoanalysis.

The patients came, in a trickle at first and then a stream which threatened to become a mighty river. He had no idea there were so many. Each time he closed his door on one, he was aware of thousands more waiting to get in. Walking the streets, he saw their faces with the nightmares still clinging to their chins. The noses looked squashed or bent or turned up too far like broken spigots. He marveled that they could breathe at all. They walked quickly, jerkily, as if picking their way through debris. Their eyes opened and closed. They crossed with the lights. Dr. Prokosh hurried back to his office and waited, restlessly, for his next patient.

"A wasteful system," his wife had said. "Expensive." She gestured toward the picture of Freud above his desk. "You really should move along, Arnold."

He had been married, briefly, to a big woman, prematurely

gray, a woman who had, almost from the beginning, carried an old head on her shoulders. She was several years older than he and twice as distinguished, with a special interest in the psychology of primitive peoples. Her father had been a well-known anthropologist and she spent a good deal of time, when she wasn't lecturing around the country, on foreign field trips, following up Daddy's data. Dr. Prokosh was never quite sure why she had married him, unless it was to share his office and his tape recorder. He enjoyed escorting her to lectures and meeting her famous friends and seeing her name above his on the door, though Dr. Leslie Hamish sounded more like a colleague than a wife. But it had not been there for long. She had left him after a year, not for another man but for an African village, to broaden her experience and narrow her hips. "Don't know how long I'll be gone, Herr Doktor," she said, patting his chin. "But don't wait up. Though you might move around a bit yourself. See more than one patient an hour and more than one pigmentation. It's a big world, Arnold. Take a look. If not to Africa, at least as far as Harlem. Vary the perspective and the color scheme. Everything's group-minded and technicolored now." And she left to apply modern psychiatric methods to the natives of Mozambique.

He went as far as Mexico and Latin America, collecting pre-Columbian art, which he hung in his office and interpreted freely to patients and guests. He made slight forays into the study of drug therapy and intensive researches into the psychology of primitive art, publishing for his own pleasure—and unexpected profit—psychoanalytic studies of blankets and bowls and masks and cups. He acquired a reputation.

Otherwise he was content behind his desk, fascinated by the vagaries of human behavior that appeared on his couch. Mrs. Altchek, who went through life with her head down lest her face be worn away. "I have sensitive skin, doctor," she said. "Too many people looking too much, it peels." Mrs. Finletter, who had lived for ten years in the cedar closet of her huge house to avoid so much empty space. And Mr. Kruger, who, recognizing the importance of beginning well, had spent twenty years on his memoirs and had two hundred and eighty pages of first lines. He had been a rich man once with a whole string of drugstores inherited from his father.

"Tell me, please, why I can't get past the first line."

"Fear of your own hostilities, perhaps. Hidden too long behind cotton and cough syrup."

"So prescribe, please."

"For repressed hostilities there are no pills," Dr. Prokosh said. Mr. Kruger gave himself up, full time, to psychoanalysis and his opening sentence. And Dr. Prokosh cleared his mind for his next patient.

Once he dreamed he was a mechanic. He was all alone in a huge garage with the stock neatly arranged around the walls according to size and clearly labeled. On one side were the small parts in divided drawers like nuts and bolts in a hardware store. Only they were marked "Phobias" and "Talents" and "Aggressions" and "Needs." Farther along, the parts became increasingly bigger and easily identified: eyes and toes and hands and heads. As he waited, boxes on wheels rolled in with their lids up and he could see the bodies in various stages of disintegration, mental and physical. It was up to him to decide what was lacking and supply the missing parts. But though he worked smoothly and efficiently, he worked in terror, for he knew that sooner or later some of the parts would be used up. Then he would have to send some bodies out with two heads and no hands or five obsessions and no talents. But the boxes kept coming long after most of the needed parts were gone. He stood shaking and weeping, unable to work, unable to mend the broken people, while the boxes continued to pile up around him, long boxes with their lids up.

After that he kept his lights on all night and spent many evenings playing over, for distraction and reassurance, the tapes of the past, a practice he continued in the tower. His old patients, he told himself, were far more appealing than any he had now. Except, perhaps, Terence Drew.

But he did not want to think of Terence Drew, who reminded him so much of an earlier patient, Toby Downes. He had been Dr. Prokosh's last private patient, young and fair like Terence and handsome enough to charm the masks off the walls. He had been a schoolteacher too and Dr. Prokosh sometimes had the odd feeling that Toby was examining *him,* allowing twenty-dollar pauses to stretch out between them, waiting, like any tolerant teacher, for Dr. Prokosh's response.

Toby Downes was a high-school teacher who had suddenly gone dumb and become a lifeguard at the Westside Community Pool instead. But he wanted to teach. It had happened on a Wednesday, a perfectly ordinary, yawn-filled, once-a-week type Wednesday at the beginning of the second period. He had opened his mouth to ask a routine question about the Intolerable Acts when he realized that his voice was not there. It was a ghastly, obscene, degrading feeling, like putting his hand to his brow and finding that his head was gone. He stood there in front of the class, panting and gasping and silent as a fish. In the end he could only close his mouth and flee. He had gone back once more only to have the same thing happen again.

"It happened only in school?" Dr. Prokosh said.

"Yes."

"And always in the same class?"

"The same subject and the same room. Yes."

"Ahhh. Tell me about it."

It was a perfectly ordinary third form class in American history. "Nice kids," Toby said. "Mixed boys and girls. I knew some of the boys quite well." For he coached the swimming team and the track team. "It was a good class. One of the best." He closed his eyes and began to describe the room. He could see it all so clearly. He had spent from 10 to 10:50 A.M. in that room every morning and two periods in the afternoon. For over a year.

A pleasant room with a view of the playing fields, green and smooth, ending in a border of trees. There was an aquarium at the back of the room full of fish and spitballs, and one wall carried prints of the death masks of Shelley and Keats, the contribution of some long-retired English teacher. He could see the bulletin board crowded with clippings and a color picture of President Truman over the door.

"President *Truman?*" Dr. Prokosh said.

"No. Oh, no." Toby Downes opened his eyes. Yet he could see it so clearly, that picture above the door, the stern face looking down at him through steel-rimmed spectacles like some super-principal guarding the exit, watching him constantly. Toby remembered how afraid he had been of him as a boy. But of course. That had been long ago, in his own ninth-grade classroom when he had been a shy student, terrified of Miss Bray with the red face and the fiery tongue. But she had had, thank God, weak eyes. Toby always sat in the back of the room, last row, last seat on the left next to the window. He knew that he had been very unhappy that year but he could not remember why. Only that he was lonely and miserable and had taken up swimming and poetry and crosscountry running. He had memorized yards of Kipling and Macaulay and Omar Khayyám which he could still remember. He had never talked to anyone about his misery, had probably never understood it himself. Perhaps that was why that year, and the boy who lived it, remained so vivid and so detached in his mind. As if the boy, Toby, had stayed there, was sitting there still, in that ninth-grade classroom. And he realized that when he had thought of teaching, it was that room he had visualized, with Harry Truman watching from the door. And it was that boy, last row, last seat on the left by the window, whom he would teach.

"And did you?"

"Did I what?"

"Teach him. That boy in the last row by the window."

Toby sat up suddenly and whirled around to face Dr. Prokosh. "But that's *exactly* what I did. Of course. I never realized it before. Directed most of my remarks to that seat. Ever since I began to teach. Of course, that's what I did."

"And last Wednesday?"

Toby stared. There was a long pause. "The seat was empty." He leaned back and rested his head on the back of the couch. His face was covered with sweat.

"And the next time?" Dr. Prokosh said softly. "It was empty again?"

Toby nodded in silence.

He left full of smiles and wonder and gratitude. "My God," he said, shaking his head and Dr. Prokosh's hand. "My God. My God. Any time you want to swim in the Westside Community Pool, let me know. I'll see you have it all to yourself."

But later, when Dr. Prokosh suggested it was time to go back to school, he blanched.

"I think you're ready," Dr. Prokosh said.

"Ready?"

"To try again."

"No. Hell no."

"You're frightened, of course. But you'll always be frightened until you try it."

"It will happen again. I know it will."

"No. Now that we know *why* it happened, I feel quite sure it won't."

"But I *don't* know why."

"I think you do. As much as you can know now. But there's something else you must find out."

"Something else?"

"I think it's important to know who *really* sits in that seat."

"But I've no idea. Lots of people, in fact. I have three classes in that room and we don't have assigned seats."

"Nevertheless," Dr. Prokosh said, putting the tips of his fingers together, "I think it's important to know who they are. Think about it. And when you go back, make a point of noticing who is in that seat. At each class. We'll talk about it next time. It is essential that we know."

"But I can't go back," Toby said. He was perspiring. "I'm not ready. It will happen again. I know it will. I can't go back."

"Yes you can. Of course you can. And it will not happen."

Later he was to wonder why he had been so insistent. And so impatient. Was it simply that he had never before had a patient who was also a teacher, used to giving directions and structuring the hour? Who knew all of *The Rubáiyát* by heart and American history well enough to teach it and swimming well enough to guard others? And run crosscountry besides? He had even made the masks smile. But they were not smiling now. For Toby Downes was not exuding charm now. He was sitting on the couch, staring at the rug.

"Remember," Dr. Prokosh said, "we want to know who sits in that seat. We'll explore it next time."

"I'm not ready," Toby said. "It will happen again. I know it will." He got up, picked up his coat, and, for the first time, left without saying good-bye. Dr. Prokosh never saw him again.

Toby did go back to his classroom and this time the seat in the back near the window was not empty. But it happened anyway. He had stared steadily at the seat, trying to make out who was sitting there, and opened his mouth. But no voice came. No voice of his anyway. What he heard instead was a terrible roaring in his ears, and Dr. Prokosh's voice shouting: "Who sits in that seat? Who *really* sits in that seat? It is essential that we know." Toby tried very hard to see who it was but his sight was blurred as if from the vibrations of that thundering voice. He stood there for a long time, staring and panting, trying desperately to get his own voice out over Dr. Prokosh's and to see who was sitting there. For some reason, though he did not know why, it was terribly important to know who it was. "Who? Who? Who?"

Dr. Prokosh shouted. And Toby realized that he could find neither his voice nor his vision in that terrible din. He closed his mouth and fled.

They found him later, fully dressed, face down in the Westside Community Pool, with a copy of *The Rubáiyát* in his pocket. The boy in the seat by the window that day was a new student whom Toby had never seen before.

That night Dr. Prokosh sat behind his desk as usual but he could not work on his current book or read the latest article on drug therapy or even listen to the tapes of the past. For the only voice he could hear was Toby Downes' saying over and over: "It will happen again. I know it will. I'm not ready." Dr. Prokosh had never failed a patient so completely before.

He sat behind his desk for a long time, thinking about his patients and his past. Until he remembered his wife, that large, active, courageous woman who had let her hair go white and could afford to face facts, telling him briskly that he should move along. Two months later he took down Dr. Sigmund Freud and packed up his old tapes and his primitive art and moved to the tower apartment of the Mayflower Memorial Hospital, to be the director of its new experimental psychiatric ward. And to institute a new system.

He worked hard, harder than ever before, though he rarely left his suite. But he told himself that the move to Farnsbee South had taken him farther than any African village. Had, in fact, made him an explorer in the heart of Manhattan. Sometimes, in the evenings, he would stand quietly, unnoticed, in the doorway of the solarium, watching the patients dance and sing and flirt, a tourist in his own ward, observing, with interest and pleasure, the youth he had never known. But he avoided, as much as possible, the sight of Terence Drew, who was young and blond and a teacher too. Terence Drew with his hair faded and his insides burned away. But at least he was walking the ward, not lying, face down, in the Westside Community Pool.

CHAPTER EIGHT

"*I'll* tell you what it is with you, Daphne," Beverly Ann said at Family Meeting. "You don't *want* to get well. You never had it so good. Right, Vince?"

In a far corner, a thin man in a green suit nodded miserably. He had never known anyone in a mental hospital before. He told his friends his wife was having "female trouble."

"No cooking. No cleaning. Like a hotel," Beverly Ann went on. "Right, Vince? With lots of people around all the time—like students and interns and doctors and patients. Like a resort. Not just the goddamn kitchen curtains and the towels on the rack. And Vince after five. Right, Vince?" And Vince nodded again as though he could, somehow, intercept the flow of words with his forehead and leave his pride intact.

"After 4:40," Daphne said. "They give him time off for good behavior. Or maybe they just can't stand him around too long. He wears bifocals, don't forget."

In the corner, Vince stopped nodding. He took off his glasses and covered his eyes with his hands.

"I told him from the very beginning," Daphne said. "No kids. Not now. Maybe never. But that's no reason, is it, Dr. Fensterer, to lock me up in the broom closet?"

In the corner Vince, in the green suit that made him look desperate, exploded. "My God, Daphne. My God. I never did such a thing. You know I didn't." He looked around helplessly, hands out, offering a defense. "I come home for supper and there she is, sitting in the broom closet with her arms around the mop and a carton of empty Coke bottles on the ironing board. And the table still set for breakfast. She said she might never come out. Unless it was to go to Fort Lauderdale, Florida. That's all she ever talked about. A married woman. Fort Lauderdale, Florida."

"Just wanted attention," Beverly Ann said. "Like she always does. That's why she hides."

"Maybe she just felt safe in the broom closet," Terence said.

"Safe? Safe from what?" Vince said.

"You," Daphne said.

"Life," Hartley's mother muttered, sitting in the back. Hartley was picking his nose and wondering, she knew, what there would be for refreshments. He could sit through a thousand Family Meetings and Group Therapy too, for that matter. It wouldn't cure his mind any more than his arm. Probably wither *that* too. Better to pick his nose and dream than listen to the usual dirt they served up here. As bad as the stuff in the books she sold. She wondered if he even knew she was there and she had driven for an hour through the thick Jersey smells with the fog pasted to her windshield. She was sweating now, under the heavy coat she refused to unbutton. It was the only gesture left to her. To keep herself buttoned up and sweat for her son.

"I wonder why, Daphne," Dr. Fensterer said slowly, hoping he sounded shrewd and incisive. Like the senior men when they asked obvious questions. Which everyone knew weren't obvious and weren't really questions. They always began with "I wonder why."

"I wonder why," Dr. Fensterer said now, "you're so afraid of having a baby."

"I didn't say I was afraid," Daphne said. "Just that I don't *want* one." She looked at Dr. Fensterer and let her eyes fill with tears. He rubbed his cheeks and thought about rocks and wondered again whether he didn't, after all, prefer them to people. It made him wonder about Rosalie too and getting married and having someone around all the time, someone who might want to explore the nightlife at Vegas when he wanted to examine the faults on Mount Monadnock. She might not even appreciate his rock collection, which was spreading in all directions from the kitchen sink.

"You wanna be a geologist?" she would scream again. She might even cry and then he would have to kiss her. He wondered if his training analysis had been a success. He was still undone by tears, even Daphne's, who cried all the time. He wrote "Daphne" on his pad, enclosed in a large tear.

At the other end of the table, Dr. Sourette was not listening. In another lifetime, perhaps, he could devote himself to the deformities and malnutrition of the mind, help confused little white Americans like Daphne and Sandra to straighten out and settle down and raise tall sons to sound the seas and patrol the world and, eventually, command the moon. Where there would certainly be little black men to shine their shoes and polish their egos and help them conquer Mars. But now he should be back in Haiti with his skin turning darker in the relentless sun. In Haiti he had been ashamed of his light skin, a reluctant, diluted black like the mulattoes of Petienville, soaking in their private pools while the rivers ran dry below. The peasant women walked miles for water, carrying it back over the rocks in heavy Texaco drums worn high on their heads. Dr. Sourette had wanted to rush out and help them.

"Go to the United States instead," his father had said. "Bring back something as precious as water. And scarcer. Something they cannot fetch for themselves." His father was a doctor but aging rapidly. At forty he was thin and dry and shaggy as an old eucalyptus. "Go quickly. Tell no one. Just go," he said. "But come back soon. We need you here."

In Haiti the mulattoes looked pale but in New York, where noise and speed and size eliminated all subtleties, there were no shades. Only black and white. And in New York, surrounded by whites, Dr. Sourette was black. His hands on the counter looked dark as gravy. His face in the mirror surprised him.

He walked the streets of New York, longing for Port-au-Prince. He was afraid of the city. In the perpetual shadows of huge buildings, he would grow paler still and smaller, squashed beneath the noise and the tiny square of sky he carried home each night. He avoided the eyes of the manikins in the shop windows and the faces of the women in the street, their chins resting on the little worn spots chipped out of Mondays and Tuesdays. The city was a sin and an embarrassment. The sun blushed and the stars twitched and a nervous tremor shook the streets. He put on weight to avoid being knocked down. But he should have gone home instead, gone before the strange white doctor in the black suit sat down opposite him at lunch in the hospital cafeteria that day. Now he might never get home at all.

The doctor had worn a black suit and white cuffs like Baron Samedi, the Haitian god who ruled over sorcery and cemeteries. He was carrying a tray with black coffee and a container of yogurt instead of a cane and a top hat. But for a moment, Dr. Sourette felt death itself coming toward him from the "Cold Snack" counter.

Dr. Prokosh sat down and stared at the smooth brown face across the table. It reminded him of his wife and her African village. "Vary the perspective and the color scheme," she had said, ". . . at least as far as Harlem." But Dr. Prokosh had no time to go even as far as Harlem, though this young Negro might do it for him, might provide him with a new perspective and broaden his clientele.

"You are an intern here?" he said suddenly.

"Yes, sir."

"You have a residency for next year?"

"No, sir."

"I have an opening in my ward. I'll speak to Dr. Purcell."

It was weeks before he learned that Dr. Sourette was not a Negro from Harlem but a French-speaking mulatto from Haiti who could give him no insight or entrée into black America. And not until it was too late did Dr. Sourette learn that Baron Samedi was really Dr. Arnold Prokosh, in charge of a psychiatric ward. The two men avoided each other as much as possible, Dr. Prokosh from embarrassment, Dr. Sourette from fear. For Dr. Prokosh, with his white hands and black suit, still suggested sorcery and cemeteries. And there were times when Dr. Sourette felt he would never be free of him, was Dr. Prokosh's permanent acquisition, as if he had put his head on the tray that afternoon at lunch. Twice he tried to tell Prokosh that he could not remain in the ward, that he was not suited to manipulating white minds. That he must go home to treat black bodies.

The first time, he stood outside Dr. Prokosh's ward office ready to knock but heard voices. He waited patiently for the visitor to leave. But when Dr. Prokosh finally came out, he was alone. He nodded briefly to Sourette and hurried off down the hall. But just before he locked the door, Dr. Sourette managed to get a glimpse of the office. He saw only the empty chair and the huge gold wristwatch, face up on the desk. And knew that he had been tricked.

The next time, Dr. Prokosh hardly waited till he was through the door. "Ah, Sourette," he said, extending a hand. "I was about to send for you. You are a great success. Especially with the ladies. Do you know that?" Joyce regarded him, the only Catholic on the staff, as an ally; Mrs. Schiller trusted him as the only other foreigner; and Daphne and Beverly Ann preferred him as being the youngest and handsomest. Dr. Prokosh smiled his odd smile —Dr. Sourette could almost hear it squeak—and took his hand in a firm cold grip. He might have taken his tongue as well, for Dr. Sourette could not loosen it except, at last, to thank him. For what? he wondered now, and smiled at Daphne crying at the other end of the table. Her tears watered his intent. It was sprouting, filling his chest.

"I don't know *why* I don't want a baby," Daphne said. "I just *don't.*"

"Afraid it will look like Vince, probably," Beverly Ann said.

"I'm too young," Daphne said. "That's what it is. I'm too young."

"Too immature, you mean," Beverly Ann said. "*You* wanna be the baby."

"And too selfish," Joyce said. "Can't stand to think about anyone else. Ever."

"Look, Dr. Fensterer," Daphne said, "I thought you were all supposed to *help* me here. Not *scold* me. Not take Vince's side. You don't know what he's like. Making me get married so young just so he could have someone to cook for him after his mother died. And tickle his feet. And now he wants to keep me shut up with a baby so he can run around with all those women he's supposed to be teaching to *drive. Driving* lessons, that's what he calls it. Valerie Minch flunked her test four times. And I know for a fact that he's been giving her lessons steadily for two years. You just don't know what he's like, Dr. Fensterer. Just because he sits there so quiet in that God-awful green suit. He only wears it to annoy me. He *knows* I'm allergic to green. You just don't know what he's like."

"Not like that, believe me," Vince moaned. "Dear God, it's none of it true. She was dying to get married. Couldn't wait to have a place of her own. And it had to be a *house.* Made me borrow money for the down payment."

"That was just to get away from Daddy," Daphne said. "So he wouldn't beat me up every time I came home from a date. Crazy jealous, he was. So I had to go and marry *Vince*. Know why he locks me in the broom closet? So I won't see the milkman. Every Monday, Wednesday, and Friday I spend with the mops. I told him if I have a baby there'll be the diaperman and the doctor and the milkman probably *four* times a week. That's when he picked up the bread knife and said he would fix *that* all right. Said he was going to slice it very thin." She stopped while her face considered it, teetering between giggles and tears. "What I really wanted was a place of my own with hostess pants and a phone by the bed. I guess I forgot Vince would be living there too."

In the corner, Vince put his face in his hands. He sat motionless for a moment, his pale wrists sticking out of the green sleeves. Then he picked up his hat and, with his head down, walked quickly to the door. Daphne, smiling, watched him leave. "See what I mean, Dr. Fensterer?" she said. "I couldn't possibly go back to him now, could I? Once he even picked all the raisins out of the Sara Lee coffee cake."

"I don't think there'll be any more mail for Mrs. Daphne Krisch," Mr. Nuffield said from the door. "Not ever. We'll just have to stamp them all 'Addressee Unknown. Return to Sender.'" He turned and walked back down the hall.

"Make him stop that," Daphne screamed. "He's always spying on me. Torturing me. Just like Daddy. Wicked, crazy, dirty old man. Tell him to leave me alone. Creeping around and watching me all the time like he was. . . ."

"Ach, he doesn't hurt you," Mrs. Schiller said.

"And just exactly how would *you* know?" Beverly Ann said. "How the hell would you know *anything* around here with your nose in a book all the time?"

"I honestly think, Beverly Ann," Joyce said softly, crossing herself, "that it wouldn't hurt you to put *yours* there once in a while. Instead of always in other people's business. You might even learn something. Maybe. And stop telling lies about things you don't know anything about. Like shrouds cut in two and Jews. . . ."

"Just exactly who you calling a liar?" Beverly Ann shouted.

"You, dear. You told me all that blasphemy about people being buried half-naked and how Jews never take a bath except on Friday night and only with kosher soap. And Mrs. Schiller takes a bath *every* night. With Ivory."

"So, stupid? What's *that* supposed to prove? Who says she's a good Jew. Could be she's just trying to pass. Ever think of that, holy Sister Shithead?"

"What?" Mrs. Schiller said. "I'm not good? No good? Why not, please?"

"*You're* no good, Beverly Ann Grumm," Joyce said.

"Who you calling no good?" Beverly Ann shouted. "You fat, lousy, two-bit. . . ."

"You have a rash tongue and an evil heart and a wicked, blasphemous spirit," Joyce said. She stood up calmly and put her hands up her sleeves. "I'm sorry, Dr. Fensterer, but my vows do not permit me to listen. . . ."

"Why you bitch. You no-good, shitty, fucking bitch." Beverly Ann jumped up and, reaching across the table, began to claw Joyce.

"Kill her, Bev," a boy among the visitors shouted.

"Ladies, please," Dr. Fensterer said.

But Rex and Bigelow had already pulled them apart.

"I'm afraid this means suspended privileges for you again," Dr. Fensterer said. He rubbed his cheek.

"Screw you," Beverly Ann said. "Because that means I'll *really* go berserk. Christ, I'll tear this place apart. And my father will tear *you* apart. Blast you right out of this nice cozy little berth."

"Our time is up," Dr. Fensterer said. He nodded good night

and hurried off down the hall. He must not be late again. His sinuses couldn't stand it.

The rest of the ward was moving now, patients and friends and relations, moving toward argument and indignation and the comfort of jellied doughnuts. "My God," a woman in a huge fur hat said. "It shouldn't be allowed. She'll kill someone one of these days. Like all those maniacs they let run around loose. Five last month, shot down in a beauty parlor. Sat there for two hours, stone dead, with the dryers on 'hot.' I haven't had my hair done since."

"I'm taking Bonnie out next week," her companion said, pulling an enormous piece of embroidery out of her shopping bag. "She can go to that nice little place on Cape Cod. You know, where the Kennedys go when they want to get away from each other. That's all she needs. A little rest and a vacation from her mother-in-law." She sat down and began to thread a needle. "This place is terrible for the nerves."

Terence sat alone, holding his empty can. Refreshments were not for him. But neither was sitting at a table, watching Beverly Ann scratch and maul. Had he spent twenty-five years—and nine months before that—for this? Kept his hair groomed and his declensions tidy, worked hard at chemistry and math and packing groceries for *this?* "Terence, this is stupid stuff," he told himself, spitting into the can. He remembered his feelings as a boy, reading the headlines: "DANCER FOUND DEAD IN LUXURY APARTMENT." And there she was, smiling off the front page, a young girl who might have graduated from the local high school just last week, except for the bare shoulders. And he would imagine her growing up in some small town, playing house and learning to ride a bike and, later, curling her hair every night and studying *Evangeline* and the causes of the Civil War. She'd gotten through it all so well too, with her parents pushing so proudly from behind, had gone right through high school and maybe even ballet school and on to New York. And the front page of the *Daily News.*

Rex, carrying a cup of coffee, sat down beside him: Rex with his coffee, Terence with his can. Outside they were drinking beer and whisky and blood. And spitting each other's bones into the street. Outside "Thou *Shalt* Kill" had become the eleventh commandment. Otherwise you went to jail. Except yourself. For trying that you went to Farnsbee South. To hold your own spit.

The voices of the others bubbled up in the coffee urn and rose through the holes of the doughnuts, even hissed at him from the bottom of the can.

"I don't think I can take much more of this," he told Rex. "And it can only get worse."

"Worse?"

"I guess Fresh Meadows *is* worse."

"The state mental hospital? Christ, they're not really sending you *there?*"

"It really doesn't make much difference where I go. All I want, all I ever think about, is being someplace quiet. And you know what? There isn't any. Not now. And not later either. Not here and certainly not at Fresh Meadows. Or with Marlene and the baby and the January White Sales. Or the James Buchanan High School. And Dr. Fensterer says I mustn't be alone. So there's no place. No place at all. Except for ten minutes in the bathtub. And the grave."

"Not planning to go there yet, I hope," Rex said.

"I don't know." He stared into the can. "I overshot it once already. And now I'm stuck here, on the far side. But it can't be any worse over there. And my aim may be better next time."

"Jesus," Rex said. He saw the can shake in Terence's hand, saw the faded gold hair and the pale cheeks and realized how much of Terence was being burned away. "Jesus," he said again. "Jesus." He stood up. "I'll be right back." Someone must tell Prokosh. And he must listen. After Mrs. Hunnicutt, at peace beneath her pillow. He banged on the office door and heard, again, the familiar shuffling and shutting sounds.

In his swivel chair Dr. Prokosh looked calm and satisfied, as though he'd just finished a good dinner of depressions and manias and compulsive obsessions taken on a tray at his desk. Rex reached for his notes.

"Ah, Rex. Sit down. But leave your pad in your pocket, please. How are you getting on?"

"The only way I can. By reporting." Rex put his notebook on the desk.

"You are a man as well as a reporter. Put the notes away."

"And are you a man as well as a doctor?"

"You wish to talk to me as a man? To *talk*, not to report?"

"I wish to *plead*, for Christ's sake. If necessary. For Terence. He's in a bad way."

Dr. Prokosh swiveled slightly to the left. "Then *he* should come and talk to me himself. Not send you."

"He didn't send me."

"Can you be sure? He didn't tell you to come in so many words, perhaps. But didn't he, in fact, make sure you would come?"

Rex stared at him. Was Dr. Prokosh right? Dr. Prokosh with his theories. While Rex had only his feelings.

"If you really want to help Terence, don't run interference for him. He's got to help himself. You've been here long enough to know that. He's got to take responsibility for himself. With an assist from us."

"Such as shoving him into Fresh Meadows?"

"Perhaps."

"Into total despair? Christ, he's threatening. . . ."

"I know what he's threatening. We are, after all, very used to such threats."

"Christ. You keep him here till he can't pay his bills then shove him into that state inferno for *debt?* Why in hell don't you let him out so he can make some money if you're so damn anxious to be paid?"

Dr. Prokosh sighed and swiveled to the right. "Because he's not ready."

"Not ready?"

"He doesn't even really want it."

"Not *want* it?"

"Of course not. He tells us that every minute of every day. He is, after all, still clutching his can. As you, Rex Bannister, still cling to your notebook. Think about *that,* if you please. And leave Terence to us."

Rex nodded slowly and stood up. Of course. Dr. Prokosh was right. He had to be. It was a professional disease, this need of Rex's to snoop and pry and distrust the facts; to report and expose. Everywhere. "OK," he said. "I'll try." But just before he reached the door he remembered his notebook. He picked it up and put it carefully back in his pocket.

CHAPTER NINE

Marcus Mishkin put on his hat, arranged his features, and prepared to venture out into the public domain for his visit to Farnsbee South. He still hated hospitals, though the Mayflower Memorial was more like a hotel than a hospital, with a lobby full of plants and rugs and modern furniture, the kind designed for arrogant women with crossed legs and very long, very slim cigarettes. But upstairs there were little carts filled with jars and tubes and long silent stretchers and strange bells. And a disembodied voice summoning "Dr. Passmore, Dr. Edgerton Passmore," to heaven or the operating room. Marcus lived in terror of the day he would hear "Mrs. Mishkin, Mrs. Sandra Mishkin." Until then, he walked quickly through the halls, covering as much space with as few steps as possible. Avoiding contact. The thought of twenty floors of occupied beds filled him with guilt. There seemed to be so much of him and all of it healthy and so little of everyone else. Two men could easily wear his trousers if willing to go in the same direction. He even had the upper regions of the subway and the street to himself. And the comfort of his pockets. While the sick were pinned down to six feet of bed and an empty stretch of sheet. Hospital gowns, he suspected, had no pockets.

In the elevator, the car stopped to admit a young nurse with a full life plumping out her uniform and a guarantee of more to come strapped to her wrist, a watch to determine other people's heartbeats and her own lunch break. Tonight she would dance with Rick at the Cheetah. But now she was pushing an old man on a stretcher toward Radiology. He was flat on his back with his eyes open and the sheet up to his chin. Death was covering him like a white tide. Only his face was still above water. He did not move at all but kept staring above him, at the ceiling and the intravenous bottle suspended from the stretcher. He could look nowhere *but* up. Marcus, whose head was on a level with the bottle, saw the old man's eyes shift slightly, saw him smile.

"Come at last, eh?" the old man said. "Knew they couldn't keep you away." His voice was feeble and dry, as if he'd already taken a mouthful of dust. He stretched out a hand. "Good boy," he said. "And big too. Like your daddy and your granddaddy. Knew they couldn't keep you down. Good boy." He nodded and closed his eyes. The elevator stopped and the nurse pushed the stretcher out. Marcus, holding the old man's hand, went too. The stretcher bounced slightly and Marcus saw the head with the closed eyes bounce too.

"Nurse," Marcus said.

"Sorry. He's always worse when he has to go for treatments."

"Nurse," Marcus began again. "Do you think . . . I mean, I wonder . . . well, I don't think he'll be needing treatments anymore."

She stopped pushing and stared down at her patient's face. Then reached for his pulse. "You're right," she said, disengaging Marcus' hand and putting the old man's back under the sheet.

"Right back upstairs for him," she said, turning the stretcher around. "Nice you could come. Just the right height too. He's been waiting all week." She rang for the elevator. "Unless it was the shock that killed him." She bent over him again. And Marcus knew that the tide was about to rise. The stretcher would look flat and empty then except for the glucose bottle, still dripping, sweetening the old man's death. Marcus tipped his hat and hurried off in the direction of Maternity.

When the stretcher had gone, Marcus got back into the elevator and rode up and down for a long time, a huge perpendicular man in an upright coffin. Though far too big to be buried standing up. Yet he might have been just that, standing motionless in that small box, riding up and down between "20" and "B," between heaven and hell. With death, perhaps, still beside him where the stretcher had been. But death had not harmed him, had not so much as brushed the sleeve of his coat, had merely stretched out a hand in greeting. Had taken the old man instead, had taken him gently, merely closing his eyes and covering his face, and carried him back upstairs. And provided Marcus for solace. Otherwise the old man would have had nothing but the glucose bottle. The nurse had been too busy watching the floors and balancing the flowered handkerchief in her left breast pocket. Only Marcus had seen the old man's death, leaning across the stretcher, waiting for his eyes to shift slightly, to take in Marcus as well as the glucose bottle before closing them forever. The wonder of it carried Marcus up to the twentieth floor and down to the basement, to be lifted up again by the realization that he, Marcus, bigger than life, whose head brushed canopies and whose feet hung over the curb, had, for once, been just exactly the right size. Had reached just high enough. Had filled a gap between life and death and helped an old man across. It was his calling, not his size, he realized, that was at fault. He should have been a doctor or a priest, not an accountant, helping people with death not taxes.

He pushed the button for the seventh floor. For the first time in his life he felt comfortable inside his own body, felt he could stretch enough to fill it completely. A big man who had held death itself in his hand. A big man with a big man inside. But with less room than ever, perhaps, for Sandra.

At Farnsbee South he realized that he did not want to see her at all. He wanted to talk to Rex, who knew all about death: death by flood and fire and the bullets of righteous men; by accident and design and carefully selected disease; in the name of God and Law and Motherland and Fatherland. Deaths that came too soon or too late. And bizarre deaths that carried a hint of frivolity: to the man in a helicopter observing the traffic; to the lady in Dallas unscrewing the cleaning fluid. But no one, surely, had seen death as he had, a fellow passenger in an elevator who had shaken hands with him between the first and fourth floors.

Rex met him in the hall. The big man, he thought, looked shaken. As though someone or something had finally gotten to him, way up on his mountain peak. Enough to start a landslide. "Come sit down," Rex said, to halt disaster.

Marcus sat in Rex's only chair and stared at Rex's face with its look, like one of Millicent Carr's pots, of having been fired but with the thumbprints still visible. An embarrassing face. Marcus coughed and rattled his coins. Rex sat on the bed with his head against the wall and his arms stretched out beside him, palms up. The old man's hand, Marcus remembered, had been cold.

"I just saw someone die," he heard himself say. "First time in my life. A man I didn't even know."

"You watched someone die?" Rex said it with awe. "I never have, you know. Not really. Because they didn't really die. They were killed. It's not the same thing."

"Not the same thing at all," Marcus said. "Not at all." It was a distinction he had never considered before. And now, suddenly, he longed to consider it, that private personalized death which had so clearly been chosen and expected and greeted like a guest.

Daphne, the monitor for the day, stuck her head in the door. "Sandra's in the therapy room," she told Marcus, "having her portrait painted." She giggled. "By Bigelow."

Marcus did not get up but jingled his coins again. "They tell me she's better," he said.

Rex nodded.

"But not with me."

Poor damn Marcus, all alone on a mountain peak and yearning for the coziness of a house in the valley. Tied to a wife who could not climb up, even part way, to meet him. "She's better *here,*" Rex said. "where she's never alone. Where there are lots of us. Always. We keep her stimulated but make no demands. She's the darling of the ward, you know. We've given her a pose, at last. And she doesn't have to go all rigid to keep it. But outside. . . ." He lifted his palms for a moment, then let them drop. Ever since Mrs. Hunnicutt, he had been limp and tired, far too tired to talk to Marcus Mishkin clutching his coins, married to a wooden wife and unable, himself, to bend either toward or away from her. Unable to do anything but sit in misery on the straight hard chair he had been offered, with his feet and his hands and his rump nailed down.

"But she *is* much better."

"Not with me," Marcus said. "She hates me." He stared across the room and saw his own face and one side of Rex's head in the mirror. "She hates me," he said again.

"No," Rex said. "Afraid of you."

"It comes to the same thing." He paused. "What should I do?"

"Stop being afraid of *her,* maybe. She's just a poor sick girl who happens to have a pretty face." And has therefore, he thought, been permanently flawed. In her case, looks *had* killed. "But she doesn't need to be worshiped," he said.

"I don't know what she needs," Marcus murmured. "Or even wants."

"To be petted and protected, I suspect."

"But not by me." He was looking at the mirror again. And realized, suddenly, how much they had in common: Marcus with a wife he couldn't keep and Rex with a wife who couldn't keep him.

"Cheer up," Rex said. "Who knows? Sandra may fool you yet. May be ready for a new pose. May even decide to sit as a housewife with a grocery list in her pocket."

"And you? Found a 'custodian' yet?"

Rex smiled and shook his head. "I shall probably explode someday and spill my chemicals all over the ward. Maybe they could use them to balance someone else's glands. I rather like the idea of keeping someone else calmed down. And give my eyes to the blind." For they were still perfectly good, his eyes, in spite of having seen so much. "Look out of someone else's head for a change."

Marcus, rising to leave, knew that Sandra would never relax. Not for him. Would not even turn her head and smile. Though, surely, it was not too late for Rex, who seemed to know so much. And needed so little. But Sandra needed the crowded rooms of Farnsbee South, which he, Marcus, could not provide.

At the door of Rex's room, he took his hands out of his pockets to say good-bye. There was something else he wanted to say but the words were all jumbled up with the coins. He was not yet ready to sort them out.

"Don't worry," Rex said, holding out his hand. "Sandra's just scared like everyone else. They'll fix her up. Don't worry."

Marcus relinquished his coins to take Rex's hand. "Thanks," he said. "Thanks for taking me in."

Walking down the hall he allowed himself, for the first time, to glance into the rooms. He saw a girl on her knees and a young man practicing forward passes. Seeing Marcus, he smiled. "Catch," he said, and tossed him an invisible ball. Marcus smiled back and hugged it to his chest. An old man, walking up and down the hall, stopped for a moment to say: "Sorry. Nothing for you today. But tomorrow, you know. Maybe tomorrow."

In the elevator, Marcus remembered the old man who had died on his way to Radiology. Marcus had forgotten all about him. At the door of the hospital, he slipped the memory on again with his hat, holding it tight against the wind.

That night, for the first time in months, Marcus had the sensation, just before falling asleep, that he was aboard his ship again. Beside him stood a young man in white and behind him the silent passengers read and prayed and tossed footballs into the sea. There was no figurehead on the prow and no course to follow. But the sea was calm and he floated gently into sleep.

Rex, walking slowly back down the hall, passed the room where Mrs. Hunnicutt had spoken her last lines and the therapy room, where Benson had accompanied her on the piano. Perhaps he was accompanying her still, a boy whose skill reached beyond the grave and a woman eager to perform anywhere at all. Sometimes, waking in the night, Rex would imagine he could still hear Benson playing that small slice of Rachmaninoff's concerto over and over, the only piece of music he had ever learned. Just as he was playing the same limited part over and over in his uncle's tawdry drama. Even his second sight gave him no vision, except of the grave. And Dr. Prokosh had provided no light, had merely sent him back with his white stick and the memory of a few measures of music to entertain him between spirits. But what had Prokosh done for any of the others, Rex wondered, looking around the solarium—at Garrick and Terence and Verna, with her head still bent beneath His hand? And Clay bouncing his ball. They were, each, still clinging to their special symbols, the only valuable possessions that had not been locked up in the hospital safe. So Garrick wrote and Terence spat and Verna hung on the words of the Lord. What in the world did He say to her? Rex wondered. And why were there never any commands to act?

No "Thou Shalts" apparently. Only "Thou Shalt *Not*."

"He wants to do all the talking, so why doesn't she bring Him to Family Meeting?" Beverly Ann said in Group Therapy. "Husband substitute like."

"If Joyce doesn't object, that is," Daphne said. "Don't forget, she was married to Him once. Engaged anyway."

"That's blasphemy," Joyce said. "But you'll be down there for eternity anyway. You sure have a nice long hot future ahead."

"You're just jealous," Clay, the boy from Miami, said. "Probably nothing but babies and old maids in the other place."

"Yeah." Daphne giggled. "That'd be the *real* hell."

"Well, I doubt if there'll be much of what you want in hell," Joyce said. "Even if you're holed up with the biggest wolves in history."

At the word "hell," Verna turned her head and stared, for a moment, at the group around the table. Her lips moved slightly and she raised her fist. Then she turned back to the corner of the ceiling.

Why *doesn't* she invite Him down? Rex thought. Since Prokosh refused to budge from his particular heaven.

"She'll never get well, sitting by herself all the time, staring the paint off the wall," Beverly Ann said. "You'd think someone in this lousy community would *care* about getting her to interact."

"I wonder why, Beverly Ann," Dr. Fensterer said slowly, drawing circles on his pad, "I wonder why *you* care so much." She had been caught in the phone booth last night with Clay and a bottle of Scotch. Her bangs seemed to be bushier and higher than ever.

"Could be she feels insecure," Joyce said.

"Yeah. Needs to feel the group's always right there," Bigelow said.

"If the group doesn't seem to care about Verna, it may not care about her either," Terence said.

"Needs reassurance," Daphne said.

"Needs love," Rex murmured.

"You all nuts or something?" Beverly Ann shouted. *"Me* need *reassurance? Me* need *love? Love?* My God, I've been getting it from everyone in pants since I was twelve. From the corner butcher right on up the block. Both sides of the street. And right across Route 1 too, for that matter. Christ, I'm probably the only one here who *doesn't* need it. The rest of you are too old or too crazy or too faggoty. Except Clay." She gave him a long slow smile.

"That's right, baby," Clay said.

"And me," Daphne announced. "Don't forget about me."

"You call that *love?"* Joyce said.

"Ever wonder why you were getting it?" Terence said. "From everyone in pants all up and down the block?"

"She's just bragging," Daphne said.

"Or did you just assume it was your devastating, irresistible charm?" Terence said.

Beverly Ann smiled. "Yeah, professor. That's *just* what I assumed. You got a better explanation?"

"You bet I do," Terence began.

"Then why all the 'trips'?" Bigelow said suddenly.

"Because I'm turned on. That's why. Like everyone who isn't too old or too square or too scared."

"Or too stupid or too sick to stop," Bigelow said. "Or do you just like mental wards?"

"I was just unlucky, that's all. Had a bad trip."

"Five," Joyce said.

"At least it's not crazy. Like trying to burn off your tongue or kill yourself with kitchen equipment. And missing at that."

"You missed too," Garrick said suddenly. "Unless you were *trying* for Farnsbee South."

Beverly Ann leaned over and spat on his pad.

But the session was over. Dr. Fensterer hurried out. He had promised to call Rosalie at three and he was ten minutes late already.

Dr. Sourette, still sitting at one end of the table, saw Verna, absolutely still, with her head bent, listening. She reminded him of a zombie, one of the dead who have been revived and enslaved to do some sorcerer's bidding. He longed to sprinkle her food with salt so she could break the spell and run away. But Verna, he remembered, refused to eat. And there were no *loa* here to possess her, no gods to mount her and ride her back to sanity. Only that strange white Father and His weak, sad Son who kept His hand on her head and His finger on her lips. Dr. Sourette, watching, saw Beverly Ann pinch Verna's arm. But she did not move. He got up and started down the hall to the nurses' station. As soon as he was off duty, he would check the cost of a one-way ticket to Haiti.

In the solarium Garrick sat against the wall, writing with his left hand.

"Right hand still paralyzed?" Rex asked.

Garrick nodded. "A message from Grant," he said. "I know it."

"Why not phone and check?"

Garrick shook his head. "Oh, no," he said. "They won't allow it. Fensterer says I must learn to function on my own. Not be so dependent on Grant. But I'm not, you know. Even though he's my twin. Not at all. I just want to be sure he's all right." That he was still sitting in East Harlem, doling out the welfare while Garrick remained sheltered in Farnsbee South, writing down his poems.

"Where's his office?" Rex said. "I'll phone for you."

"Ninety-sixth and Lex. But they won't let you phone either. They listen in, you know. And if they catch you phoning Grant, they'll take my pad and pencil away. Thanks just the same." He smiled his slow jagged smile. He'll cut his lips, Rex thought, waiting for the sight of blood. Garrick bent to his pad again, a poet hiding behind his illegible script. Though he must have known that nothing so loosely woven could ever protect Grant. Was rather a net to trap himself.

"What makes you think he's in trouble?"

"My right hand, which will not move. And my left, which writes what it wills and not what I direct." He handed Rex his pad. For once the words were legible: "Oh, how sick and weary I/Underneath my mirtle lie." But they were none of them Garrick's. "Like to dung upon the ground/Underneath my mirtle bound."

"See what I mean? If I could only get out. I'd go up there. See for myself. Ninety-sixth and Lex. With green walls."

"I'll remember," Rex said. "If I ever get out."

"Have you seen Sandra?" Miss Reed said, appearing at the door. "She has an appointment with Dr. Prokosh in five minutes. She's his next patient."

"Tell him he's needed *here,"* Rex said, looking at Garrick. "Never mind his next patient."

"Yeah, I need him," Hartley murmured, coming up. "Here."

"Me too," Daphne said. "Honest, Miss Reed, I've hardly seen him since I came. Nothing but interns and residents and third-year students. I feel more like a blind date than a patient. Tell him I want to see him. Now."

"Message for Dr. Prokosh," Mr. Nuffield announced from the hall. "Special delivery for Dr. Prokosh."

"Message for Prokosh," Hartley shouted.

"Calling Dr. Prokosh. Calling Dr. Arnold Prokosh," Daphne chanted down the hall. From all parts of the ward the others took it up. Terence and Joyce and Bigelow and even Garrick joined in, participating for the first time in Farnsbee South, in a community sing. Everyone but Sandra, who could not be found.

"She went out on a pass but she should be back by now," Daphne said. But Sandra was always doing things to attract attention. Away from her, Daphne. Because she was jealous. They all were. Of her lovely hair and her big eyes and her soft, free-flowing tears. She looked around for a place to hide.

"Sandra's the one person who *doesn't* need to see Prokosh," Rex said.

"OK," Bigelow said. "But where is she?"

The others took it up, shouting: "Where is she? Where is she?" They began to rush through the ward, looking for Sandra. All except Garrick, who stayed where he was. Mrs. Schiller hurried out to the balcony and peered over the rail; Hartley rushed into the pantry and began to search in the fridge. Daphne, watching the others race past her, ran into the utility room and sat down on the floor with her arms around a broom and her thumb in her mouth. She stayed there until dinner, when Beverly Ann came and pulled her out.

Rex found Sandra, at last, in the staff room, posed in front of a mirror in which, he knew, she saw absolutely nothing.

"I don't want to go," she told him. "I'm afraid."

"Then don't. You don't have to do anything you're afraid of. Just tell him."

"That's right," someone shouted. "Don't do anything you're afraid of."

"Don't do anything you don't want to."

"Fuck the bastard."

"Be yourself."

"Be free."

They formed a protective line across the door, chanting: "Be free, be free, fuck that bastard, A.P." The uproar continued until nurses and orderlies and aides came to lead the patients away. The solarium and the lounge were closed. Dinner, that night, was served in the rooms.

That evening Rex knocked on Dr. Prokosh's door. If he was not in, Rex thought, he would storm the tower. For Garrick, too gentle to raise his fist even against a closed door, and for Sandra, too timid to ask for anything, even the time. Rex would have to do it for them. But Dr. Prokosh was telling him to come in. Not inviting. Just telling.

"Come in. Come in. Sit down."

Rex put his notebook on the desk.

"Not another interview, I hope."

"You know what happened this afternoon?" Rex said.

"I know."

"Sandra's scared."

"That I know too."

"Of her husband."

"Of many things."

"Then why don't you do something about it?"

Dr. Prokosh sighed and swiveled to the left. "Such as?"

"Tell him not to come any more."

"So that she can feel rejected again? As she has been all her life. By her father and her mother and now her husband. So that she will have no one at all?"

"But she's terrified. . . ."

"He's a frightening man, her husband?" Dr. Prokosh swiveled to the right.

"Not at all."

"Exactly. So, removing her husband will not remove her fear. Her *real* fear. But I must remind you again that I am not free to discuss the other patients with you." He smiled and gestured toward the notebook. "And I'm certainly not free to give interviews to the press. There is only *one* patient you and I can talk about: Rex Bannister. So if you will excuse me, I have a conference in five minutes." He picked up the notebook and handed it to Rex. "When you are ready to come out from behind your notes, to start looking *in* instead of around, let me know. Perhaps then we can really talk."

He was gone, locking the door behind him. With the light still burning. As if someone were still there: Dr. Prokosh, who was both walking down the hall to his conference and sitting behind his desk in the office, swiveling to the right and to the left, rocking the ward to soothe it and breathing over it gently to warm it or cool it as the occasion demanded. A man who could be two places at once. While he, Rex, could barely cover one. Had failed, again, to give his report, so that Prokosh, skillful as he was, was still ignorant: of the longings of Bigelow, who wanted only to be a farmer, and of Joyce, who was still a nun; of the torments of Mrs. Schiller and the true agony of the Mishkins.

He remained standing in the middle of the hall and felt his own heart beating beneath his notebook.

Upstairs, in his tower suite, Dr. Prokosh felt the agitation below. Sandra, he realized, was becoming a storm center. And Rex was stirring up the ward. It was beginning to slop over the edges. He got out the tapes on Sandra and Rex and listened for a long time with his eyes closed and his fingertips together, swiveling gently.

CHAPTER TEN

At the ward party, Rex remained seated, tilted gloomily against the wall, watching the Farnsbee guinea pigs dance to order. Just as they ate and slept and hallucinated as prescribed. But tonight there were even nurses and students and doctors and visitors, staring or strutting or twisting together, all dancing to the same tune. Proving what? Solidarity? Frivolity? Humanity? All but Verna. And Dr. Prokosh. Rex's list of demands was still in his pocket. It had gotten longer. It made a bulge. But there was no one to give it to. Certainly not poor Dr. Sourette, still waiting for the beat of his native drums and dancing, doggedly, to electric guitars. Even Mrs. Schiller had bravely left her corner and her Dante to be guided across the room by him. The first time in years, Rex thought, she had felt anyone's arms around her.

"Do you paint?" she asked. For Dr. Sourette was smiling down at her with his head slightly tilted, like her brother Rheinhold.

"Only in Haiti," he said. "And only walls. To cover up the bloodstains after the soldiers leave."

"Ach. You are homesick. No?"

"Yes. A little." He looked around the room at the white faces bobbing on the surface of the music, white faces and white necks and white hands—like eggshells. White, the absence of color. And they were *all* white, wrapped up in trousers and skirts and whatever they could buy to provide substance. Their *things* possessed them as the *loa* possessed the Haitian peasant. No wonder they needed them so desperately: the cars and the hair coloring and the electric toothbrush. They became not gods but blondes and junior executives. He hated their things. He hated his white uniform and his shoes with tongues and eyes. When he took them off at night, his feet wore the marks of the laces.

"But you are learning much here, yes?" Mrs. Schiller said.

"Yes. Quite a bit." Not enough but more than he would ever need about the customs of the North, where the white men went, one by one, down the steps of the subway, sucking their individually wrapped Charms, clutching their private, personal tokens; where there was no marketplace and no *combite,* no drum calling men and gods together to dance through the night. Only Dr. Prokosh, twenty floors up, who had ridden him, like one of the Divine Horsemen, into Farnsbee South.

He helped Mrs. Schiller back to her corner and thanked her and saw her plunge back down into her Inferno. He wondered just how far down she had gotten. He crossed the room and sat down beside Rex. "You're not dancing?"

"Never learned how."

"Nor I. Not this kind." Dr. Sourette mopped his brow. He had rarely talked to Rex before. He knew only of his "incident" in Haiti. Rex seemed to avoid him.

"When do you go home?" Rex asked. As if it were his home too.

"July, I guess." July would be hot and dry, with the yaws thick as berries. He looked at Rex and saw the fringes of the palms on his lashes. His eyes were dark. They had seen the dry hills of Haiti and the burned maize and the bananas and mangoes dropping too soon. In Haiti, man, they're starving to death, the eyes seemed to say. No wonder they avoided him. July was much too late.

"Going back without learning our native dances?" Rex smiled.

Dr. Sourette smiled back. "There are many things I have not learned," he said. Like how to carry a black skin through a country of whites. Until he went to the university he had never shaken hands with a white man. He imagined it would be like gripping a boiled egg. On his day off, he walked in Harlem. "Perhaps, in this case, my skin protects me."

"Armor couldn't protect you," Joyce said, sitting down beside them. "Not in this crowd." They were, indeed, getting noisier and wilder. Beverly Ann, in a man's straw hat, was kicking and twisting with abandon. Her partner had an expression of stupor on his face and a bulge in his back pocket. "I'm not going back there," Joyce said. "I don't have to interact with my hips. And I think Beverly Ann is smashed. Or stoned. Or something. Even more than usual."

"I thought all American girls liked to dance," Dr. Sourette said.

"I'm not really an American girl," Joyce said. "I'm a nun." She slid her hands up her sleeves. "I never really learned anything worldly. Except typing."

"And will you be a nun when you leave here?"

"I'll always be a nun. No matter what I do. Even if I have to go back to Mr. Looney's typing pool. Which I probably will. You see, they don't want me at St. Ursula's. But I really hate typing." She bent her head and looked at her arms with her hands gone.

"But surely there are many other things you can do?"

She shook her head. "No. Nothing else."

"Come to Haiti," he said. "There are very many things you could do there."

"Really? What?"

"Help in a clinic or teach school, for example."

"But I don't know anything. Except prayers and *The Lives of the Saints* and touch-typing."

"You could teach little children to read and write, certainly. And to wash their hands before eating."

"Yes," she said slowly. "I could do that. Would they really want me to do that? I'd *love* that."

She looked at him and smiled. But the music rushed in to fill their pause and she became aware of the others: of Hartley, sitting alone beside the record player, beating time against his ribs with his withered arm; of Sandra, walking stiffly through the steps with a new patient from MIT, her head turned away, keeping her pose from the knees up. Bigelow was dancing six feet from Daphne, with his arms folded across his chest and the expression of a man skirting a cesspool. And two girls in serapes were dancing together. Near the door, Garrick, his ski cap pulled down, sat alone, a pad on his knee. And beside the refreshments, Dr. Fensterer consulted his watch. He had promised to take Rosalie to her high-school alumni dance. "Two bands," she had said. "And all those bitchy little cats who act like they think they're Princess Margaret. Just because they're *married*. And you know what they married? Hardware and delicatessen and dental supplies. I want them to meet you, Merv, Dr. Merwin Martin Fensterer, M.D." When he told her about the ward dance, she cried. "So marry one of *them*," she had shouted. "See how you like having breakfast every day with a maniac." He had promised to come as soon as he could but he was half an hour late already. He would have to rush from the ward dance to the high-school dance, a man who hated to dance.

"But they won't let me go," Joyce said to Dr. Sourette. "I don't know why. But I know they won't."

Beverly Ann passed, in a straw hat, pulling Terence. "Come on, professor. Loosen up. You're just a nut in a nut house like the rest of us. Even if you do know Latin. Put down that damn can and turn on."

"No thanks," Terence said. "Nice of you to ask, but no thanks."

"Why you goddamn snobbish son-of-a-bitch," Beverly Ann said. She spat into his can. "Maybe you'd like to dance with *that* instead."

"Excuse me for a moment, please," Joyce said. "I'm going to slap Beverly Ann. She's always spitting at people."

"You know what will happen if you do," Dr. Sourette said. But sat still.

Joyce stood up, took her hands out of her sleeves, and crossed herself. "She has a hard, uncontrite spirit, that girl. Besides, I haven't had a single wicked thought all day."

"To seek out punishment willfully is, itself, a form of arrogance," Reverend Mother had said. "It is against the entire spirit of our Order." But Joyce was sure He would forget her, stuck away in Farnsbee South, unless she reminded Him nightly beneath her crucifix that she was still there, a wicked sinner needing to be saved. Reverend Mother did not understand. She was safe with a whole community of holy sisters around her who sang His praises constantly and attracted His attention. But she was all alone, surrounded by atheists and renegades and Beverly Ann Grumm. She might so easily be overlooked. She put her hands back up her sleeves and walked sedately, through the jerking crowd, to Beverly Ann.

Dr. Sourette watched her go, aware that he should have stopped her, reminded her to think of the others. But how could she remember, poor girl, obsessed as she was by the need to preserve her own soul? It was all she had in a society where possession was nine-tenths of the law. He would allow Joyce her scrap of soul. Besides, it was too late now anyway. He watched her remove Beverly Ann's straw hat and slap her, very calmly, across the cheek.

"What the hell?" Beverly Ann screamed. And slapped back. "Holy Mother, the great big plaster saint herself." She kept slapping while Joyce stood perfectly still with her hands up her sleeves and turned the other cheek. Beverly Ann slapped that too. "Look at her, great big overblown cow, acting like she's scared she might get diseased or something from us miserable sinners. And then goes around slapping people for no reason at all." She began to hit and scratch and pull Joyce's hair. "You looking for martyrdom, is that it? Well, here's a piece of it. But it won't get you into heaven. Heaven? Jesus, a straitjacket in solitary would be more like it." She kept scratching and pulling. But Joyce, Rex noted, could hold her own.

Across the room he saw Beverly Ann's latest cousin pulling Sandra onto the floor. Her face was white and her body rigid. She might have been posing again. For the Rape of the Sabine Women. Rex jumped up and hurried over. "Leave her alone," he said.

"Says who?" He went on clutching Sandra's hand.

"Says I. And Me. And Mr. and Mrs. Mayflower Memorial. And all the little Memorials."

"You nuts or something? Yeah, that's it. You're nuts. An inmate."

"I said leave her alone. Now."

"Sure. You said it. That's all right. You can say it. It's a free country. Even for looneys."

Rex grabbed the boy's arm and twisted it. "What the hell?" the boy shouted, dropping Sandra's hand. He swung at Rex but missed. Rex swung back, connecting. They went at it in earnest while the others crowded around: Hartley jumped up and down, cheering for Rex, and the others stopped dancing and stood in a circle, shouting and laughing while the music rocked and rolled. Even Joyce and Beverly Ann gave up their private fight to watch the main bout.

"Kill him, Stew," Beverly Ann shouted. "Blast him, Stewie baby." Stewie, who was getting the worst of it, reached for the bulge in his hip pocket. But the bottle slipped and smashed, spilling bourbon on the floor. There was a sudden silence, except for the music.

"Turn that thing off," a voice said. Then it too stopped abruptly.

Rex turned and saw Dr. Prokosh and felt he was seeing him for the first time. Not tucked down behind a desk beside the utility room but standing tall and firm, surrounded by his patients as if ready to touch for the King's Evil, subduing disturbance by the mere display of a bit of white cuff. His hair, Rex realized now, was not gray at all but still black, still thick above the black suit and white shirt. A man accustomed to contrasts. But able to distinguish all the subtle shades between, from Sandra's stricken silence to the screams of the daily press. Not like Rex, who saw *only* the extremes. Which was why he was the patient. And yet, what a misnomer. For it was Prokosh who was patient, standing perfectly still now and waiting. Not questioning or commanding, just waiting. Willing to spend his life waiting, waiting and watching, directing slow difficult cures from twenty floors up. Chewed on by Beverly Anns and Rex Bannisters. Accepting into his tower suite all responsibility and no gratitude. Unseen as a prompter in his box with the entire production in his hands and no script at all, except what he might improvise himself. His pockets lay flat against his hips, not to be stuffed with the reports and recommendations of one of his own patients. For he knew it all, even twenty floors up. His face was calm, with his eyes straight ahead and his ears steady, keeping his patients always within view and earshot. Even twenty floors up. Rex, ashamed, put his hand over the notebook in his breast pocket. The walls of the solarium moved in, enclosing perfect silence.

"All visitors will please wait outside," Dr. Prokosh said. "Except that one." He pointed at Stewie. "Who will leave at once. The rest of you will sit down."

The patients sat in a circle around the room, with Dr. Prokosh in the center, speaking quietly and turning slowly, keeping them all in sight. As he kept them all in mind, exposed as their case histories in the files, inhabiting his conscience. A comforting thought to Rex Bannister, who had roamed the world alone, absorbing other people's agonies, reporting other people's histories. Now, at last, he could retire to being just a patient, full time, responsible only to his own symptoms. When he so much as itched, Dr. Prokosh would tell him where to scratch.

"I regret that this is necessary," Dr. Prokosh said. "But I'm afraid it is long overdue."

At last, Rex thought, the ward will be reorganized and the needed changes made. Dr. Prokosh's face was calm and his creases sharp. An orderly, decisive man, he would know how to control the anger and the delusions and the splintered personalities crouched beneath the sills. As he controlled himself. Dr. Prokosh began to look at each patient in turn, speaking to each individually.

"You have created a disturbance for the third time in as many days," he told Beverly Ann. "You will go back to half-hour checks." And move out of Mrs. Schiller's room, Rex thought. "And you will have no visitors," Dr. Prokosh continued, "for two weeks."

"The hell I will," Beverly Ann said. "Just try that and I'll have my father and the whole damn city council down here within twenty-four hours. My father'll fix your wagon. So fast you'll be sorry you didn't learn the catechism instead of Dr. Sigmund Freud. So fast you'll damn well never get another chance to fuck up another patient. . . ." But two nurses at the end of the room moved in quietly beside her. Dr. Prokosh turned to Mrs. Schiller.

"You have persisted in hiding behind your books," he said. "It's time, you know, that you came out of Dante's hell and faced your own. Perhaps we have been delinquent in leaving it entirely up to you, in not helping you to get more involved in the life of the ward. Only *you* can effect your own cure, after all. And the only way to do that is to help with the cure of your fellows. We are *all* patients here, and all doctors." He smiled slightly.

Ah, yes, Rex thought. Yes. Yes.

"So, I shall begin to help you by asking you to help Beverly Ann. We shall expect you to be responsible for her half-hour checks."

"Ach, nein!" Mrs. Schiller said.

"She'll go mad," Rex said.

"On the contrary," Dr. Prokosh said. And smiled again.

He doesn't know about Elsa's room and her roommates and Beverly Ann, Rex thought. I never told him about Elsa. An intellectual woman shut up with a set of lurid comics.

But Dr. Prokosh was speaking to Terence. "Your throat, as you know, is entirely healed. Now you must make an effort to heal your mind as well. Accept the fact that you are, physically, completely fit."

"If he could only start teaching again," Rex said. "But Fensterer keeps canceling passes."

"And I shall have to cancel passes too," Dr. Prokosh said. "After this incident tonight."

"Not again?" Rex said.

"Not again?" Hartley echoed.

"You know the rules," said Prokosh.

"Fuck the rules," screamed Beverly Ann.

"Fuck *you,*" shouted Daphne.

"Shut up," said Rex.

Dr. Prokosh raised his hand. "This does not include Sandra, who is to be discharged on Thursday."

Sandra, sitting calmly beside Bigelow, gave a start. The disk on her head stopped revolving. Across the room, Rex saw her face go white and stiff and knew she had sunk down inside her own womb. They would never find her again.

"Sent home?" Bigelow said.

"But she's just beginning to like it here," Rex said.

"There's always that danger," Dr. Prokosh said.

"You're really going to send her back to her husband?" Rex said.

"That creep?" Bigelow said.

"But you know she's afraid of him," Rex said. "For whatever reason."

"She'll get sick again," Bigelow shouted, jumping up. "I know she will." His hands were hanging at his sides, his fists clenched. He had dropped the football at last. "It's damn cruel to send her back."

"You don't know how terrified she is," Rex said. "Even if it is misplaced."

"I'm afraid there are some things that you, patients, don't know," Dr. Prokosh said. "But we can't go into them now."

"And I think, maybe, there are some things that you, doctor, don't know," Rex said. "Some things you evidently haven't been told. You wouldn't let me tell you and obviously no one else has."

"Any patient is free to come and talk to me at any time," Dr. Prokosh said. "I'm always on call. In fact, I shall be in my ward office for the next hour." He smiled slightly. "Good night." He watched for a moment while they dispersed, some to the refreshment table, some down the hall. He might, Rex thought, have said "At ease" or "Dismissed." Rex watched while Prokosh stopped at the door to talk to Miss Reed, giving permission for the guests to return, self-assured and poised as always in his sleek black suit, unaware of how much he did not know. Like a funeral director whose function it is to bury the dead, not mourn them. Watching Prokosh walk away, Rex found himself wondering about that beautifully cut suit. Wondering if, inside that perfect grooming, there was, perhaps, only half a man. The front half. He got up and followed Prokosh down the hall.

Dr. Fensterer, escaping quickly, knew he would have to endure Rosalie's recriminations tonight and Prokosh's questions in the morning. "Tell me, please, Dr. Fensterer, as the physician in charge. . . ." But Dr. Fensterer would be able to tell him nothing, for he had observed nothing. Only the face of his watch, which told him only how late he was. Tonight, he thought, he would tell Rosalie, firmly, irrevocably, that he had decided for rocks. Silent, still, stable rocks, patient and predictable, possessing their secrets with dignity but revealing, to those who cared, the nicks and fissures of the ages. Tonight he would tell her, try to make her understand. "You don't know what it means to me to have something I can touch and feel and even pick up. Something that will stand still and let me examine it. And then I can be outdoors most of the time, working in a field or a hillside instead of a ward. Trying to find out what nature's up to instead of Dr. Arnold Prokosh. Don't you see?" If she didn't, she could marry Popoff, the druggist, and get her bubble bath free. Which was as close to medicine as she would ever want to be anyway. Tonight, he told himself firmly, the declaration of independence. Tomorrow revolution. And soon he would be crossing the Delaware on his way to Conshohocken schist.

On the narrow bed in his room, Dr. Etienne Sourette took off his socks and stared at his feet. They were beginning to look quite different from wearing shoes all the time and sitting down so much. Was *he* beginning to look different too? Tonight he had allowed something to happen that he should have stopped. Because he had grown tired of the Daphnes and the Beverly Anns? And had therefore failed the others—Rex and Garrick and Elsa and Terence—the innocent who would now suffer because of him. By July the marks of the laces might be permanent. By July his feet might no longer be able to drive a jeep up the mountains or support him fifteen hours at a stretch. By July it might be too late. His bag was packed. By midnight he would be in Port-au-Prince, where the moon, full as a mango, would drop into his open arms; where there might, someday, be a native girl with her hair shy about her ears and her skirt swinging.

Sandra, holding her pose in her room with her hair down and her eyes on the left knob of the second bureau drawer, waited for her fifteen-minute break. She had been perfectly happy these past few weeks, sitting with Bigelow, living, like any work of art, a timeless existence while the hours flowed, unused, around her, protected from erosion by the walls of the ward and the routine of Farnsbee South. But now, with Dr. Prokosh's announcement, she could feel time swirling by, rising to her chin. It would sweep her away, out into the roar of the city and the silence of the apartment off First, where the river lay like a damp rope ready to drag her in. Marcus' empty shoes would follow her down the street to the supermarket with the spreading heads of lettuce and the naked little chickens with holes where their necks should have been. And the fish frozen solid. And in the apartment only silence and Marcus' broad back. She sat motionless, staring for safety at the knob on the bureau drawer, a drawer which, as long as she held her pose, would never be opened, would never reveal its sinister contents.

Dr. Prokosh, walking slowly down the hall, saw, through the open doors, Joyce at her devotions and Sandra rigid on her bed and Bigelow practicing forward passes. As though they did not know that the crowds were gone and the easels covered and that God Himself had rolled His head farther to the left, leaving a gap in the heavens over Farnsbee South. Leaving Dr. Arnold Prokosh to cope, alone, with the scraps tossed into his ward, with no sky above him and no limit to the errors he might commit. With infinity gazing down and Rex Bannister, ace journalist, to sneer and snoop and report assorted horrors to a waiting world. Banner headlines without explanation or qualification. Because Rex's whirling eyeballs avoided the fine print.

But how, except in the finest of print, could Sandra's story be told? A girl like a Greek vase, completely empty and not to be used or touched but kept forever in a glass case for others to admire. To send her back into the world, he knew, was like using an amphora for a shopping bag—the jab of an elbow, the ring of a cash register, might crack it forever. But he could hardly set her up in a permanent display case in the ward. He was a doctor, not a curator.

Or was he even a doctor any more? A doctor who did not touch his patients. A director. A captain who plotted courses but descended only rarely from the bridge to mingle with the passengers and crew. A captain who was now about to abandon a passenger on the high seas. For her sake or his? Because her very presence, as he had realized almost from the beginning, threatened to rock the boat? His boat, which, he was determined, would run smoothly and steadily along the coast.

He walked faster now, eager to get back to his tower rooms, eager to avoid Rex, champion of lost causes and gadfly to the world. Dr. Prokosh felt covered with welts. He hurried down the hall to the elevators and the tower to play the old tapes, which reminded him of the days when he had sat quietly with a single patient for fifty minutes, when he was a light in a dark week and his couch was a refuge.

Near the door of the ward, he passed Mr. Nuffield, carrying his invisible pack. The old man stopped for a moment and looked at him sadly. "Sorry," he said, extending a hand. "Terribly sorry. Returned for postage due. Hope it's nothing urgent." He nodded and moved on. Dr. Prokosh's fingers closed around an imaginary message. He stood there for a moment, clutching it tightly. Then he turned and walked back to his ward office. For he had a sudden feeling that it was, indeed, urgent. Terribly, terribly urgent.

CHAPTER ELEVEN

In the solarium Terence watched Rex's back move down the hall and wondered where he was going. Rex could go anywhere, was afraid of nothing: guerrilla warfare or Southern racists or even Dr. Arnold Prokosh. But Terence was afraid of his own saliva. No matter how many times they told him his throat was healed, he dared not swallow. And he knew he would never get well here with Beverly Ann stripping off someone's skin at every meeting and Mrs. Schiller clawing at her conscience and Dr. Prokosh watching constantly from above and ready to pounce. He must find someplace else, anyplace. Walk the streets, maybe, with his can extended, collecting something better than his own spit.

The room seemed to be getting hotter and the noise louder. He felt the voices throb at the back of his sore throat and slide down the scorched passages. They had intruded into his life and probed at his mind and now they were invading his body. He got up, clutching his can, and started down the hall.

Rex, following Prokosh, stopped outside his office. He was about to knock when he heard a voice. Prokosh was there but had someone with him. Rex turned to go. But the voice, he realized, was his own. He stood there for a moment, listening in fascination to himself talking to Prokosh. For there he was, taped and ready any time Dr. Prokosh cared to turn the knob. Like a crooner in the night. But there was more to it than that. For what Rex was saying had been said, originally, to Dr. Fensterer. Dr. Prokosh was eavesdropping. Rex stood there listening in growing fury and fascination to himself informing on himself. Not only to Prokosh and the noon clinic and whatever classes or seminars or lecture groups Dr. Prokosh cared to invite, but to as many of posterity as cared to listen. His voice would be as much of a curiosity as Neanderthal man's bones. His unconscious, like Sandra's face and form, was public property now.

At last the tape ended. There was a moment of silence and then he heard Dr. Prokosh's voice, a voice that stood up to speak and strutted around the room, pausing for applause. There must be someone with him, Rex thought, and turned to go.

"Rex Bannister," the voice said—Rex stopped to listen—"presents symptoms which, due to a certain verbal facility and an ingratiating manner, are easily masked and peculiarly deceptive and require a good deal more exploration. His manic phases are still potentially dangerous and show elements of unresolved. . . ." The voice went on and on. There was, evidently, no one else. Dr. Prokosh was playing back his own tapes, had carefully recorded his own interpretation of Dr. Fensterer's sessions so that he could listen to himself, could analyze his own analysis. Narcissism compounded. Endlessly. Prokosh analyzing his own analysis of an earlier analysis. *Und so weiter*. It made Rex's head whirl. He took a deep breath and knocked.

"Yes?" There was a click and a squeak: the voice boxed up again. "Come in." Dr. Prokosh was sitting behind his desk. "Ah, Rex. Come in." He glanced at his watch, that enormous gold watch riding his thin wrist, its face to the world. "You wish to discuss . . . ?"

"Lots of things."

Dr. Prokosh sighed. "In that case," he said, "you'd better sit down."

But Rex remained standing. He felt suddenly very uncomfortable in that office, that bare little office with the blotter and the desk and the tape recorder in the corner. And the lights always burning. That small stripped office with Dr. Prokosh on one side of the desk asking questions that had no relevance at all to his own needs. And the patients giving answers that brought him no comfort. His own analysis must have been over years ago. Who listened to him now? Only the tape recorder and himself hearing the echo of himself. And upstairs, there was the apartment where Dr. Prokosh worked and slept and dreamed his dreams—with no one to tell them to—inside the walls of a hospital and above the heads of his patients.

"Yes?" Dr. Prokosh said, and folded his hands on his desk.

"I thought you knew all about this ward," Rex said. "But, obviously, you don't. There's a helluva lot going on here you don't seem to know anything about. It's time you read my notes." He patted his breast pocket.

"Oh?" Behind his desk, Dr. Prokosh seemed to stiffen. He looked quite angry now and Rex remembered that he was, after all, the director, giving orders, not taking them. His hair was flat and his ears steady. No terror stirred his locks or shifted his eyeballs. A neat, controlled man whose very creases stayed where they belonged. Rex imagined him hung up at night inside his suit with his thoughts neatly folded in the drawer.

"I thought we'd been through all that," Dr. Prokosh said.

"No. I've never had time. And it's a long list. Full of facts you damn well ought to know."

"What kind of facts?"

"All kinds. And all having to do with gross injustices—among your very own patients."

"You've come to talk about the other patients *again?*"

"About Sandra in particular right now."

Dr. Prokosh swiveled quickly from right to left and back again. "But you know I can't listen to that. You know the rules. . . ."

"Yes. I know the rules. But there's something you should know. . . ."

"About Sandra?"

"Yes, dammit. About Sandra." He remembered her face as he had last seen it across the room: the face of someone disappearing forever behind her own defenses.

"Then *she* has to tell me."

"But she won't."

"In that case, I prefer not to know." He stood up and folded his arms across his chest. His buttons, Rex noted, were shiny and his cuffs stiff, ready to shoot onto someone else's wrists. He reminded Rex of that Haitian colonel who commanded the prison in Port-au-Prince. Rex had seen him daily from his cell, reviewing the guard and directing the executions. "For Sandra's sake," Dr. Prokosh continued. "If there's something that concerns only her, she must be allowed to tell me herself. Otherwise, I have no right to know. The patient must make the choice. For his own good."

The Haitian colonel had lined up the "traitors" and given them a short lecture before shooting them down. "You have lived like dogs," he said. "Now I will give you a chance to die like men." And gave the order to fire.

Dr. Prokosh, staring at Rex standing beside the desk, noted how big he looked—and strong, with a face that seemed all bone, set, at the moment, in anger. A basic face. The face beneath the mask. Yet in some strange way, it reminded him of the faces on his tower wall. Called "masks," they had obviously been designed not to hide but to express, to reveal. Rex's face, he thought, was all revelation. An interesting face. He would probably miss it when Rex finally left, that bony face with its profile sharp enough to pick locks. They had much in common, though Rex would never acknowledge it. His own profile, Dr. Prokosh thought, resembled a key.

He sighed and sat down again. There were times when his old dream still haunted him, the master mechanic searching frantically for the missing part. He hoped desperately that this time he would find the right one.

"Sit down," he said again. "We should talk, you and I. But not about Sandra. We should talk about Rex Bannister."

No wonder those cuffs slid in and out so easily, Rex thought. There were no bumps on Prokosh. He had been rubbed smooth to fit the theories he had fashioned and the groove he had cut for himself. No wonder his eyes looked straight ahead and had no need to roll sideways into corners or pockets. His life held no distractions. And no purpose except what his patients provided. My God, how he needed his patients. Even their disembodied voices. Otherwise he might feel alone and forgotten, dumped down beside the utility room.

"You're angry, of course," Dr. Prokosh went on. "I've just been playing over your tapes. You are still, obviously, unable to handle authority of any kind on any level. Even the most elementary. You continue to resist routine, regulations, restrictions. You are, in short, still uncooperative. So," he paused and smiled slightly, "let's talk by all means. But let's talk about Rex Bannister." He gestured toward the empty chair.

But Rex remained standing. The colonel had raised one hand when giving the order to fire. Rex felt his eyes somersault and his ears, facing backward, caught echoes. "I like it here," Sandra had said, ". . . except when Marcus comes." "Except the grave," Terence had said, ". . . except the grave."

"Look, you arrogant bastard," Rex said.

"Yes?" Dr. Prokosh stiffened and put the tips of his fingers together carefully. The prisoner at the end of the line, Rex remembered, had fallen seconds before the soldiers fired. But he was dead. The colonel turned him over slowly with his foot. "Next time," he said, "we save the ammunition." And smiled sweetly at his men.

"I've got enough evidence here of what you don't know to fill a Sunday *Times Magazine* article. A long one. You want to read it or should I file it?"

Dr. Prokosh stood up. He felt terribly tired. Rex was, after all, merely a patient. A difficult, recalcitrant patient who persisted in his pattern of withdrawal and aggression. There would be no shortcuts, no sudden flashes of mutual understanding between them. Merely the old routine of hard work, conducted mainly from the tower. Even this much personal involvement had, clearly, been a mistake. "Tell Sandra I'll see her in the morning, if she wishes."

"She won't wish. And the morning may be too late, for Christ's sake."

"That's a risk I'll have to take."

"No, goddamn it. It's a risk you don't *dare* take."

"*I'm* the judge of that. Not you. You seem to forget that *I'm* the doctor no matter what you. . . ."

"No, dammit. You're *not* a judge. How can you be when you don't know the facts and don't want to? And you're certainly not a doctor when you don't even know your own patients. You're just an administrator and a technician with formulas and a certain number of drugs to fool with. And tapes to keep you amused. And a chance to play God. Christ, you send Sandra back to a setup you know damn well she can't handle and you keep Terence locked up till he's desperate. And refuse to let Garrick see his brother, the only relative he's got in the world, the only human being he gives a damn about. What the hell kind of a sadist are you?"

"And you, I'm afraid, are neither a judge nor a doctor," Dr. Prokosh said calmly. "Nor even a competent reporter. A reporter should, at least, have all the facts. Which you don't. You know nothing at all about Garrick and his brother, for instance. A brother who has been dead for almost forty years. Who died, in fact, at birth." He paused and smiled faintly at Rex.

Rex hardly heard the words but noted the smile. Like the colonel's sword, he thought. Ornamental and symbolic. The colonel always drew his sword when he gave the command to fire.

"So you see," Prokosh went on, "I can hardly allow Garrick to visit his brother, as you keep demanding. And you can hardly expect to play *all* the roles at once: patient and reporter and doctor and judge. At the moment, I'm afraid, you are simply a patient in a mental ward. And a very arrogant one at that. My treatment of my patients is no concern of yours."

"No!" Rex shouted. "Not your patients, dammit. Not anymore. I'll see to that. I'll report you to the AMA. I'll expose you to Health, Education, and Welfare. I'll denounce you to WHO and UNESCO and the SPCA. I have a whole goddamn dossier on you."

Dr. Prokosh came out slowly from behind his desk. "And I think I should, perhaps, prescribe a sedative for you. Come, I'll speak to Miss Reed. Besides, any further discussion between us now would clearly be dysfunctional."

"Dysfunctional," Rex thought. Not right or wrong or good or bad but "dysfunctional." One of those words indicating a member of the ruling class. Dysfunctional for *whom,* by God? He watched as Dr. Prokosh came toward him with his little pellet eyes and the handcuffs ready, Dr. Arnold Prokosh accusing him from behind his glasses, damning him with his small, flat, recording ears. Rex felt his own eyes begin to whirl. He no longer saw the well-groomed Dr. Prokosh who might have slept beneath his mattress, keeping himself in press for the deranged patients of Farnsbee South. He no longer saw Dr. Arnold Prokosh, lord of the ward, commanding his office, but all the other masters he had confronted all over the world: officials demanding passports and policemen brandishing guns and soldiers aiming bombs. All the way back to his father lounging against a tombstone in a deserted cemetery with one hand out, commanding him to eat. Men who turned people into commodities and corpses. Rex felt his glands burst and the chemicals, once so carefully controlled, seemed to flood him in a riot of imbalance. He lunged at Prokosh, wanting to punch him hard, so hard that the doctor's eyes would bounce in their sockets and his ears come unstuck and his smooth slick hair drip like wet paint on his forehead. Rex lunged—for the inmates of Farnsbee South and the prisoners in Port-au-Prince and the inhabitants of "enemy" villages forever in the line of fire. Rex swung for them all, and missed, sideswiping merely a split second and a swathe of air. And landed, at last, in the chair.

Christ, I fight nothing but delusions, he thought. A madman spending his anger wantonly, fecklessly, leaving him too weak to hit the right target, leaving the Prokoshes always in command.

"Tell Sandra I'll see her tomorrow at ten," Dr. Prokosh said softly, opening the office door. He held out his hand.

Rex looked down at the hand, another outstretched hand. Not a begging hand this time, nor even a helping one. For Dr. Prokosh was, clearly, neither seeking nor offering salvation. Just extending another open hand. Into which Rex, for once, felt no desire to empty his pockets. Or place his own. He merely looked down at it. *"Sieg Heil,"* he said.

"I was fighting Nazis while you were still nurturing your neuroses," Dr. Prokosh said. And turned to lock his office door.

CHAPTER TWELVE

In the solarium the patients and their visitors were still eating and drinking. Beverly Ann and her current cousin were still squeezed into one chair while Mrs. Schiller huddled in another with plenty of room for somebody else. Around her the other patients and their guests laughed and talked and ate: chicken salad and potato chips and doughnuts, devouring the holes. In the center of the room Hartley's mother, tall and bulky, divided the scene, all buttoned up. She held a steaming cup of coffee into which she cried intermittently. Hartley had started shock treatments and had passed her without knowing her. "Go away," he said when she tried to kiss him. "I don't have to obey you any more. I'm not on your squash team any more." But he seemed happy now, eating doughnuts with his good hand, the other tucked up at his side like a spare. While his mother watched. And perspired.

The room was hot and noisy with the patients, Mrs. Schiller

thought, going up and down and around. Like the animals on the carousel at the end of the Wilhelmstrasse. The night the soldiers came they made old Herr Steinfinkel go round and round on a donkey until he fell off and lay face down, with his blood flowing beneath the hooves and his neck caught in the stirrup. They found him the next morning, still revolving slowly, with the donkey still going up and down above him, jerking his head, making it nod incessantly, acquiescing in his own death. Mrs. Schiller closed her eyes.

When she opened them, she saw Verna standing in the middle of the room with her right arm raised. " 'Behold,' " she said in a loud firm voice. " 'The Lord has put forth His hand and touched my mouth; and the Lord said unto me: Behold I have put My words in your mouth. . . . To root out and to pull down, and to destroy and to overthrow.' "

Garrick, sitting against the wall, felt a thrill of horror at that tiny intense woman who had lived so long with those terrible words beneath her tongue. No wonder she had refused to speak. She had guarded them fiercely, maintaining her own silence to preserve their purity. No trivia had been allowed to cross her lips to contaminate the words of the Lord, kept for safety inside her sealed mouth. While he spilled words all day, justifying his isolation, allowing Grant to live his life for him. Verna dropped her arm and Garrick felt another stab, of recognition this time, of that other small intense woman with her arm raised and her finger pointed: "Didn't you almost kill me?" she screamed. "Racing selfishly to get out?" He felt the pain in his left hand and wondered if it too was becoming paralyzed.

Daphne was screaming now: "Shut her up, somebody. Shut her up. Make her stop that crazy talk." She jumped up and started toward Verna, followed by Beverly Ann and her cousin as if they were about to shut Verna up by force. Then, suddenly and completely, the lights went out. There was a moment of stunned silence.

"My God," someone screamed. "What the hell?"

"Who's fiddling with the lights?"

"Lemme outta here. I don't belong here. I'm only visiting."

"Hey, Nuffield," Beverly Ann called. "Cut the crap and turn those lights back on. You're supposed to be playing post office. Not God. On second thought, though," she said slowly, "never mind, Nuffield, never mind. Right, Rudy? Just plain never mind."

Ach, Mrs. Schiller thought. It is the Inferno. Only which circle, please? For it implied horrors not mentioned in Dante.

"Power failure," Mr. Nuffield announced from the door. "Can't stop now. Mail must get through. Especially now. No phones now. People must communicate."

"My God, he's right," Hartley's mother said. "The streets are all dark." She sat down suddenly and slowly unbuttoned her coat. She might even take it off now.

The other voices rose as if to make up for the absence of light.

"It's all out. Even across the river."

"Communist."

"Sabotage."

"Treason."

"Milt'll be stuck in the subway for days. In Queens yet."

"The kids are all alone. I thought I'd be back in an hour. For an hour you don't pay for a sitter."

"My freezer!"

"My furnace!"

"My God!"

The largest city in the most powerful country in the world had been blacked out, brought to a dead stop: underground, on the ground, above ground. No light would shine, no wheels turn. Buildings would grow cold and ice would melt and dead bodies would begin to decompose. Time itself was stuck to the wall, Pacific time and Mountain time and Prairie time, not lost but forever unused, and unusable, piled up now like a slag heap in the center of the city. A memorial to those twelve hours when men sat down with humility and lit candles in the dark and remembered, for a little while, the light of the moon.

Terence had hurried down the hall and through the door at the end of the ward. No one tried to stop him. No one noticed him. They were all too busy eating and drinking and talking about the dance, holding off bedtime with the tips of their tongues. The nurses were all in the solarium keeping an eye on Daphne and Joyce and Beverly Ann, keeping the atmosphere calm. At the nurses' station, Dr. Sourette, busily calculating the distance in time and money between Port-au-Prince and Farnsbee South, did not raise his head. Terence had no idea where he was going: under a bus or into the river or down an elevator shaft. But out of Farnsbee South, clutching his can for comfort.

As he stepped off the ward, he realized that he did not even know the way. He could see nothing ahead but corridors leading to more corridors and closed doors that would open, most probably, not on the street but on operating rooms and delivery rooms and other wards. He forced himself to walk more slowly, carrying his can casually at his side as if it were just another empty container and he merely another visitor looking for the trash. Nurses and visitors and doctors passed him and he felt the saliva gather in his mouth. He ducked into a men's room to spit and consult the mirror. It showed him a young man who needed a haircut and, possibly, a chance to swallow his own humiliation. Whatever else he needed did not show.

He started down the hall again. Straight ahead was a set of swinging doors. He remembered that strange ward where he had spent his first week, with the stretchers and the wheelchairs and the little carts of bottles and tubes. With the patients stretched out by day, requiring no more space than a corpse, and hung up at night like so many empty robes. "To get the blood circulating again," he could imagine the nurse with the covered trays explaining. He stopped walking.

There was nothing ahead but the swinging doors. He held his breath as though even an exhalation might blow them open. Behind him there was only Farnsbee South. He was back where he had started, had, in fact, merely gone the straightest route between two horrors. And what now? Was he supposed to begin all over, step forward and push the doors and lie down between the cold sheets, beside a dead man's bed, to be removed again to Farnsbee South? He could only stand and stare. Until suddenly, as if in answer—a mysterious, mocking, sinister answer—the lights went out. He stood still, holding his breath while the darkness filled his mouth like cotton wool. But the darkness changed nothing. Up ahead, behind the swinging doors, the patients still lay on their backs, still growing, without the aid of light, the hernias and the lesions, the cancers and the ulcers and the clots, in the still dumb flesh beneath the sheets. And behind him the old delusions would penetrate the dark, steadying Mr. Nuffield's pack and Joyce's faith, bringing Mrs. Schiller the relentless comfort of Dante. And suddenly Terence remembered Rex, remembered him jumping up, striding from the solarium with his back straight and stiff like a man on constant guard duty. Where had he gone? Terence wondered. Toward what? Prokosh and another incident and total darkness? Because Rex didn't really know Dr. Prokosh. And he, Terence, had never warned him. That Prokosh was far too clever to be caught, unawares, by a patient in his office. Had probably turned out all the lights so that right now Rex might be wandering about in the dark, roaming up and down the halls, pushing against strange doors. He might even push against a swinging door and be caught in that terrible ward, to be hung up at night with the old men, his head on one side and his feet dangling.

Terence turned and felt for the wall. He could not go out into the streets tonight. Tonight he must go back to Farnsbee South and find Rex. He began to grope his way back, the long dark way back, feeling for the wall with both hands. Not until he reached the ward and had passed the closed door of Dr. Prokosh's office, did he realize he had lost his can. He must have left it in the men's room or dropped it when the lights went out. He had been swallowing steadily, painlessly, ever since.

In his room Dr. Sourette closed his bag and felt the wheel turn. A huge movement, going full circle, carrying him home. For he was going at last, quickly, secretly, as his father had advised long ago. He felt a lurch beneath his feet and a giddiness in his head and the warmth of the Haitian sun hissing at him through the radiator. His head was in the clouds but his ticket was in his pocket and soon his feet would be in the dust of Port-au-Prince.

He had packed quickly, hurrying around the room in his bare feet. He would buy sandals as soon as he landed. He would have to learn Creole all over again and cultivate a taste for *clairon*. When he had finished packing, he swept his room and made the bed and put fresh water in the pitcher. He felt strangely happy, as he had when a boy, helping his father. He took one last look around and picked up his bag. It felt very light. Like the coffins of the poor, he thought.

He opened the door and stepped softly out into the hall. And then, suddenly, the lights went out. He stood staring into the darkness, holding his bag, waiting for the lights to come back. He stood there for a long time, long enough for the wheel to turn again. But the hospital and the street and the whole city remained black. And he knew that, once again, Baron Samedi had outtricked him.

Marcus Mishkin, terribly late for the party at Farnsbee South, had been kept by a client who insisted on deductions for everything, including each breath she took—a singer with weak lungs. He had caught a cab outside his office and sat watching the crowds in the streets, envying the men who spent the evenings with friends and relations in bars and movies and the nights with their wives, women whose beauty was purely private, to be found only on the rim of a cup or the wrinkle of a sheet; men who stayed within normal proportions, who did not care to travel the seas at night or limit their intimacy to the coins in their pockets. As the cab turned a corner, Marcus stooped to retrieve a dime.

When he lifted his head, the streets were completely dark.

"Jesus," the cabby said. "I knew I shouldda stood in the garage. Out ten minutes and this."

"What is it?"

"Who knows? In this town, buddy, it could be anything. You name it, we got it. Junkies and Commies and hippies and kooks. Who knows, maybe Con Edison's gotta identity crisis. Maybe the mayor wants a nice quiet rest and don't wanna go all the way to them Virgin Islands. Maybe he don't like virgins. Just wants it nice and quiet right there in Gracie Mansion. And switched the whole goddamn mess right off."

Marcus got out near the hospital, shocked to see that it too was dark, like a huge shadow beside the river, a shadow that seemed to be listing somewhat, like a great ship going down with a full moon coming up behind. The lobby was full of shadows and noise and confusion; of visitors who longed for home and the reassurance of a dry martini and a double bed.

Marcus hurried up the stairs and the moon met him at the landings. On the seventh floor he walked quickly down the dim hall where shadowy figures passed occasionally and the voices of the patients rose, without conviction, to stir the night. He hurried on, refusing to acknowledge what lay behind the half-open doors where the sick waited in darkness and isolation, forced to sit up and live out the night in whatever position their mechanical beds demanded, staring at blank televisions and reaching out for silent bells, frozen in a world where nothing moved except the slow progress of each individual disease.

He hurried on to Farnsbee South and into the solarium, well lit now by an arc light and a sense of community. Visitors and patients were still eating the remains of the buffet supper, making the darkness more palatable with potato chips and a few shreds of lettuce. In one corner, where the shadows remained heaped on the couch, Verna sat with her hands in her lap and her eyes fixed, not on a corner of the ceiling now but straight ahead.

Daphne and Beverly Ann and some of the other patients were huddled together in a semicircle at her feet. Marcus, moving closer, realized that she was talking, talking steadily in a clear even voice. "'Therefore I will not refrain my mouth;/I will speak in the anguish of my spirit./I will complain in the bitterness of my soul.'" She was talking back to Him at last. As if the darkness had given her a new vision and a new courage. "'How long wilt Thou not look away from me,/Nor let me alone till I swallow down my spittle? . . . Why hast Thou set me as a mark for Thee,/So that I am a burden to myself?'" As if the darkness had finally brought Him down to her level and enabled her to argue with Him, in bitterness and reproach, through His own words and the words of His people. Beverly Ann, Marcus noticed, was crying quietly and nodding. Was she, he wondered, addressing *her* father, able at last to scold the biggest secondhand car dealer in Babylon, Long Island, through the words of Verna and Job? "'Is it good unto Thee that Thou shouldst oppress,/That Thou shouldst despise the work of Thy hands?'"

But Sandra, he realized, was not there. Or even Joyce or Bigelow. Joyce was undoubtedly on her knees in her room, not fighting with her God but praying to Him, for light, not justice. Bigelow, he learned later, had been withdrawn quite suddenly by his father, an important man in merchandising who expected results. A product that would not move was dropped. And Bigelow, obviously, was not moving. Unless pushed. His father had, therefore, pushed him firmly out of his room and down the hall and back into the world, though Bigelow had threatened, every minute, to turn and run fifty yards in the wrong direction. He avoided the other patients, though he shook hands with Mr. Nuffield, who told him not to worry, he would deliver Bigelow's message to Sandra and personally forward his mail. Bigelow dared not say good-bye to anyone else. He did not even take his football with him but left it hidden in the utility room. He followed his father slowly, sadly, down the hall, as if he had just fumbled a forward pass.

So Marcus found Sandra alone in her room with her pose and her hair running down her back. She was, Marcus realized, terribly afraid. For the moon, which spotlighted the bureau and the sketch hanging above it, did not quite reach to her bed and she had always been afraid of the dark. What good, after all, was a model in the dark? When she saw him, she did not turn away as usual but smiled expectantly. As if she had been waiting for him. And then, suddenly, Marcus knew what to do. It was easier in the dark, where his height was blurred, where he might have been a smaller, more self-assured man with his features spread out, ready for a smile. And in the darkness he recognized Sandra's expression: it was not hostility but fear. What pose could she possibly take alone in a blacked-out room? What was it Rex had said? That she needed only to be protected and petted? Marcus smiled at her, placed her hands gently in her lap and tilted her head toward him. Then he sat down beside her with his arm around her shoulders.

She sat silently, listening to the voices of the others up and down the hall, loud voices that sounded afraid, as if they were trying to shout down the darkness. Poor people who did not know what position to assume, what attitude to strike, when the darkness came and filled up all the hiding places and covered the retreats. Poor people to whom no nice man had come to tilt their heads and fold their hands. Such an easy pose. She stopped trying to think, trying to remember where she was and why, and what had frightened her so. She had taken her hair down right after Dr. Prokosh announced that she was going home and had thought of nothing since but holding her pose. As long as she did that, she thought, she was safe. But the darkness had come, jolting her so that it wobbled uncertainly. Until this nice man came and secured it.

"The clock's stopped, you fool," someone shouted down the hall. "It's electric, nitwit."

Time has stopped, Sandra thought. Then what about the breaks? For she could not hold even this easy pose forever. She would go rigid, would spend the rest of her life sitting up straight with her head at a slight tilt, as if questioning the strange gentleman's left ear.

Marcus, glancing at his watch, saw that it was quite late. They might send him away soon, to sit with the other stranded visitors in the lobby, crowded and complaining, angry at him for being so big that he seemed to cast a shadow even in the dark. He patted Sandra's hands.

"Time for a break," he said softly. "We've done enough for today. Wouldn't you like to go to bed now?"

"Yes, please," she said.

In her room, Joyce got up off her knees and carried her candle across the hall. "It's a punishment," she told Marcus. "For all the wickedness in this ward. I wondered how long He would wait. But not against her." She nodded at Sandra. "She's the only real innocent here. She should have been a nun. The sisters would have taken care of her, protected her from all the Clays and Daphnes and Beverly Anns—inside and outside the ward. God's chosen always have to be protected from the others."

Marcus stared at her, a big girl who looked more suited to labor in the vineyards of the Lord than to be His bride; a girl with large eyes that glowed in the candlelight but seemed meant to examine the contents of a saucepan rather than the mystery of the Trinity.

"I used to think *I* was one," Joyce went on. "One of the chosen, I mean. But He wouldn't have me. Reverend Mother said I didn't really have a calling. That He meant for me to serve Him in the world. In Mr. Looney's Type-Rite Pool, I guess." She sighed.

What, Marcus wondered, did she find to say during those long periods on her knees to a God she seemed to imagine as some grandiose usher telling her just how far up she might sit?

"But He would accept *her,*" Joyce went on. "I know He would. Take her to St. Ursula's. And then, maybe, I could visit her sometime. And I could teach her. I know she doesn't know anything about praying or penance or polishing the vessels. But I could teach her."

She was right, of course, Marcus thought. It was what Rex had said. A quiet protected life, carefully stripped and rigidly controlled. The life of a nun—without the religion. She was sitting on her bed now while Joyce brushed her hair. She sat perfectly still, with her hands crossed in her lap and her eyes raised. A perfect madonna, a youthful madonna who would never have a child or stand beneath the cross. A madonna who existed only to be admired and copied. Only he, Marcus Mishkin, so big he could be nailed down in the dark, had attempted to possess her.

He sat there for a long time, reluctant to go out into the black city, back to his own dark empty apartment where he would be alone from now on and which would remain gray even after the lights went on, with the grayness of monotony and failure. No hope, now, that Sandra would ever walk with him beside the river or voyage with him to the islands of the night. Instead, they would sit side by side on Sunday afternoons, in some small sanitarium in Brooklyn or Queens, staring out a window, waiting for the afternoon to drag its slow length across the path. He had no idea how he would manage it, the cost of a private home, but if Sandra needed it, a home without him, a place to be herself, whatever of herself was still left, she should have it. He had, after all, seen death itself, had actually shaken hands with it one afternoon in an excess of friendliness. And had witnessed the Lord listening patiently at one end of the ward. He could certainly manage a sanitarium.

He got up, at last, and walked slowly down the hall toward Rex's room. He wanted to tell him about Sandra, to tell him he had been right. Rex, who had traveled so far and flown so high to be confined, now, to a bed in Farnsbee South. A man who had accepted the whole world as his assignment. But Rex was not there.

Terence and Hartley were asleep, with a candle burning on the table between them. Hartley, the blanket covering his withered arm and his mouth at peace, looked like any schoolboy between Tuesday and Wednesday. Terence's head was turned and a trickle of saliva hung, like a thin white string, from his mouth, tying him to his past. But Rex was not there.

Marcus lingered in the doorway, wondering why he was waiting, wondering why he did not go home and climb the twelve flights of stairs in the dark, fumbling for his own lock and feeling his way through his own apartment. There would be no light unless he borrowed a votary candle from Joyce, in which case he might feel obliged to spend the night on his knees, giving thanks that this strange day was over, had in fact ended prematurely. A day in which he had heard Verna raise her voice to her Lord and seen darkness descend, and had consigned his wife, permanently, to the suburbs. A terrible, exhausting, lopsided day which left him tired and stooped, forcing even his huge bulk closer to the ground. He leaned against the door and stared at Rex's empty bed. It was in a dark corner, farthest from the candle. But where was Rex?

He thought of Rex's life as it had been and might be again: Rex flying to Biafra and Tel Aviv and Vietnam. He imagined a great plane landing and the crowds gathered and the dark hair lifted in the wind. And himself waiting beyond the barrier to say "Welcome home." For he would be all alone again, with no responsibilities except weekly visits and monthly bills. He could easily sign whatever chit was necessary to release Rex from Farnsbee South. And Rex might go with him, occasionally, to visit Sandra and stand with him, someday, beside the grave of his parents. He would give Rex back his world with a tiny corner reserved for him. Marcus took off his shoes and lay down on Rex's bed. Soon he closed his eyes, raised his sails, and slept.

Miss Reed, on duty in Farnsbee South, looked around the solarium and saw, by the light of the arc lamps, that all, at last, was calm. Most of the patients had gone to bed. A few still lingered over coffee and doughnuts with their visitors, stirring old complaints, swallowing old doubts, and nibbling at the slices of light. Only Mr. Hunnicutt was alone, bouncing a library book on his knee.

It will be *The Little Flowers of St. Francis* for Joyce, Miss Reed thought, or the latest study of Dante for Mrs. Schiller, or maybe another movie biography for Beverly Ann. She wondered what Mr. Hunnicutt took out for himself. And thought how lonely he must be, spending his days with books and his evenings with the patients of Farnsbee South. And the weekends. She sat down beside him as if he were a patient needing to interact.

"Are you all right?" she asked.

"Oh, yes. Of course. Don't bother about me, please. Unless you have nothing better to do."

"Everyone seems to be taken care of."

"Good. In that case, let me get you some coffee."

She sat still and watched him in the dim light, walking back slowly, carrying her coffee in a paper cup, carrying it carefully, watching it steadily. She was not used to being served. He might have been holding her future in his hands, offering it to her in a paper cup, filled to the brim.

"Sugar? Cream?" he was saying, bending over her. "How stupid. I forgot to ask how you take it."

It seemed, suddenly, a terribly intimate question. How do you take your coffee? How do you take your life? With a little sweetening, perhaps? And a little cream? To cut that austere taste? "Just as it is," Miss Reed said. "Just as you brought it. But where's yours?" While he went to get it, she looked at the book on his chair. It had nothing to do with St. Francis or Dante or Hollywood. It was a life of Alexandre Dumas.

"It's a new one," Mr. Hunnicutt said. "I thought it might interest you. I understand you're a student of Dumas."

A student. She laughed and looked at him, this sober man with a preference for quiet ties and used books who had, like her, chosen to spend his life inside the walls of institutions. It suggested, at least, a certain permanence. He would surely be less likely to disappear than the others. And he had brought her a book and a cup of coffee. Her first real gifts since *The Count of Monte Cristo.*

"I used to read Dumas by the yard," Mr. Hunnicutt said.

Soon she would have to get up and check on the patients for the night. But for the next few minutes, she would allow herself to sit beside Mr. Hunnicutt, drinking coffee and discussing Dumas. Thanks to the blackout, she was aware, for the first time since Dr. Curran Harte, of a glimmer of light.

CHAPTER THIRTEEN

When the lights went out, Garrick groped his way back to his room and his typewriter. The others stayed together in the solarium, waiting for the candles which they knew would come to relieve the darkness. But Garrick had no such faith. He knew that light was a miracle, dispensed by God and Con Ed, not to be created by little men with short wicks. He felt his way to the straight-backed chair and sat down with his typewriter, Grant's electric typewriter, on his lap and his hands on the keys. Even without light he could still type. But now when he pressed the keys, nothing moved. He pressed again, harder and harder. But the keys remained locked, immovable. As if the world had stopped dead in the middle of a spin and everything on it had stuck fast, with the lamps dark and the typewriter still. Or as if some huge gap had opened and swallowed up not only the light and the type but something more important. And he knew that something terrible had happened to Grant.

He had disappeared again as Garrick always feared he would, as he had at birth, when Garrick, his own brother, had kicked him aside in his hurry to get out and be born. Though Garrick had re-created him every day of his life since then. But Grant had begun to fade away again even before the lights went out, when Verna rose, with courage and the Lord's words in her mouth, to defy the ward and the lies that were harbored there. To defy *him,* Garrick Troy. Reminding him of that other tiny tense woman who had screamed at him periodically: "Brother-killer! Murdered his own brother before he was even born. Kicked him out of the way, that's what he did. And killed him in the process." And Garrick knew why the sight of Verna had pained him so and what ghastly secret lay buried beneath the elaborate syntax and symbols of his poems. The secret of Grant, his twin brother, whom Garrick had killed and re-created to inhabit the life he had renounced. Garrick's head whirled and he knew he had lost far more than he, half a man, could possibly afford.

For a long time he sat in the dark with his hands on the keys and the entire alphabet stretched out beneath his fingers. Grant's alphabet, which would no longer form words. He could not even type his name. And realized, suddenly, that he could not even remember his name. He felt absolutely alone and empty, a long hollow tube of a man whose very blood had deserted him. He sat in the dark, bent over the typewriter, while the snow inside his head began to fall. But it was black snow this time, making not a curtain but a solid wall, not only closing the world out but closing him in. It was a blown snow, whirling and drifting, freezing the inside of his temples and the back of his eyes and the passages of his ears and nose. Soon it would blow down his throat and through the empty corridors and crevices of his body, forming, in the absence of blood, a long thin icicle beneath his flesh.

Finally, he struck a match and looked at his face in the mirror, a long sad face with deep-set eyes, a face divided against itself by a thin bony nose. It was a face he did not recognize. He struck more matches and read the words on the sheet still wound in the typewriter: "While the leaves of the trees grow dog-eared/ And the face of the sun is smudged." It told him nothing. He struck match after match, frantically examining the room, the drawers, even opening books for possible clues. But he knew he was not Shakespeare or Milton or Blake or Donne. Or even Webster or Roget. He knew only that something terrible had happened and that he must find another haven for his poems: someplace on Ninety-sixth Street between Park and Lex with a plate-glass window and green walls. He put on his coat, picked up his typewriter, and with his palm on the wall to guide him, walked out of his room and down the hall and into the night.

Outside it was brighter, with headlights and a full moon and the stars stretching long shimmering legs, spinning out the night. He walked carefully lest he break a thread, a man with no past and no future and only the words ". . . the face of the sun is smudged" inside his head. He walked instinctively, unknowingly, carrying his typewriter and those words in his head while the moon followed closely behind as if about to whisper in his ear. He was aware of the sentence spelled out by the stars, if only he could decipher the code. Which might tell him who he was and where he was going in a burned-out city, carrying a black box and feeling a terrible emptiness at his side, as though someone who had been forever linked to his arm had, quite suddenly, walked away.

At last he turned into a small café with green walls and a familiar look. He sat down at the far end of the counter with his typewriter at his feet and stared at the soup cans and the pie rack and the Coke ads above the mirror. He sat there for a long time, stirring coffee and staring, until he noticed, above the ketchup and the mustard and the salt and pepper, a strange face staring at *him:* a long sad face, thin as an old crust and spread with grief. And he knew that this was the face that went with the words in the typewriter, a face blown and battered and clinging to the slopes, a face that only he would recognize as the face of a poet. He put his head down between the mustard and the ketchup and wept.

Outside his office Dr. Prokosh had locked the door, turned his back on Rex, and walked quickly down the hall, rubbing his palm. The elevator was empty and waiting. He stepped inside and watched the door close with relief. Then he leaned against the far wall and shut his eyes. He was glad to be there in that small box, alone and rising gently with no noise and no emotions to be stirred and smoothed and folded carefully inside the proper limits; no minds to be rolled out like so much dough for the cookie cutter, as though a white coat denoted not a doctor but a pastry cook. He had discarded the coat soon after medical school.

"Return to the womb," he might have called it, this peace he felt in the elevator, in the old days when such a phrase still seemed significant, still capable of helping Mrs. Finletter to leave that tiny dark furnished room and go back to her family and three stories. "Infantile regression," he had thought, remembering just in time not to suck the tip of his pen between notes. Mrs. Finletter had gone home at last, to live in the third-floor closet. Until she died and was conveyed to an even smaller, darker, quieter place. Longing for the womb, was it—or the grave? Did it matter? Escape backward or forward? It was, in any case, a distinction Mrs. Finletter could not use.

He opened his eyes to watch the indicator, hoping that it would not stop, that no one else would get on. It kept sliding silently, steadily, past five and six and seven, indicating time and place and motion so clearly and economically and efficiently. He was very tired. He leaned against the wall, a target for the delusions that wandered through his ward every day. But he was safe here, confined in the even light of the elevator. Safe and moving steadily toward the tower. He closed his eyes.

But the elevator gave a sudden jerk and stopped. He opened his eyes to total darkness. He began to pant. He hated the dark. He was a man of science, of reason, and the light burned steadily in his tower apartment, where the irrational intruded only as decoration, as masks on the walls. The dark was alien. "Let there be light" had been, after all, the first act of creation. He could hardly breathe. He stood glaring into the black space, telling himself it was only a temporary failure. But he knew this would be a long sojourn in the dark, in that small confined square meant only for the briefest of trips, quick forays into pain and disease and death. It occurred to him that if he had stayed to listen to Rex he would not now be stuck he knew not where: between Urology and Obstetrics perhaps, with the women in heaped-up mounds, waiting to give birth—from darkness into darkness, which would be no birth at all, no delivery, but merely a shift from the evil within to the evil without. He had hardly been aware before of what lay along the corridors between Farnsbee South and the tower, of what lay on the other side of the closed door of the elevator. And now he hung suspended in that unknown territory, sealed in by darkness and the door that would not open, a trespasser in his own hospital.

He groped along the wall until he felt the panel of buttons. He pushed them one by one, then pounded them all together with his palm. But they no longer had any power to give light or motion. He banged the walls and the floor. But nothing happened, nothing changed. The sounds died away and there was nothing.

He leaned back against the wall in panic, waiting for the light and the motion to return, to carry him to peace and privacy and the safety of sanity. He groped hopelessly in his pockets but he did not smoke and had long ago given up carrying matches to light his wife's cigarettes. She had smoked incessantly, had, in fact, left him an apartment full of dirty ashtrays. It had been a relief to breathe clean air again. Which was, at first, almost the only difference in his life. Until he gave up the couch and moved to the tower of the Mayflower Memorial, with Farnsbee South like a tight little ship beneath him, and Family Meeting and staff meetings and patient interviews like the bells of the watch. With the cargo safely stowed and the crew all aboard and the passengers coming and going. If he sported too much braid in the eyes of Rex Bannister, no matter. In his own eyes the queue waiting to embark had somewhat diminished. And sometimes, remembering his wife, he thought of it as his African village, though he believed it was something more—a small sample of the world, perhaps, with himself at the head. And he flattered himself that now "Dr. Arnold Prokosh" all alone on the door had its own distinction.

But, thanks to his wife, he carried no matches. The elevator was becoming hot now, the darkness thicker and his breathing heavier. If this was, indeed, like the womb, it was a hostile uncomfortable place. Why had one always assumed otherwise? Wasn't it more like the grave? Though a crowded grave, he began to realize, filled with voices, familiar voices, voices from the past. One by one they came to wait out the night with him, the voices he had heard so often long ago: "But I *must* keep my head down, doctor," Mrs. Altchek said once again, "to protect it from the crowd. Otherwise my face will be all clawed away."

"That's selfish," Mr. Kruger said. "No wonder I spent my whole life looking for perfection. And in the very first line. Why should it matter so much how one begins? It is the end that counts. Only in this country no one has time for the end. So perfection must come right away. Must be presented on entrance. Like you, Mrs. Altchek. A beautiful baby from the start. But selfish. It ruined my life."

"Not my selfishness," Mrs. Altchek said. "Your fear. Ask the doctor."

"I asked the doctor. For seventeen years I asked the doctor.

Now I'm sixty-five and all I have is canceled checks. Soon it will be all over. And I haven't even begun."

The elevator was becoming unbearably hot now as more and more voices crowded in. Voices that had, for the most part, lain low behind a permanent profile with only one eye exposed. Except on his couch, where the patients raised their voices and their full faces. He heard them now.

"I can't sleep, doctor. It's not my nerves. It's my alarm clock. It goes off every half-hour. All night long."

"My husband left me two years ago, doctor. But every Tuesday his shirts turn up in the wash."

"I have to keep eating, doctor. Otherwise I'll be too empty. People will see right through me."

What if all the others were coming too, tired of waiting in line so long? Thousands and thousands of them whom he had never treated at all, never invited to Farnsbee South with their aberrations on the end of a leash.

"I knew it would happen," Toby Downes whispered. "I wasn't ready. I told you I wasn't ready. Why didn't you listen? And now, if you ever want to swim in the Westside Community Pool, I can't promise to let you have it to yourself. Not any more. Because from now on, you know, I'll be there too. From now on I'll always be there." And spat into Terence's can. What was it Rex had wanted to tell him about Terence? And Sandra? If only he had stayed to listen he would not now be stuck all alone in a stalled elevator, jostled by voices. He would have been safe in his office when the lights went out. With Rex to companion the darkness.

It was Rex, of course, who had herded all these patients into the elevator: Rex Bannister, who recognized no authority, no reality but his own; Rex Bannister, who was undermining Dr. Prokosh with his own patients. It was undoubtedly Rex who had cut the electricity so that Prokosh was stuck forever between two floors. A sick man, Rex, dangerously sick, the kind of man who, every few generations, shakes the world and turns men's heads and shifts their vision to the edges of the crowd. Except that Rex was shut up in Farnsbee South, where he could shake nothing but Prokosh's authority and the peace of the ward.

Suddenly, Dr. Prokosh saw him high above, seven feet tall with a faint light on his face. When there was no light anywhere, there was light on Rex. He was holding Terence's can and looking down on Prokosh. The voices were suddenly still, as if waiting for Dr. Prokosh to speak.

"I wonder why," Dr. Prokosh began quietly, in his best professional manner, "you chose to do this strange childish thing. Was it revenge? Against me? The hospital? The whole city? But you realize, of course, that we're simply trying to help you, don't you? Don't you?" But Rex said nothing.

Dr. Prokosh began to perspire. "You don't like Farnsbee South," he said. "But then the patient rarely likes his medicine, does he? You don't like me or my methods, do you? You think I'm manipulative, even dictatorial. Heartless, perhaps. But you don't know about the queue, do you? The long gray queue stretching from one river to another. Waiting. Of course not. You prefer to ignore it. Disregard it. Because you are irresponsible. Arrogant. You simply sit and stare at a wall all day, feeding your guilt. You see nothing but your own needs, your own unconscious. Of course you can't understand my methods. Because you are a patient. A *patient,* not a doctor. To be a doctor you would have to give up your own obsessions and concentrate on other people's. But that requires effort and discipline and sacrifice. And that you won't do. Then why do you try to act like a doctor?" He had raised his voice, looking up at that pale pained face. Rex looked down and said nothing.

"And you're angry, of course," Dr. Prokosh went on, "that we want you to start going out. You, who feel responsible for the whole world, are afraid to be trusted with yourself. Prefer to be watched and protected and restrained. But how can you save the world when you can't control *yourself?"* He paused, waiting for Rex to answer. But Rex said nothing. "Why don't you speak?" Dr. Prokosh demanded. "You're a patient but not *like* a patient. Then what are you? *Who* are you? And why are you silent with me, who's trying to help you? With me, your doctor?"

Still Rex said nothing. And Dr. Prokosh began to be afraid, not of the elevator and the darkness now but of the mystery of that pale dim face far above him. The face was weeping huge slow tears that fell with a plop into Terence's can. "Who are you?" Dr. Prokosh shouted. *"What* are you?" But there was no answer. Only the sound of tears falling slowly, steadily, into an old can. And Dr. Prokosh knew that Rex would never answer, was, perhaps, too far up even to hear. Yet for a long time Dr. Prokosh kept on talking, Dr. Arnold Prokosh, who had spent his whole life listening. But still Rex said nothing.

"It's all wrong," Dr. Prokosh shouted. "*You* should talk and *I* should listen." Otherwise it was all confusion and role playing and no one would know who was the doctor and who the patient. In this terrible darkness he, the doctor, must keep his head, must hold on to reality. But he could not move a finger. Only his lips. So he went on talking, shouting. "You, Rex Bannister. *You* are the patient. You must talk. I am the doctor. I listen. Speak, damn you. You *must* speak. I command it."

But Rex said nothing.

After a while, Dr. Prokosh grew tired, too tired even to move his lips except to breathe in that terrible black box. Besides, he knew now that the elevator would never rise again, even with the power restored. Not with all those voices screaming and shouting and causing a great wind, enough to rock it like a cradle and send it crashing to the bottom. And the voices with it, splintered voices to go with the fractured minds. Minds that had never been properly restored. And now, without their voices, never would be.

Gradually the voices, which had been silent while he spoke,

rose again. Only now they were all mixed up—Terence's voice speaking Garrick's lines and Mrs. Schiller's voice with Hartley's complaints. As if his old nightmare had, in a sense, come true and he had not so much run out of parts as mixed them up. He slid to the floor in terror.

He lay there stretched out like one of his own patients on the couch long ago. And kept his eyes on that pale dim face far above.

Mr. Nuffield sat on his bed in the dark. It was the first time he had sat down for more than ten minutes since he retired to carry the mail for Farnsbee South. He had never delivered the mail in the dark before. He was an old man and he would not start now. He was used to walking in daylight, when the curtains twitched as he approached and the children bounced down the steps and the doors opened. He was welcome everywhere. Why should he hide behind the night? So he sat in his room, though he knew that if the light did not come soon, his feet would grow heavy, would turn into lumps of stone, and he would never walk again. They would send him to the dead-letter office then, a special place for old postmen, where they sat at long tables redirecting the mail to the deceased. But the letters they forwarded never reached their destinations. They merely came back stamped "Addressee Unknown," so that no matter how fast they worked, the piles of undelivered mail got bigger and bigger. In the end, Mr. Nuffield knew, they would bury him. He preferred to die on his feet with the mail on his back.

"Ach, Mr. Nuffield," Mrs. Schiller said from the door. "Such a shame you cannot deliver the post today. I might, perhaps, receive something. You see, it is my birthday today."

Mrs. Schiller did not seem to mind the dark at all. She was a brave little woman holding a light in the doorway. And a kind one, with an extra candle for him. She had evidently known worse things than sitting in the dark. Or maybe she preferred it. He remembered Mrs. Birdsong, 202 Salisbury Road, who refused to open her door in broad daylight, even for him; a woman whose life was punctuated by tragedy: telegrams and registered letters and special delivery and postage due. He hated to carry them. Even air mail, he felt, was irregular. He considered postcards an insult and picture postcards a frivolity. But now he could deliver nothing, not even a circular.

"Your birthday, is it, Mrs. Schiller?" he said, getting slowly to his feet. "Congratulations. We shall have to see to it that *your* mail, at least, gets through." He shook hands with her and began his long steady tramp down the hall.

"So kind," Mrs. Schiller murmured, and, carrying her candle, wandered out on the balcony. The Pediatrics wing across the way was completely dark and she wondered what the children made of it, this sudden absence of light in the grown-ups' world. Though for her, the darkness was a comfort. There was nothing she wanted to see. Even the stars looked reluctant, a faint spatter against the black. She sat down in a canvas chair and remembered the night she and Rex had talked out here. She had told him about her brother Rheinhold who, being a painter, had never learned the law of falling bodies and so had wasted a perfectly good dinner on the sidewalk. It had been dark like this, a darkness Rheinhold evidently wished to preserve. There had been a little balcony just like this where it had suddenly become *verboten* for couples to sit or children to play or laundry to hang or even plants to grow. But Mr. Weissgard, two floors up, had hanged himself there one Monday morning as less offensive, perhaps, than the wash. And Rheinhold, without regard for technicalities, had simply used it for his final leap. It was so dark that he hadn't been seen, lying there in the street with a piece of charcoal in his fist and his head turned. In fact, they had not discovered him until the next morning. For months afterward Mrs. Schiller lay in bed through the night, thinking of Rheinhold lying helpless just below her window, appealing to her, perhaps, in German and Greek and Italian, for he was a scholar, Rheinhold, though a painter. And maybe even in Hebrew. But softly so as not to wake Theo, who was, after all, not a Jew and might be offended by such a crude display of non-Aryan flesh and bone.

She sat there for a long time watching the moon rise, big and pompous and brighter than ever, as though it had gathered to itself all the lights of the city for its own greater glory. Like the huge spotlight that had shone, suddenly, that night on the fifth-floor apartment, catching them all in its beam, Mutti and Vater and Giesele and Ernst. Only Rheinhold had escaped, had rushed "from light into the kingdom of eternal night." Rheinhold and Frau Professor Theodore Friedrich Schiller, née Grossbach. But it had found her at last, as she always knew it would, had found her even in this strange faraway city, thirty years later, across an ocean and a river, even with the lights out and the power all gone, found her alone on the balcony of the Mayflower Memorial Hospital with a tiny candle in her hand and the darkness at her feet, waiting. For she was not afraid any more. She merely sat there thinking about Theo, and Rheinhold lying alone in the street all night. Even now, she thought, someone might be lying down there in the dark, alone and helpless, while she sat in comfort, defying the moon. Overhead the stars formed one half of a long pale swastika.

She got up and peered over the railing and saw something white on the pavement below. "Rheinhold?" she called softly. "Rheinhold, is it you? Wait, please. This time I come too. Right away. Only wait a minute. Please." She hurried back to her room and snatched up the *Inferno* from under her pillow and rushed back to the balcony. There was no one there. Clutching Dante, she stole along the railing, searching for the little black fire escape that ran in twists and turns to the street. She had raised geraniums there and recited Dante there and had even been courted there, in the days before the *verboten* signs appeared. She had never used it as an exit before. But Rheinhold was waiting. Besides, she was not sure who else might soon be waiting—in the building behind her or on the street below—with armbands and boots, waiting to test the blood, to make sure that no good Aryan blood was running into the sewer before calling for the hose and the garbage can. She must not wait any longer.

"Ich komme schon, Rheinhold," she whispered, and put one leg over the rail in that long descent, that long journey toward Rheinhold and Theo, from darkness into eternal light, with the *Inferno* under her arm.

Mr. Nuffield, wandering out on the balcony a few minutes later to give Mrs. Schiller her birthday card, found no one there at all. Only the little canvas chair and a burned-out candle and the full moon. For the first time in his life, Mr. Nuffield had failed to deliver the mail.

Dr. Merwin Martin Fensterer was in his car halfway to the Orpheum and a Technicolor spectacle with Rosalie on the seat beside him when the lights went out.

"We could go back to my house," Rosalie said. "We've got lots of candles. If you *want* light, that is."

He thought of the hospital with the lights and the sounds off—no bells summoning nurses or voices paging doctors or elevators going up and down. Even the beds would not move now, forcing the patients to sit upright as judges through the night, examining the darkness.

"Maybe I should go back and check on the ward," he said.

"Are you God, you can make light when Con Edison can't? At least you can see to get to my house. After that you won't need much light." And Dr. Fensterer, with her lips on his ear and advancing across his right cheek, could only swallow and swerve to avoid hitting a truck.

He found himself wishing often, in the years that followed, that he had gone to Farnsbee South that night the lights failed, had gone to be with them, the twilight people who live on the edge of reality with their nightmares stitched to their backs. But Rosalie, snuggling against him, had hinted at choices never offered before. "Of course, if you *prefer* crazy people, even off duty. . . ." And so he had made his choice, made it during that long blackout, and no amount of light would ever show him any alternative again. When dawn finally came, he knew that his rock collection would be used to edge a border and that the closest he would ever get to a field trip would be taking the kids to the Bronx Zoo. *That* Rosalie could understand. That and marrying a medical man. But he could teach her nothing else. She would go on writing his name with a "Dr." in front and an "M.D." behind—and laughing at him. "Rocks," she had said between giggles that night, pulling his hair. "Haven't you enough in your head, Dr. Merwin Martin Fensterer, M.D.? And your crazy patients?" Dr. Fensterer sighed. She would never understand about his patients, any more than about his rocks. And she would never understand him.

He drove back through the dawn, a rumpled, unwashed dawn that would become a sullen day. In the lobby of the hospital, he saw the hands of the electric clock on the wall begin to jump. The power of the city had finally been restored. But his own blackout, he knew, had only just begun.

CHAPTER FOURTEEN

Rex was in the hall outside Dr. Prokosh's office when the lights went out. He stayed there, leaning against the wall, for a long time, feeling as if he had just awakened in the middle of a long night, still surrounded by darkness but with the promise of morning ahead. His anger was gone, as if he had dropped it into Dr. Prokosh's waiting palm. And his outrage. For he knew that wherever Dr. Prokosh was now, he was as much in the dark as Rex. Even the perpetual light in the little ward office was out. There was no salvation there. But Rex felt no regret and no fear. Only a great curiosity. The cultivated curiosity of the trained reporter.

He began to cover the hospital, from top to bottom, noting the crowds huddled in the lobby, getting ready to sleep on chairs and couches and the floor—like the crowds once packed together in the steerage, except that this, a stationary crossing, led to nowhere but morning and hunger and a stiffness in the limbs.

They would have gained nothing. Only lost: time and sleep and, probably, even wages. And a sense of security. How could they ever feel absolutely certain again?

In the cafeteria huge arc lights had been turned on for the visitors, who had eaten and drunk the last scrap of food while Puerto Ricans and Jamaicans and blacks from Harlem and Alabama, men and women, swept and mopped and carted away mountains of dirty dishes. Many of them had been on all day and would stay on all night, leaving their children alone, locked up in the dark cold flats. The night shift and the day shift became incorporated into one, and in the kitchen, standing before the huge sinks, a tiny black couple spent the night side by side for the first time in twenty years.

On his way up, Rex found the stairs crowded by a water brigade: teen-agers in jeans and cowboy boots, boys and girls, with high heels and sharp toes, were standing quietly on the steps, passing water buckets to the floors above. Who were they? Rex wondered. And where had they come from so suddenly, connecting top and bottom, becoming integrated at last into a system they had, until now, merely kicked with scorn? They pulled him into line and stuck a pail in his hands. He stood on a low step between two blonds in jeans who kissed over his right shoulder, passing buckets steadily, forced to be a link in a long human chain. Until all the full buckets had gone up and the empty ones had come down. Then he continued his way upstairs, twenty floors or more.

He lost count, distracted by the moon, which hovered above his shoulder at the landings, as if for a glance beneath the blankets to discover what went on down there, among the horizontal people over whom the days and nights passed, flattening them still further into their beds. Up he went, past Obstetrics and Pediatrics, past Neurology and Cardiology and Epidemiology and Geriatrics. Past the ingenious variety of shocks that flesh is heir to. And mind also, dragged on a string to Farnsbee South, to be nursed and drugged and rested and sent spinning into the world again at a new angle. On to that room at the top, that small barren room which probably holds nothing but a bed and a sputum cup and a urinal in the nightstand. Once he stopped and looked down at the blot of the river, which, for all its silence, he knew, was still running, in spite of the power failure, through the darkness and out to sea.

On the tenth floor a woman screamed steadily for a "needle" and on the twelfth an old man, clutching his abdomen with both hands, shuffled in and out of all the rooms, searching for his missing gut and his empty bed. On the fifteenth a young man sobbed and on the twentieth he heard a strange laugh, a laugh that had torn loose from its moorings and was floating alone through space. Rex peered through the doorway and saw an old man silhouetted against the moon, bolt upright in bed, laughing to himself in an empty room. A shocking sight. For only tears are private. Laughter is a public matter. The old man looked sinister, sitting up so straight in bed in the middle of the night, laughing to himself, open-jawed against the moon. Dangerous too, for the laughter loosed so carelessly raced toward the door and assaulted Rex standing there. And, as he listened, he felt a terrible urge to laugh too. The impulse was irresistible and repulsive, like the need to vomit. Finally, he submitted—laughed or retched, he could hardly tell which—he and the strange old man laughing together in the darkness, high up in a turned-off city. A city that had left an old man to meet his own death sitting up. Laughter, at least, was less banal than tears. But when Rex finally stopped, the tears were running down his face just the same and the taste of vomit was in his mouth.

He moved on, hearing the whispers and the groans and the silences. Not one vast silence but many individual silences, distinguishable as speech: the silence of fear or pain, of hope or despair, of thought or sleep. And the long final silence of death. Rex, climbing through the darkness, heard them all.

Halfway up, he met two men carrying a stretcher covered with a sheet. Death, in the absence of the freight elevators, was being taken down the back stairs. Rex remembered his father's coffin. Too wide for the narrow hall, it was lowered out of a fourth-story window, twirling slowly in midair with his father inside, still jaunty, still entertaining the neighbors.

"This one goes all the way down," the man at the head of the stretcher said.

"Christ amighty, why? He feels like he's twins that died of overeating or maybe elephantiasis. This one we leave in the stockroom like the rest."

"No."

"For Chrissake, why?"

"Cause he ain't like the rest. This one's got connections. I'm not taking any chances. We don't dump this sweetheart with the others. He goes all the way."

"Well, I'm warning you. One more like this and you'll be lugging them down yourself. And maybe me with them. You know damn well I got a double hernia, plus my duodenal ulcer ain't enjoying this. I don't care if Lord Snowden himself is on this stretcher."

"You can be damn glad we don't have to carry them *up*."

"Might be easier. At least they're *alive* going up. They weigh more this way. What with *rigor mortis* and the blood freezing up solid. And to think I couldda had a job sweeping out the Music Hall and got holed up with them there Rockettes instead of a lotta stiffs." They turned the corner and Rex could make out the tops of their heads, the big man up and the little man down, with the stretcher tilted between them.

Back at the door of his own room, Rex paused. Marcus Mishkin was asleep on Rex's bed, with his shoes beside the chair and his head on Rex's pillow. His features, relaxed, seemed to have expanded so that his head no longer looked too small for his huge body. In the dim corner he seemed, for once, to be resting in peace and in proportion. There was no need to disturb him. He might be happier where he was, surrounded by people instead of figures and ledgers and maps on the walls. Among the aberrations of Farnsbee South he might be able to accept his size, might even explore it and recover the emotions he had stored away long ago.

Rex stood there for a moment, staring at the wall. But it showed him nothing now, except his own shadow created by the candle on the bedside table. It had nothing else to reveal. It was, after all, designed to shut *out,* to limit space and perception, enabling men to read books and drink beer and make love while the executioner takes his stand and the soldier his aim—somewhere else. A protection, Rex realized, that he no longer wanted. Not with the city waiting helplessly below, caught in its own nightmare. Not with Marcus occupying his bed, implying that he, Rex, was free to be a reporter again, free to take his place in the world again. To cover the story of the city with its streetlights black as gibbets and the wires hanging still between the poles, where no messages flowed and nothing moved but arms and legs and the private, independent circulation of the blood. While Marcus covered for him. Turning, Rex wished Marcus joy of his bed and immunity from his dreams.

He walked quickly down the dark hall and out into the black town, a town dipped in ink with all its sins blotted out; a strangely decorous town now with the bars and the ads and the "Walks" turned off. Young men stood at the intersections directing traffic. In the light they might be students or clerks or sneak thieves again. But now they gave orders and were obeyed and the traffic lights stared with wide blank eyes. The cars moved slowly, like beasts in the night.

People walked erratically, like parts that had come loose, wondering how to fit back in again. They spoke of "Them" and "They," the powerful ones, the privileged ones who had run things for so long and had now run one huge city to a dead stop. It seemed to lie nose down in the earth with a few black spars rising up against the sky. The torch of the Statue of Liberty was out but in the Automat the candles burned above the corned-beef hash.

As he walked, Rex had the sense that he might, for once, do more than cover a story. He might, in fact, *create* one. Might become an actor instead of a spectator, redeeming the chance he had missed long ago. Might even be a leader, leading the people of the city, the *other* people who did not shout orders or push buttons, who did not sit on boards or corporations with their hands folded over important documents; people who stood up to their work and bent their backs, whose power lay in their arms and legs, independent of Con Edison and the SEC. They seemed to be walking with him now, rushing out of the buildings to fill the lanes on Park, all going one way. The cleaning women mopped as they walked, sloshing the darkness. The doormen stopped whistling for cabs and stepped out from under the canopies to carry the pails. Waitresses without trays and beggars without legs, garbage men and moving men and latrine attendants. They came pouring out of the stricken buildings, leaving them to the dead machines and the helpless owners. They walked up Park with Rex. And the trees dividing the lanes walked with them, forgetting that they had been donated by a philanthropic lady for the benefit of the residents of the Waldorf and the Ambassador and the canopied apartments. Forgetting that they were intended to stay on Park. Not march with Rex and a mob to Harlem.

It seemed to Rex that he walked miles that night, way up to where the canopies stopped and the numbers rose and the skins turned dark; where too many people filled the streets, accepting, on a November night, still another deprivation; where the trains, coming up to take the air and violate the streets, brought the smoke and screech and soot of high adventure to the fire escapes of the ghetto. He walked softly with his ghostly followers behind him. Taking them . . . where? He had no idea. He would walk until he found light. Or it found him. Only not too far into the suburbs, not to Audrey and the little fox and the patio with the steaks grilled medium rare. For the doctor and the lawyer and the club champ who was also in textiles. Audrey's world. He would stay with the long ragged line on Park. Would lead it, in fact. Up ahead someone was whistling and far above a great blister of a moon sat in a corner of the sky. Underfoot, his sneakers, treading broken glass, made a soft crunching sound.

He thought of that other march long ago, when he was only a boy. Not a leader then, merely a follower. The only follower. Following a man who whistled through the horrors of the night and ripped open a grave as easily as he might have slit an envelope. And his son had grown up with the taste of dry tacos and the odor of decay and the years sidling along the edges of catastrophe.

He hurried on, faster and faster. Behind him the trees stopped, as usual, at Ninety-sixth Street and the canopies lingered over elegant doorways and the landscape retained its old appearance. But Rex did not look back. The tracks of the train rose up beside him, dividing the street, black and menacing and solid, a dire reminder of the strength and persistence of things as they are. At One Hundred and Twenty-fifth Street an empty car-carrier rattled across his path like some prehistoric monster, scurrying from one river to another before the light returned. He forced himself to walk even faster, racing to lead his followers out of the dead city, out of the slime of past and present that flowed together beneath the bridges and round and round the shores, hemming in the town, forcing it to move up and up, defying heaven. And down. Until He, disgusted at last, leaned over one November night and blew it all out.

Just before dawn Park stopped abruptly, exhausted, having covered it all: from the bargain basements of Ohrbach's to the expensive women at the Waldorf, and the long filthy fringe at the edge. And buried itself, in shame, in the arms of One Hundred and Thirty-third Street. Rex turned left and found the Harlem River waiting and the light just beginning to rise.

Glancing behind him, he realized there was no one there. Only the empty street with the dawn strolling past the shops and only the sidewalks on Madison to watch. The scrubwomen and the doormen were still on Park, squeezing out their mops and blowing their whistles for the tenants waiting for cabs. Who dared not turn the corner to Lexington.

Ahead of him the drawbridge was open, leaving a great gap in the middle of the river, separating Manhattan from the Bronx, fathers from families, and Wall Street from the candy stores on Jerome. As if the Lord, who had once divided the waters, had suddenly repented and divided the bridges instead, isolating the children of Manhattan with one snip of His shears. Cutting off all escape, for vehicles and pedestrians alike. Rex leaned against the railing and stared into the river and imagined the traffic racing off the bridge: the taxi meters clocking the descent and the shopping bags filling with sewage and the Cadillacs nosing through slime. He stood there for a long time.

When he looked up again, he saw that the bridge was back in place, reuniting the boroughs, joining secretaries to second vice-presidents and housewives to Macy's. The power failure was over. Subways would begin to move again and church bells to ring. And up in Connecticut there would be enough current to operate the electric chair. Everything was back to normal. Except, possibly, Rex Bannister.

He felt the notebook in his pocket, pressing against his chest. He took it out and tossed it into the river.

About the Author

Helen Hudson is the author of TELL THE TIME TO NONE, a first novel, which received extraordinary acclaim; MEYER MEYER, which *The New York Times* Book Review singled out for special attention; and THE LISTENER AND OTHER STORIES. Her stories have appeared in the *Ladies Home Journal, Mademoiselle, Quarterly Review of Literature, Virginia Quarterly, Antioch Review, Northwestern Review,* and *The Reporter, Sewanee Review, Best American Short Stories*—1968.